Quest for Evil:
The Magic of the Key

Quest for Evil:
The Magic of the Key

Jenna Lindsey

iUniverse, Inc.
New York   Bloomington

Quest for Evil
The Magic of the Key

Copyright © 2009 by Jenna Lindsey

All rights reserved. No part of this book may be used or reproduced by any means, graphic, electronic, or mechanical, including photocopying, recording, taping or by any information storage retrieval system without the written permission of the publisher except in the case of brief quotations embodied in critical articles and reviews.

iUniverse books may be ordered through booksellers or by contacting:

iUniverse
1663 Liberty Drive
Bloomington, IN 47403
www.iuniverse.com
1-800-Authors (1-800-288-4677)

Because of the dynamic nature of the Internet, any Web addresses or links contained in this book may have changed since publication and may no longer be valid. The views expressed in this work are solely those of the author and do not necessarily reflect the views of the publisher, and the publisher hereby disclaims any responsibility for them.

ISBN: 978-1-4401-5347-1 (pbk)
ISBN: 978-1-4401-5345-7 (hc)
ISBN: 978-1-4401-5346-4 (ebk)

LCCN: 2009930583

Printed in the United States of America

iUniverse rev. date: 7/3/2009

For my husband, Jerry.

Acknowledgements:

"Thank you very much indeed" to Rose Harris for her patience and opinions.

Many thanks to my many Editors and to Thomas at Author Assistance for helping me find my way. Special thanks to my mother, Joan Bruce Stalker, for getting me started.

Prologue

Fahgerdahl crouched in the tall grasses and listened. No voices alerted him to his pursuers. Ahead of him, across the field of flowers, the Hall of Doors stood unguarded, waiting to take him to his new destiny.

Fahgerdahl clenched his right hand into a fist, concentrating the Dark Magic within him. He must approach the hall unseen. The Dark Siskis Magic roiled within Fahgerdahl's body. For a moment, the enormity of what he had done touched him and he felt sick. Then the Siskis swept through his body and mind, cloaking him.

Invisible, Fahgerdahl rose and strode purposefully to the Hall of Doors, climbed the stone steps, and walked beneath the entry arch without pausing. The destruction of his twin sister, Fahdra, was necessary, he told himself. He should have been the one to *zinahday* with the powerful Eras Magic of their world.

If it were not for the people uniting against me, thought Fahgerdahl, *I would now be ruler supreme over all Atla. Not a fugitive seeking refuge.*

Content in his madness, Fahgerdahl moved down the endless corridor of doors. Once, he hesitated, sensing a malevolent presence behind a door. Fahgerdahl stepped up to the door and looked through the keyhole. A blue world spun before him. It glimmered occasionally against the stars, indicating to Fahgerdahl that the benign-looking world was a host for Siskis. He turned away. It was not strong enough.

Fahgerdahl continued his search. Far from the entrance of the hall, Fahgerdahl stopped at another door. He didn't need to look through the keyhole. His Siskis Magic recognized the taint of its kind.

Lifting his right hand, Fahgerdahl pointed at the door's keyhole. Blue light shot from his fingertip. The door opened.

Outside the Hall of Doors, five Atlan men and women rushed up the steps and into the distortions of Magic beneath the entry arch. One of them, a man taller and older than the rest, knew they were too late.

He turned to his companions. "Fahgerdahl has escaped us. We must wait."

"For how long, Ezamiah?" asked one of the women.

"Until a Key can be found."

Chapter One

As black clouds elbowed gray ones aside, rain streaked the horizon. A bolt of lightning spotlighted the ocean waves for an instant.

Nigel reached for his turpentine. He had to get this incoming storm just right. The owner of the small shop that sometimes accepted his seascapes had said a painting of a dramatic storm would probably sell. Or at least get displayed in the window.

Desperate for the opportunity, Nigel painted faster. The storm was his competitor in a race … and winning. It cheated, using thunder to startle him and wind to splay the colors on his palette until they merged into one.

Nigel held his ground, unaware of passersby abandoning their Sunday afternoon strolls. He concentrated on his painting, compelled to finish.

It needs a line of purple, he thought. Nigel looked across the vacant beach and out to sea. Purple?

Purple clouds rushed across the churning waves. The wind made him stagger back even as it knocked his painting from the easel.

"No!" Nigel ran after it and stumbled in the sand. Looking up, he saw his painting sail into the surf, bob for a brief moment, then sink. Nigel's heart sank with it. "Damn storm!"

A wild, rushing noise accompanied a deluge of rain. It bit Nigel's arms and beat him about the back of his neck. He scrambled to collect his palette, supplies and haversack.

I've gotta get out of here, thought Nigel. A drum roll of thunder deafened him. Everything went black. Nigel stood still, alarmed by the silence.

The pitch around him lightened to gray and soft shapes solidified under a growing overhead light, too dim for sunlight, too sudden for the dispersal of the storm clouds.

Nigel felt the dizziness he reserved for heights. He looked down.

One step further and he would plunge twenty feet into the ocean. Nigel backed away from the cliff's edge. He hated heights. A retreat of several feet bolstered his nerves and he turned to race up the beach. Nigel froze.

The land dipped a little from where he stood. A spongy, teal-colored moss glimmered in the moonlight. There wasn't a grain of sand in sight.

He stared at the strange landscape. Several yards away dark trees bent their branches against a darker sky. Far above them, an exquisitely white full moon lit the night. It was flanked by a smaller full moon.

Nigel stood still, heart pounding. Two moons? What was happening? And what was with that cliff? Where had the trees come from? Where was he?

"Where's the beach?" Nigel shouted. Breathing fast, shaking, he removed his glasses, wiped them carefully with his wet handkerchief, and returned them to their perch. He looked up. Two moons.

"Okay." Nigel nodded his head. "Okay." He stretched out a hand as if to hold the moons at bay and plunked down on the mossy turf.

Moss not sand. Night not sunset. Nigel waited for it to make sense. It didn't.

Pulling his haversack off his shoulder, Nigel rummaged in it for his flask of Southern Comfort. He twisted off the cap and took a short swig.

The strong liquor warmed him. Heartened, Nigel looked up. Two moons.

"I'm sure there's a perfectly logical explanation for you," he told them. "And for all of this." He waved the flask at his peculiar surroundings. "But I was never any good at logic so I'll be damned if I know what it is."

He shivered. He was soaked to the skin. Two moons or a dozen, he had to get moving. Taking another swig for medicinal purposes, Nigel capped the flask and returned it to his haversack. At least it had stopped raining.

Nigel ran his hand over the moss that should have been sand. Soft, springy, and dry. It definitely hadn't suffered a recent deluge. Nope. No rain today.

Pushing himself to his feet, Nigel protested to his lunar audience, "I'm supposed to be on a beach, you know. There was a storm coming in and I was painting it. That's what I do, see? I'm an artist. Nothing in Mr. Sanderman's display window yet, true, but I did sell a small beach scene. Once."

Snatching up his haversack, Nigel strode away from the ocean toward the trees, hoping for a road sign or a phone booth.

The moonlight cast a shadow caricature of his lanky frame and Nigel frowned at it. Thirty-six years old and he still hadn't grown into himself. He had neither the gracefulness of a dancer nor the sports skills of an athlete. Nigel had only his talent for blending colors.

His pursuit of capturing on canvas the joy he felt when he painted seascapes still eluded him. Sometimes Nigel wasn't certain it was an achievable goal or a goal other people would appreciate. He was certain, however, that he was an artist.

Nigel painted because he had to paint. The only time he didn't feel awkward or out of place was when he was painting. His favorite subject was seascapes because he adored the ever-changing colors of the ocean and its sky. As long as he didn't have to look at it from a height.

Nigel stopped walking. He had reached the trees.

Forest, Nigel decided, noticing how it grew parallel to the coastline. As far as he could see, to his left and his right, the trees formed a dense barrier of thick, auburn trunks and queerly shaped leaves.

Trudging away from the wood, Nigel positioned himself halfway between the forest and the ocean. He scowled at the moons and swung his haversack over his right shoulder.

He started to walk, the ocean on his right, the moons and their forest on his left.

"Sooner or later this will all make sense," Nigel told himself. "I mean, how lost can you get in a thunderstorm?"

Apparently, very, he thought. Of course, it had been a really nasty storm. One minute he had been painting its approach and the next, wham! It was on top of him like a cat on a mouse.

Nigel stopped walking. He recalled a moment of complete silence, absolute dark.

"Then I was on the cliff." He shuddered. "Geez, maybe I was hit by lightning. Maybe I'm dead. Just a dead guy walking along talking to himself."

He glanced around. This was the afterlife? Neither heavenly nor hellish, just incredibly odd? Nah.

"Maybe I fell, hit my head and I'm in a coma." Nigel shook his head.

He continued his walk. "Maybe"—Nigel forced himself to think about it—"just maybe I have some weird kind of tumor that makes you hallucinate."

He considered this seriously for about a minute then discarded it as too dramatic. Nothing dramatic ever happened to Nigel Nessel.

He had managed, barely, to sustain his existence and his choice of occupation by doing whatever part-time employment was available. Paper routes as a boy, burger joints as a teenager.

When he qualified for a management position at a supermarket, Nigel switched to stock boy. He wasn't interested in any kind of advancement. Nigel Nessel was not searching to improve himself in the food industry or any other industry. He was not the industrial type. If he was any type at all, it was creative.

An advertisement for a flower delivery man answered Nigel's need for a steady income. Paint supplies were expensive. So was romance. Unhappily, both pursuits were unsuccessful at the moment. Few women were interested in a guy who lived over a thrift store and smelled of turpentine and roses.

He had no friends or family to either introduce him to prospective dates or encourage him to continue painting. Not even a rich, long-lost uncle to appear out of the blue. Sea-blue. With maybe a tint of aquamarine.

Nigel hunkered down into his wet shirt and indulged in feeling miserable. The night air was cool, his socks were soggy, and he was sure he had sand in one shoe. He stared gloomily at his sneakers and trudged on.

The forest was dropping away on his left and Nigel became aware of a gradual descent. He paused and looked around.

Not more than fifty feet away, someone was tending a campfire.

"Hey! Hey, hello!" Nigel waved and broke into a happy jog.

The figure beside the fire watched Nigel's approach with interest.

"Hello!" Nigel repeated, arriving breathless and smiling. "Boy, am I glad to see you. I've been walking for miles. I must have got lost in the storm. Can you give me directions? Tell me where I am?"

The figure took a step toward him and Nigel saw it was a man. A short, stocky fellow with blond hair and a round, friendly face. *"Deshah,"* he said. *"Cooma stali va?"*

Nigel's smile drooped. "What'd you say?"

A look of puzzlement crossed the man's face. Lifting a hand to his forehead, he stared at Nigel for a long minute.

Nigel flinched. A strange, tingling sensation crept along his scalp from front to back and front again.

"Hel-oh," the man said. "I am Padwick. Welcome." His quiet tone of voice was warm and pleasant. "Please join me. You are tired and in need of rest."

"Well, you're right there." Nigel took a step forward. "I'm really stressed, too. Was that French you were speaking? Oh, by the way, my name is Nigel. Nigel Nessel."

Padwick bowed his head and motioned Nigel to sit by the fire. The two sat across from one another, polite and expectant, like chessmen on a board.

With the unconscious attentiveness of all artists, Nigel studied Padwick. His buttercup blond hair fell over one shoulder in a long, thick braid that reminded Nigel of a plaited horse's tail. His skin, while extraordinarily pale, had a healthy pink hue, which accented the eerie brightness of his blue eyes. In spite of Padwick's cherubic features, Nigel had the impression that he was older than himself.

He wore a long-sleeved gray jumpsuit that appeared to be completely covered with pockets of all shapes and sizes. Short brown boots fitted loosely at his ankles and snugly over his feet like baggy velvet socks.

Nigel cleared his throat, suddenly aware of Padwick's equally curious regard.

"What is your planet of origin?" Padwick inquired.

"My what?" A twinge of anxiety lifted Nigel's voice. This was not how the conversation was supposed to go. He had hoped for a return to normality now that he wasn't alone. Instead, he felt his sense of reality slipping further away.

"My what?" Nigel repeated, hoping he hadn't heard the question right.

"From what world have you traveled?"

"What world?" Nigel knew he sounded like a parrot, but he couldn't help himself.

Nigel looked up at the moons. They shared their halos, paired in the starless sky like conspirators. He shuddered.

"Are you ill?" asked Padwick.

"Ill?"

"I feel your unease. Have I offended you somehow? Your language is strange and you are the first other-worlder I have ever met."

"Other-worlder?"

"Is there some custom which requires you to repeat the end of my sentences? Perhaps it is rude of me to ask them. I apologize."

Nigel shook his head, bewildered. "No. I'm not offended. Padwick, is it?"

"Yes."

Nigel nodded. "Padwick. Um, I'm either very ill or very lost." Taking a deep breath, Nigel cast a chagrined eye at the moons. "How many moons do you see?"

Padwick glanced up. "Two. Do you not have two moons where you come from?"

Nigel stood up. "What do you mean 'where I come from'? Where the hell do you come from? Where am I?"

Dismayed by Nigel's fear and anger, Padwick tried to reassure him. "I come from the Province of Penkas. We are in that province now. This world is Atla."

"What? No." Nigel held up his hand. "Don't say it again." He walked around the campfire. He had a headache. Finally, he gestured at the moons, the moss, the trees. "All this is real?"

"Yes."

Nigel returned to his haversack and sank down beside it. "So, I'm not crazy and I'm not dead. I'm just a billion miles from home on another world in another galaxy."

"I do not know how great the distance is which separates our worlds. Ezamiah says distance is not a concern for the bearer of a true Gift. Such a person can cross the ocean between worlds as easily as one walks through air."

"You mean space? I've traveled through space? Without a ship. Just me."

"So it would seem. You truly had no intent to come to Atla?"

"Nope. I was just trying to get out of the storm."

Padwick leaned forward. "Tell me."

"There's not much to tell. I was painting a seascape. I'm an artist." Nigel paused for comment: disbelief was the norm. Padwick only nodded.

Encouraged, Nigel continued. "I was adding the finishing touches to the sky. It kept changing because of the weather and I wanted to get it just right before the storm hit."

"Before the storm hit what?"

"Me." Absently, Nigel reached into his haversack for his flask. "But I was too slow. It started to rain. No, pour. Torrential, wrath of God, build-yourself-an-ark downpour.

"And the wind …" Nigel took a drink, remembering the ferocity of the blast that destroyed his canvas and easel. "The wind was so cold it hurt.

"I grabbed for my stuff"—Nigel nodded at his haversack—"and it got dark. Like someone turned off a light. Then all of a sudden, boom!"

"Boom?"

Nigel nodded. "Yeah. A storm like that is loud, right? But when it stops, the silence is even louder. I mean, one minute I'm in this horrible storm and the next"—Nigel snapped his fingers—"absolute black and freezing cold. I look around and I'm on the edge of a cliff."

Padwick considered all that Nigel had described. "What were your thoughts when you were painting the storm?"

Nigel shrugged. "Getting my painting completed. Then I was thinking, I've got to get out of here. I remember, I yelled at the storm."

"You yelled at the storm," Padwick mused. "An incantation?"

"Incantation? Like a wizard or something? No. Be serious. Nothing like that. Just a yell. When you live alone, you'll talk to anything.

"Anyway, I yelled at the storm and then …" Nigel thought for a minute. "Then I felt dizzy. I get dizzy when I'm near heights."

Nigel looked around him, forcing calm onto anxiety. His gaze turned to Padwick. "Care for a sip?" Nigel offered the flask.

Still reflecting on Nigel's narrative, Padwick reached to accept. Their fingers brushed.

"Ow!" Nigel jerked his hand away, his fingers stinging from an electric shock.

"By the Light!" Padwick set the flask aside and flexed his hand. "My apologies, Nigel. How careless of me. I did not intend to intrude on your Aura."

"What?" Nigel blew on his fingers and glowered at Padwick.

"I did not intend to intrude on your Aura," Padwick repeated loudly.

"I heard you; I just don't understand what you said. What's an Aura? And why did I get a shock from you?"

Padwick composed himself. "An Aura is a Magic. The Magic of the Soul."

"A Magic," repeated Nigel.

"Yes. You received a shock from me because I was unprepared for physical contact. Our Auras met in a brief, insubstantial *zinahday*."

Nigel sighed. *I am definitely in way over my head here*, he thought.

Padwick felt his fatigue. "You should rest. We can talk more of this tomorrow."

"Tomorrow!" Nigel doffed his lassitude like a cape. "Can't you get me back tonight?"

"Get you back? To your world?"

"Of course, to my world. You can't expect me to stay. I mean …" Nigel grappled with the mind-boggling concept of life on another world and settled for something simpler. "I don't even have my toothbrush."

Snatching up his flask, Nigel swallowed a mouthful of liquor.

"What is a toothbrush?"

Nigel looked askance at Padwick. "It's a very small brush with close-set bristles that humans use to keep their teeth clean."

"You brush your teeth?" Padwick was incredulous.

"Well, what do you do?"

"We rinse our mouths with *carba*. It is a cleanser for the mouth and teeth; it bubbles pleasantly."

This appealed to Nigel. "No dentists?"

"Pardon?"

"People who drill holes in your teeth."

Padwick blanched. "By the Light! You come from a violent world. No, Nigel. We do not have dentists."

"How about lawyers? Politicians? Used-car salesmen?"

Padwick was shaking his head. "As far as I can understand your language, these words have no meaning in Atla."

"And you said something about magic?"

Pleased that Nigel was calmer, Padwick smiled. "Yes. All worlds have Magic."

"I used to think mine did," Nigel confided. "I used to believe I could paint magic. Sometimes I thought I saw the magic in my paintings, but I'd just accidentally switched colors and was using pink instead of green, or purple instead of beige."

Padwick thought a moment. He could recall images from the sudden *zinahday* when his fingers touched Nigel's hand. Vague impressions of a world going mad.

"Ezamiah says all worlds have Magic. It may be asleep, perhaps even dying, but the Magic you painted is still there."

"You think so?"

"Yes. I believe the storm roused the Eras Magic of your world. It must have combined with your Aura and your desire to get out. It would be a potent blend. Indeed, it has catapulted you through space. Is it not exciting?"

"Actually, it's a little nerve-wracking. I was just trying to paint the best seascape I could, hoping it would be displayed. Purchased even. Now, poof! I'm in a world of Magic and good dental hygiene." Nigel took his glasses off and rubbed his eyes. "And no way home; a one way trip."

"One way." Padwick looked thoughtful then his face brightened. "You traveled safely once. I am certain you will again. For now, you are in Atla. Is it so distressing?"

Nigel looked at the blur which was Padwick, replaced his glasses, and thought about his life. It didn't take long.

"You know"—Nigel put the cap on his flask—"now that I think about it, I guess the only thing that's distressing is that it's not distressing. Does that make any sense?"

"Yes. You do not feel the way you think you should feel."

Nigel nodded. "Exactly." He looked around him. "I've always wanted something extraordinary to happen to me. Now's a hell of a time to make a fuss. It's just that, well, I'm not good at anything except art. And even then, only seascapes really. If there's any logic in the universe, someone really goofed up bringing me here."

"You think you were brought here?"

"I don't know. Maybe. I've painted storms before and never gotten farther than my apartment. What do you think?"

"I think you are here because, as you said, you wanted something extraordinary to happen. There is a special magic in the air, my friend. I feel it. Perhaps there will be an adventure." Padwick looked excited then his voice dropped to a whisper. "Or a quest."

"What's the difference?" asked Nigel.

"An adventure is for amusement. A quest has a purpose."

"Well, I can't see what possible purpose I could serve on a quest. All I can do is paint seascapes."

"And travel from one world to another," Padwick said.

"Oh, yeah."

"Whatever your purpose or adventure, Nigel, I will be happy to help you prepare. I am not a teacher, but I can help you learn how to evoke the Eras Magic. I am to meet Ezamiah at the Inn of Sunderland four days from this day. This gives us time to teach you of Magic and Atla."

I gotta be out of my mind, thought Nigel. *I'm certainly out of my element. Quest? Adventure?* Nigel decided he preferred the word adventure. It sounded like the less perilous of the two possibilities.

"What makes you so certain this is my adventure, Padwick?" Nigel asked. "Maybe it's your adventure and I just happened along."

"Perhaps it is an adventure for both of us."

"Sure, why not? Kind of a 'two for one' sort of deal," Nigel said. "Coupon day."

"What is a coupon?"

"A piece of paper that you carry around with you and forget to use."

Tilting his head down, Nigel rubbed the back of his neck and stretched.

"Nigel?"

Nigel looked at Padwick. "What? Oh, sorry, Padwick. What did you say?"

"I said you must accompany me to the Inn of Sunderland. Please."

"Oh. Okay. I don't seem to have anything pressing on my social calendar."

"Excellent. We will start at first light. Now you should rest. Sleep is what you need, not conversation."

Nigel yawned. "You've got that right. I could sleep for a week." He stretched out by the fire.

"I am delighted we will be traveling together," said Padwick. "Company makes a long journey short."

Nigel's eyes closed, opened, closed. "Company," he murmured. "Short."

He thought he heard Padwick talking to himself. Then a soft blanket was draped over him and Nigel snuggled into its warmth, unaware his clothes were dry.

"Sleep well, my new friend," Padwick said.

"Uh-huh." Nigel groped for his glasses, pausing as he caught sight of the moons. What kind of an adventure had he signed up for, he wondered. Hopefully the easy kind.

Nigel stuck his tongue out at the moons. Feeling better, he took his glasses off, and the world became an indistinct shadowland of light and dark

Chapter Two

Nigel rolled over, shutting his eyes tighter against the light. His sleep had been deep and dreamless. He didn't want to wake up yet, but the light was insistent. Nigel reached for his glasses and opened his eyes.

The sky came into focus in a collage of pastel pinks and purples with shades of blue he couldn't name. The colors blended, separated, and mixed again.

Nigel watched, fascinated. As the sky lightened, the colors intensified like pieces of stained glass when the sun shines through them.

It's unearthly, he thought. "Unearthly?"

He sat up fast as he remembered where he was and what had happened.

"Good morning," a cheery voice said from behind him.

Nigel looked around. Padwick sat nearby, his round face beaming, blue eyes twinkling.

"Uh, good morning," Nigel answered. *So, it wasn't a dream,* he thought. *I'm really on another world. Funny. I don't feel afraid or out of place.*

Nigel stretched and stood up. He rolled his shoulders, expecting to feel stiff from sleeping on the ground. "I feel great," he said, surprised.

"Excellent." Padwick held out a piece of bread. "I have a delicious *lassenberry* jam. Do you like *lassenberries*?"

"I don't know. I've never tried them." Nigel eyed the bread, remembering the jolt of electricity the first time Padwick had touched him.

Understanding Nigel's reluctance, Padwick hastened to reassure him. "Have no fear. Touch only the bread."

Nigel stepped forward and cautiously accepted the bread. He took a small bite.

It was thick and soft with a mild nutty flavor. Nigel wolfed it down.

"What are lassenberries?" he asked, brushing the crumbs from his fingers.

Padwick laughed and handed him another slice of bread, this piece covered with a glaze of purple. *"Lassenberries* are the fruit of the *lork* tree," he answered, as if that explained everything.

"Mm, like blueberries only better." Nigel ate more slowly this time, savoring the flavor of the jam. "Delicious, just like you said."

"Would you like more?"

Nigel shook his head. "No, thanks. It's very filling. I'm stuffed. All I need now is a shot of caffeine and I'll be ready for anything. Uh, I don't suppose you have coffee?"

"Coffee," Padwick repeated. "No. I am sorry. I cannot think of an Atlan word for coffee. What is it?"

"It's a drink. Strong, non-alcoholic. Served hot, if you're lucky. I like it with lots of cream and sugar to sweeten the taste. It's kind of bitter."

"Then why do you drink it?"

"Good question. Guess I'm hooked on the caffeine. It perks me up, gets me going."

"Ah, a Prime ingredient this caffeine?"

"Well." Nigel wasn't sure how to answer. "The caffeine is part of the coffee bean; the coffee bean is the prime ingredient. Hey! I have a chocolate bar. It has the best of everything: sugar, cocoa, and caffeine."

He reached for his haversack. "Want to try some?"

Padwick had listened carefully. It was a strange concept: food and drink which tasted bad, but made you feel good.

"Here." Finding his chocolate bar, Nigel broke off a piece and gave it to Padwick. "Try it," he encouraged.

Padwick fingered the strange food, inspecting it closely. He smelled it. He gave it a lick. "How extraordinary. I have never tasted anything like it. Is this a common substance on your planet?"

On your planet, Nigel echoed the words in his head. Here I am, God knows where, describing coffee to an alien and sharing my chocolate bar with him. And it all feels perfectly normal to me.

Admit it, Nessel, he chided himself, *this is more fun than dodging the landlord and wondering if today is the day they turn off your phone.*

"Nigel?"

"What? Oh, yeah. I mean, yes. It's a common substance on Earth."

"That is the name of your planet? Earth?"

"You bet. Third planet from the Sun in the Milky Way."

"Milky Way. What is that?"

"Well, until I was nine I thought it was a chocolate bar, but it's actually the name of our galaxy. Uh, my galaxy."

"Fascinating. You named your galaxy after a bar of chocolate. It must be a very important substance. I will save some for *fairowing*."

Nigel opened his mouth to correct him then shut it again. Why quibble over details? He was never very good at science anyway.

Padwick stood up. "If you are ready, Nigel, we shall begin our journey."

Popping another piece of chocolate into his mouth, Nigel picked up his haversack. It was then he noticed there were no signs of a campfire. The moss was smooth, unscorched; there were no telltale ashes or bits of charred wood.

He glanced about, recalling a blanket just before he fell asleep. Nothing. Padwick wasn't carrying a backpack, either. He just stood there, hands clasped behind his back.

"Where is everything?" asked Nigel.

"Pardon?"

"The blanket, the fire, the … the knife you used to spread jam on the bread. For that matter, where's the bread?"

"Oh. I have all the Prime ingredients packed away in my pockets." Padwick patted a few of the pockets on his jumpsuit.

"What do you mean? What are you talking about?"

"Forgive me," Padwick apologized. "I forget you are unfamiliar with Magic. I shall explain as we walk. Ask me as many questions as you please."

Padwick motioned for Nigel to follow him as he began walking in the direction Nigel had come from the night before.

"We must hurry. Ezamiah said it was important."

Nigel stood for a moment, taking it all in: the sky a haze of colors, the ground a soft carpet of teal, the trees a forest of auburn trunks lifting branches high above his head. He could see the leaves now, a myriad of gold rippling in the occasional breeze.

A horticultural seascape just waiting for me to paint it, thought Nigel. *Maybe later.*

He hurried to catch up with Padwick.

They plunged into the forest. At first, they wound in and about the trees, Nigel cautious and noisy, Padwick sure-footed and quick. A narrow path welcomed them and they followed it. The trees touched infrequently above them, their leaves shaped like long, thin hearts.

Nigel heard faint, birdlike noises and the scuffling of small animals. He was enchanted. He might have walked in appreciative silence if not for his companion.

Padwick loved to talk. Eager to help Nigel feel at ease, Padwick rambled on happily about the land and its people.

Nigel learned that his dark hair and brown eyes were as uncommon as his height. Here, the women were the taller gender, with red hair and green eyes.

The men were fair-haired with blues eyes, usually shorter, too. Although not, Padwick confessed, usually as short as he.

Nigel imagined fierce Amazonian women with flaming hair and steel breastplates. *Very intimidating,* he thought.

"We are heading for the Great Road," Padwick said. "One has only to follow the Road to travel through all seven provinces.

"We are near to where Penkas, the province we are in, becomes Sunderland. By late tomorrow, the forest will thin to grasslands and the valleys will roll into gentle hills like waves that never reach the shore. The air there is tangy and warm and sometimes a strong wind will carry the fragrances of the flowers of Eshref. That is our most southern province.

"I shall draw a map for you when we stop this evening. It will help you orient yourself and ..."

"Stop this evening?" interrupted Nigel. "You mean walk all day? You can't be serious. What about lunch?"

"Are you hungry?"

"No. Not at the moment, but I won't be able to walk all day long without taking a break. I guess Atlans have more stamina than humans."

"Do not concern yourself with fatigue, Nigel. The Eras will sustain you."

"The what?"

"The Eras," Padwick repeated. "The Magic of the Land."

"More magic?"

"Yes. It is strange to me that Magic is not well understood on your Earth. Here it is not only understood, it is our way of life."

"How much magic is there?" asked Nigel. He glanced around, half expecting a magician to step out of the forest and pull a rabbit out of his hat.

"There are four kinds of Magics," Padwick replied. Eras is the Magic of the Land: the energies of the elements of Atla. It is ever changing yet constant.

"Atlans are in harmony with the Eras. The combined emanations of our Auras and the Eras Magic fill the sky with their colors. Even at night, the Magics veil the stars and only the moons can penetrate the cloak."

"And what is an Aura?" Nigel asked. "You mentioned something about that last night."

"Aura is the energy generated by each individual. We call it the Magic of the Soul. I used this Magic to touch your mind last night and learn your language. When I touched your fingers, I knew what you knew, felt what you felt. If you had been prepared, the exchange would have been mutual." Padwick looked embarrassed.

"Atlans do not touch casually or without asking permission. It was very careless of me and I apologize again. The strength of the contact surprised me, as did the strength of your Aura."

"I have an Aura?"

"All beings with souls have Auras. Yours is strong; your thoughts and emotions will be easily sensed until you develop it. I am certain, however, you will achieve harmony with the Eras quickly. Indeed, I suspect you have already established a link."

"I have an Aura." Nigel grinned. "Hey, that's only two kinds of Magic. You said there were four."

"Yes. Siskis and Agenta." Padwick lowered his voice. "Siskis is sometimes called the Dark Magic because it has been the source of great pain on our world. Some Atlans believe Siskis may even be the counterbalance of Agenta. Whatever its true nature, we have learned that Siskis is too dangerous to wield and we shun the Dark Magic.

"We call Agenta the Magic of the Light because it is the source of creativity, inspiration, even life. Only those born to it can wield this Magic properly." Padwick's tone was reverent and Nigel nodded, interested, but distracted.

"Uh, Padwick?"

"Yes?"

"I hope this won't spoil my harmony with the Eras, but I have to take a leak."

This brought Padwick to a halt. "Take a leak?"

"You bet." Stepping off the path, Nigel pushed his way past several bushes, finally stopping behind a large shrub.

"You're right about this Eras Magic," Nigel said over his shoulder. "I really don't feel tired and we've been walking for hours. It's great. If this is an adventure, I think I'm going to like it."

Nigel returned to the path. Padwick was studying him with curiosity.

"Do you do this often?" Padwick inquired.

"Whenever nature calls. Don't you?"

"Only once, at the end of the day."

"That's convenient."

"Yes."

They stood a moment, regarding each other: the tall, dark-haired human and the short, pale Atlan, their differences cloaked by their similarities.

"I keep forgetting you're an alien," said Nigel.

Padwick smiled. "On Atla, Nigel, you are the alien, not I."

"Good point. Okay, I'm ready if you are."

"I am."

Side by side now, they continued their walk. Although Nigel couldn't see the sun through the blend of Magics in the sky, he could feel its warmth and smiled up at where he imagined it to be.

"You know, Padwick, I didn't expect to like it so much."

"Like what?"

Nigel waved a hand around him. "This. Being on a strange world. Heading into the unknown. I'm hardly brave and dashing. I expected to feel nervous and uncomfortable."

"And you do not."

"Not at the moment. I'm having a good time. I'm not even homesick." Nigel lapsed into reflective silence.

"You expected to be sick for home?" Padwick asked, concerned.

"Yeah. But I'm not. I guess I don't have a home to feel sick for."

"What have you left behind?"

"Not much really. A few acquaintances. A couple of unpaid bills. A lot of art critics. I didn't realize it last night, but I don't have anything to go back to."

"This does not make you sad." It was a statement.

Nigel thought before answering. "No. Not at the moment." Nigel looked around him at the strange trees that didn't seem strange in the daylight, just different.

"Hey, Padwick, I meant to ask you. What's a *zinahday*?"

"*Zinahday*," Padwick emphasized the first syllable and Nigel repeated the word.

"It is the connection between Magics," explained Padwick. "A fusion of thoughts and energies. When we touched accidentally, I received an impression of you and your world. The images were vague and fleeting, but I remember your Gift."

"My gift? What gift?"

"The Gift of Colors. What is your word for it? Artist."

"Well, I appreciate the compliment, Padwick. Believe me, I really do. But it's hardly a gift. More like a talent for being unemployed.

"I suppose if I'd worked harder at form and structure I could have managed to make a living doing landscapes, painting pictures of cottages with ponds and ducks, that sort of thing. But I kept going back to the seashore and painting the ocean. Tide in, tide out, it didn't matter. I was always trying to capture the way the waves touched the horizon and the surface reflected the sky. It mesmerized me: all that motion, all that power and beauty. Sometimes the sky would look like the ocean and the clouds were the whitecaps."

Nigel looked up at the tree tops, imagining birds surfing the gold ocean of leaves. *And squirrels,* he thought. *If it has to be a forest, it should have some squirrels.*

Nigel wasn't sure if he liked squirrels, he just liked the saying the word. Squirrels. Sea squirrels. *Was there such a thing? And if there was an aquatic equivalent, what color would it be?*

Nigel realized he was daydreaming about seascapes again. "Sometimes everything looks like an ocean to me." He confided to Padwick. "An ocean of color."

Padwick thought it was a marvelous perception of the world and said so even as he stooped to pick up a blossom that had wafted to the ground in front of him. It was silver and white: a *lanitude*. Setting it gently underneath the tree that had discarded it, he rejoined Nigel. They continued their trek and Padwick continued talking about Atla.

Atlans were sometimes born with Gifts. If a gift was constant and natural, then it was "true" and it was expected to be cultivated and shared. Storytellers had the Gift of Words. They often worked with those who possessed the Gift of Music.

Some Atlans had the Gift of Knowledge. They had long, accurate memories and became teachers and historians.

Atlans with the Gift of Health could soothe any pain and heal any injury. The Gift of Foresight gave a person awareness of the future, but Atlans with that particular Gift were born blind. They could see only their visions.

"Sounds spooky," Nigel commented.

"Spooky?"

"Scary."

"Yes. A difficult Gift to bear. And there is one Gift that is even more difficult. It is so rare that usually only one person is born with it in a lifetime. The Gift of Agenta."

"The Magic?"

"Yes. The one who can wield Agenta is called a Venger. The Gift is the ability to *zinahday* with Atla and channel all Magics through the body, focusing and projecting the combinations. It is a powerful weapon. The Gift of Agenta, if it is true, makes the Venger responsible for the welfare of all Atlans and the protection of Atla.

"My friend, Breegan, is a Venger. She may be with Ezamiah at the Inn of Sunderland. I do not know." Padwick paused for a moment, as if he felt the burden of Breegan's responsibility.

"But your Gift, Nigel, is wondrous. The Gift of Colors, if it is true and deep, is far more than art. It is the ability to pass from one realm of reality to another, to travel from world to world no matter how great the distance, with only the effort of the thought."

"Seems like I've done that last bit already," remarked Nigel.

"Indeed. How fortunate you are. One can excel at many skills and develop one's Aura to great heights, but few are born with a Gift."

"Do you have a Gift, Padwick?" Nigel asked.

"No. I must seek my own destiny, but we Atlans are adventurous people. We live for the joy of life, content in knowing we are all part of the Light and will one day join it entirely."

"What is the Light?"

"I think you would say God. But we do not make the Light a person. It simply is. Invisible and untouchable until we interact with it: expressing love, creating beauty, honoring our noblest ideals while striving to achieve our goals and caring for our world and each other."

For a few minutes Padwick walked along, pointing out various ferns and flowers, unaware that Nigel was no longer beside him.

Nigel had been distracted by a bird swooping among the tree branches. He lingered behind to admire the sky. Framed by the leaves of the trees, the colors swirled overhead, deepening in hue even as he watched.

It must be getting close to sunset, thought Nigel. "I've walked all day."

There was a scrambling in some foliage at the sound of his voice. Nigel froze.

A small, furry face poked its head around a shrub and gazed at him, wide-eyed.

Nigel returned the stare.

The creature was a pale lavender in color. Its eyes, framed by white patches, were a rich amber. It inched forward, hesitated, and then hopped suddenly into the middle of the trail.

"It's a rabbit!"

The rabbit thumped a hind foot and bounded off the trail into the forest.

"A purple rabbit," Nigel marveled.

Noticing his companion was missing, Padwick hurriedly retraced his steps. "Is anything wrong?" Padwick asked.

"I just saw a purple rabbit," said Nigel. "Lavender, actually. Nice hue. A big, floppy-eared, lavender rabbit. Hopped right by me." Nigel pointed to the forest.

"Indeed," said Padwick. "I have always liked the pink ones myself."

"You have pink rabbits, too?"

"Yes. What colors are the rabbits on your world?"

"Oh, white, brown, black. Nothing quite as startling as pink or purple."

Nigel rubbed the back of his neck, feeling tired at last.

Sensing it, Padwick suggested they stop for the day. "And I will draw a map of Atla for you, but we will have to begin at first light tomorrow."

"At first light?" Nigel shrugged. What the hell. He sometimes got up that early to paint the sea at sunrise. He didn't like the hour, but he loved the colors. "Okay."

They left the path at the spot where the rabbit had appeared and walked through the forest for a few minutes until they came to a small glade.

"This will do nicely," Padwick decided. "We will rest here." He sat down with his back against a tree and made himself comfortable.

"Don't we have to set up camp?"

"What strange phrases your language has. Perhaps you could explain?"

"Pitch a tent, gather firewood." Nigel sat down next to Padwick and pulled his haversack off his shoulder. "You tell me. I've never camped out before. Besides, you're the guy who said he had all the ingredients."

"Oh, yes. I have Prime ingredients for almost everything. I like to travel about Atla and I try to be prepared for whatever the need might be. That reminds me, I said I would draw you a map."

Padwick reached into a narrow pocket and pulled out a small feather. From another pocket, he produced a tiny square of paper. Holding one item in each hand, palm up, he focused his attention on them.

"*Tessa, katra, nook,*" he said slowly. The feather and paper disappeared into a cream-colored mist for a moment then reappeared.

"What the hell?" Nigel whispered.

In one hand, Padwick now held a quill pen and in the other hand, a scroll of paper.

"I forgot the ink," Padwick said and felt about in his pockets. "Ah! Here it is."

He drew forth a minuscule jar. Holding it in his right hand, he repeated the incantation. Mist obscured the jar and then Padwick was holding a larger jar filled with a beige, oily liquid.

"Now that," Nigel said with admiration, "is what I call a Gift."

Padwick shook his head. "It is not a Gift. It is only an interaction of Magics. It can be difficult to get the amount correct. I am improving. Shall I explain?"

"Please." Nigel leaned forward.

"It is called *fairowing*, and there are many levels of it. You focus the Magic of your Aura on a single thought, and then project that energy into the object you wish to *fairow*. The Eras in that object responds to your Aura, the Magics combine, and you have whatever it is you were concentrating on. It is simple."

"For you, sure."

"Perhaps I could explain better by example. Let me think." He foraged in his pockets again and brought forth a tiny piece of cloth.

"Now," said Padwick, "I focus my Aura on the cloth. It will be cool tonight and I want it to be a blanket. I now project my Aura into the cloth. It combines with the Eras already there, for the cloth is from the land. I then evoke the metamorphosis with the incantation: *tessa, katra, nook*." The cloth became transparent and seemed to get a little bigger.

"I am not concentrating," Padwick said. He gave the cloth his complete attention. It disappeared into a mist and Padwick's arms were full with a large, fluffy pink blanket.

"I did not intend it to be so big," he told Nigel. "It is a good example, however, of what can happen when you do not focus your Aura properly. You must concentrate."

"Right. Got it. Concentrate." Nigel smiled. "It's kind of like an art project," he said.

"Yes." Padwick set the blanket aside. "When my Aura is more advanced I will no longer need the incantation. I will even be able to *fairow* items that have only a trace of Eras in them, but such advancement takes time and practice.

"We are taught to focus our Aura when we are very young. The first two things we learn to *fairow* are water and fire. That is because they require only a little energy and effort. You have only to say their Key Word with feeling. Look there."

Padwick pointed a finger at a spot three feet in front of them. *"Kesla!"*

Fire sprang into existence. A small, neat circle of flames blazed brightly in the center of the darkening glade, neither burning the ground nor expelling smoke.

"Fantastic! But you didn't have anything to start with. No Prime ingredient?"

"Correct. A Prime ingredient is a portion of whatever you wish to *fairow*. It is not necessary for fire and water because they are elements of Eras."

"Eras. The Magic of the Land," said Nigel, catching on.

"Precisely."

"But doesn't the Eras eventually wear out?"

"Oh, no. What we take from the Eras, we also return. *Rion!*"

The fire snapped out of existence.

"It has returned to the Eras. *Kesla!*"

Flames danced before them once again.

"It has been given back. We are in harmony with our environment. Only one tree was felled to make the paper I carry. In its place, another was immediately planted."

"I'm impressed," Nigel said. "Do you think I could learn to do magic?"

"I do. Your Gift allows you to easily interact with Eras Magic. Try to *fairow* water; it is the simplest. The Key Word for it is *alaies*."

"Alaies," Nigel repeated, accenting the second syllable.

"Correct. Now clear your mind. Focus your thoughts on a pool of water. A small pool of water. Picture it in your mind. Water."

Nigel visualized a small pool of water in the center of the glade. *"Alaies!"*

Nothing happened.

"Try again," Padwick encouraged. "Feel the flow of energy from the Eras to your Aura, from your Aura to the Eras. A continuous flow of energy. Feel it. Focus it."

Nigel stared hard at the center of the glade. His eyes bored into the teal moss. *A pool*, thought Nigel, concentrating. *A pool of water.*

He felt a sudden rush go through him. *"Alaies!"*

A small puddle appeared.

"You did it, Nigel!"

Astonished, Nigel leapt up and ran over to the puddle. He knelt beside it. Hesitant, afraid it might disappear, he reached out to touch it. His hand sank into the cool water.

"I did it," he whispered.

Fascinated, Nigel clenched the mud beneath his hand. He pulled it free of the puddle and watched it slide through his fingers, hardly hearing Padwick encouraging him to try again.

It was too fantastic. There was magic literally at his finger tips. It was almost better than painting. Almost.

***

In the Province of Eshref, Ezamiah stood by a Well of Thoughts. "He has arrived, Breegan. I had hoped to meet him first, but I did not know where he would materialize. Young Padwick is with him. I will join them at the Inn of Sunderland."

"Be wary of the Seers." Breegan's voice drifted through the Magics of the Well.

"Yes." Ezamiah turned away. "There is great trouble ahead." He took a deep breath. "I shall present your quest to Padwick as an adventure. Perhaps all will go better than we expect."

"I will meet you at the Hall of Doors," Breegan said, her voice fading. "Be wary, Ezamiah, and bring me the Key."

Her voice disappeared.

Ezamiah left the Well of Thoughts and looked up at the moons. "It has begun."

Chapter Three

Nigel lounged in a large chair, his feet stretched out to a fireplace. He held a glass of *chessit*, a warm, amber liquid which relaxed and revitalized. In a chair beside him, Padwick dozed.

They had arrived at the Inn of Sunderland just after midnight. Henna, the Keeper of the Inn, had spoken to Padwick in the soft, melodic tones of the Atlan language: the Venger, Breegan was not at the Inn. Ezamiah would arrive at dawn.

Nigel felt ambivalent about meeting Ezamiah. Padwick talked about him with such deference that Nigel was picturing a cross between a priest and a drill sergeant. *Kind of unnerving,* he thought.

He swirled the *chessit* in his glass. It had been four days since he'd been thrust into this world of purple rabbits, magic words, and multicolored skies.

Padwick was excited. Nigel was interested. He had always hoped the magic he saw when he painted existed somewhere. He just never expected to be part of it..

Strange how he seemed to fit in so easily, like a piece of a puzzle. He was beginning to feel he was meant to be in Atla, something Padwick took for granted.

Nigel glanced over at his snoring friend. Friend. He liked the word. He'd never had a friend before. Oh, a few people to greet in passing, the odd one who might join him for a beer. But not a friend. Not someone to, well, join him for an adventure.

Padwick mumbled in his sleep and Nigel tried to think quietly.

Think quietly! What a ridiculous concept that would have been four days ago. Now it made perfect sense.

Padwick had explained that because Nigel's Aura was strong and undeveloped, his emotions, and occasionally his thoughts, could be sensed by anyone near him. Nigel had to learn to "think quietly, feel gently."

He felt self-conscious at first. Having just learned he had an Aura, a psychic faculty all Atlans took for granted, Nigel resented having to look after it. He had to learn how to control the Magic and "use it well and responsibly." It was fun, but it was hard work, too. Like a toy that had to be assembled.

Once or twice, he felt resentful of the entire escapade, particularly when he was hungry. After a long day of walking and listening, Nigel had to stifle his annoyance when Padwick still wanted him to practice his new skills.

There was so much to learn, so much to remember. It was like summer camp; you knew you could have a good time if they would only allow it.

Nigel grudgingly admitted to himself that all the work was worth it. He thought back to the night he had learned to *fairow* water. He had actually created water out of thin air, no mirrors, no hats with false bottoms or coats with long sleeves. It hadn't been a trick. It had been a reality.

Nigel smiled. In his exuberance at *fairowing* water he had attempted a waterfall so he could shower, inadvertently dousing Padwick in the process.

Padwick had taken it in good humor, but suggested Nigel concentrate on making the puddle larger. Then he could bathe.

It had been a struggle. First, Nigel hadn't been able to get his puddle wide enough and then it took a great deal of concentration to lengthen it.

Finally achieving a pool of a respectable size, Nigel had stripped and stepped into the cool water. It just covered his ankles. Frustrated, he had turned to ask Padwick for help and found the Atlan staring at him in surprise.

Male Atlans did not have nipples. Or chest hair. Atlans had hair on their heads. They had eyebrows and eyelashes. According to Padwick, the only creature on Atla with body hair similar to Nigel's was a Huki, a small, thin rodent that climbed trees.

Recalling his embarrassment, Nigel rubbed the stubble on his unshaved face. Atlans didn't grow beards. The physical distinctions between Atlans and humans were so inconspicuous that when they were noticed they never failed to startle.

Equally startling was Padwick's map. Exquisitely drawn, it showed a single land mass equivalent to the size of Russia, Europe, and Asia. It had hundreds of rivers and lakes and one inland sea. In the far southeast corner of the map was a single island, about the size of New Zealand.

"You've marked the continent with the same name as your world," Nigel objected.

"Atla is both. This continent is our world. Our world is this continent."

"What about the island? What's it called?"

Padwick hesitated. "Karn," he said.

For the first time in their brief acquaintance, Padwick was taciturn. Nigel changed the subject. "Why aren't there any borders?"

"What are borders?"

Nigel thought of customs line-ups, airport security, passports, inoculations. Atlans wouldn't trouble themselves or each other with such nonsense. They were simpler in a way that surpassed any standard of civilization.

"How do you know when you leave one province and enter another?" Nigel asked.

"Ah, the climate changes," said Padwick. "See here?" He pointed at the Province of Hardisty, a place of mountains and plains southwest of Penkas.

"Gradually the mountains diminish, the plains become bare, the temperature increases. Then the sands begin and one knows one is in Jeraj."

Jeraj, Nigel remembered, the province of deserts and oases. That was where Breegan's *deshuba* was from, Padwick had told him.

A *deshuba* was a fiancée, someone who was to be a soul mate in every sense of the word. Atlans were monogamous. When they chose a husband or a wife, they made a special *zinahday* called a Pledge. It bound them together literally heart and soul, making them each other's *casielle*. If a Pledge *zinahday* was broken, for any reason, it could never be restored or made again.

Padwick's friend, the Venger, Breegan, could never be her *deshuba's casielle* because of her responsibilities to Atla.

"So, she can't get married?" Nigel had asked.

"She is bound to Atla in an unbreakable *zinahday*. Ezamiah feared a Pledge *zinahday* could interfere with it. He forbade her to make the Pledge with Judson. She must think of Atla and its people first, before her own happiness. Breegan and Judson are together in body only. It makes her very sad." Padwick, too, was sad as he explained.

"Yeah." Nigel nodded his head in sympathy. "I guess it would. Is Ezamiah her father or what? Why does he get to call all the shots?" Nigel held up his hand before Padwick could ask him to clarify the expression.

"What I mean is, why does Ezamiah get to tell Breegan what to do with her life?"

"It is not her life, Nigel," said Padwick, "it is Atla's. Ezamiah was once Breegan's tutor, now he is her counselor. He reminds Breegan of her duties. He ensures she is physically well. He guides her through the many demands of her status as Venger.

"I think that is why she likes to live in Jeraj instead of her home province of Biachin. She told me once she felt so cold inside that she needed always to be warm on the outside."

Biachin. That was the northern province. A bit like Alaska, according to Padwick's description. He had also mentioned that Atlans, unlike Nigel, had only one name and that it always began with the letter of their native province.

Having always felt cursed with his name, Nigel liked that custom very much. He checked the map, but there wasn't a province beginning with 'N'.

"A name that is so unique," Padwick reassured him, "is considered to be very special. It is rarely given and is honored by all."

Nigel only nodded. He didn't mention he had a middle name, too.

On their third day of traveling, they had reached the Great Road. On the map, it was a long diamond, its top point in Biachin, its bottom point in Eshref, the southern province. Hardisty was its western tip and Sunderland its eastern. Nigel had imagined a rough dirt trail.

When he finally saw it, Nigel had stopped, awed. Flawlessly smooth, the Great Road ran as straight as Padwick had drawn it. It was cool to the touch, silvery gray, and cast a faint glow at night.

It was, Nigel had thought, designed to be in harmony with its environment. Their pace increased.

Late that night, the trees along the road flickered with turquoise lights as Padwick and Nigel approached the Inn. Padwick had said every province had an inn: a place to rest, socialize, even to live.

The Inn of Sunderland had tall columns and long, graceful lines. Each amethyst-colored stone was set perfectly, one against the other, giving a seamless appearance as if it were carved from ice.

Inside, tapestries hung from the walls depicting whimsical and historical scenes. Soft rugs were centerpieces for clusters of chairs and tables. Every item Nigel cast his eyes upon was exquisitely carved, woven, or cut.

Padwick had told him some Atlans preferred to work with their hands and still used the ancient ways of design and craftsmanship.

Nigel drained the last of the *chessit* from his glass. *Remarkable people,* he thought.

"Thank you," a deep voice said behind him.

Nigel jumped. He peered around the corner of his chair. A tall, slender figure swathed in a long cloak and hood stood behind him.

"Uh, hi. You wouldn't be Ezamiah by any chance, would you?"

"I am Ezamiah. And you, Nigel Nessel, must not think so loudly until you have further disciplined your Aura. Already I have gleaned knowledge of your language from the thoughts I overheard. Tell me, have you mastered fire and water?"

"Well, I seem to have gotten the hang of water, uh, sir, but I haven't managed fire yet."

"You will. But not today. Today we fly to the Isle. To the Hall of Doors. Even now we are late and Breegan is waiting for us."

"Padwick!"

Padwick woke with a start.

"Yes? Pardon? Oh! Ezamiah." Padwick stood up quickly and bowed his head.

"Good day to you, Padwick. Are you prepared to assist Breegan in every way you are able?"

"Yes, Ezamiah. It will be my honor. I have all my Prime ingredients ready. I am prepared." He nodded in Nigel's direction. "And Nigel, too, is prepared. I think. He has been practicing fairowing each day since we met and learning of Atla and our ways."

"You have been his teacher?"

Padwick looked abashed. "Yes, Ezamiah."

"He is fortunate."

"Thank you." Padwick's smile illuminated the room.

"Excuse me," Nigel said, "but just exactly what are we supposed to be ready for?"

Ezamiah was imposing, true, but Nigel felt he ought to get a few things straight before they got out of hand. Like, just what the hell was going on?

"I will tell you as we fly. Come." Ezamiah turned and strode out of the inn.

"Come along." Padwick motioned to Nigel. "He does not like to wait."

Nigel's questions were squelched as the word "fly" sunk in.

"Fly?" Nigel repeated, worried.

He scooped up his haversack and followed Padwick outside and into the pale colors of dawn. As they walked down the steps, Nigel saw three large creatures in the courtyard. They looked familiar somehow.

The creatures stood ten feet tall with small heads perched atop long, slender necks; short legs and wide webbed feet supported splendid, ivory white plumage.

"They're swans!" Nigel took a step back in surprise.

"I wondered how you managed to travel so quickly, Ezamiah," Padwick said. He turned to Nigel.

"They are from the Emerald Sea. It is a great privilege to ride one."

"Ride one?" Nigel's voice cracked.

Ezamiah came up to Nigel. He pulled his hood back. Hair as pale as his skin framed a long, gentle face. Deep-set sapphire eyes riveted Nigel's attention. They were old eyes; they held hope, sorrow, and great wisdom.

Nigel stood still, waiting.

"Nigel"—Ezamiah's deep voice was soothing—"we will ride these birds to the Isle. Have no fear. You will not fall. Padwick and I will flank you, and you will be able to talk and to hear us. You will not be afraid."

"I won't?" Nigel felt calmer, but when he looked away from Ezamiah's gaze and sized up the swans, he grabbed onto the first excuse that came to mind.

"I can't fly. I have to hold my haversack." He held it up.

"It has my paints in it," he continued. "I can't leave it behind. It's very important to me. Really." Nigel fidgeted as he spoke, feeling very human and vulnerable.

Ezamiah smiled, as if he watched a child telling a story so as not to get in trouble. "It is important," he said. "Hold it up before me."

Nigel did as he was told.

Ezamiah raised his right arm above his head then brought it down in a sweeping motion. "*Aliov!*"

Nigel's haversack was now the size of his wallet.

"Why couldn't we do that?" Nigel asked Padwick. He recalled when Padwick had tried to create the same metamorphosis the day before and, upon failing, suggested there wasn't enough Eras in the bag.

This had been particularly disappointing, as Padwick had been trying to *fairow* the piece of chocolate Nigel had given him and Nigel was hoping he could then *fairow* the last of his Southern Comfort.

"My Aura is not as advanced as Ezamiah's," Padwick said now.

"Keep it safe in your pocket," Ezamiah commanded. "You will have need of it later."

He turned and hoisted himself up on a swan's back. Padwick did the same, nestling in among the feathers and placing his hands upon the shoulders of the bird.

Nigel took a deep breath. He walked over to his swan.

"Hi, there!"

The bird looked at Nigel, fluffed its feathers, and then settled itself on the ground.

Nigel got the impression that the bird had formed a quick and unflattering opinion of him. He reached gingerly for the bird's neck and, when it did not protest, swung a leg onto its back.

The swan stood up. Nigel clung frantically to it, trying to arrange himself as he had seen Ezamiah and Padwick do.

"Let us be off," said Ezamiah.

"No! Wait! I'm not ready!" Nigel panicked. The swan rose up and beat its wings. There was a sudden lurch and a sickening swinging motion as the bird took flight.

Nigel squeezed his eyes shut, clinging with all his strength. Cool air blew in his face and he became aware of a soft, swishing sound: the beat of the swan's wings.

It's okay, Nessel, he told himself. Nigel opened his eyes. He looked down. The land was hundreds of feet below him. His stomach churned.

"Nigel?" It was Padwick.

"What?" Nigel managed to choke out, not daring to look over in Padwick's general direction.

"Are you ill?"

"No, no. I'm fine. Really. I'll be okay. I've just never flown before. I mean, I've flown. Once. But it was on an airplane. Sure it was coach, but at least it had a floor."

"Nigel." Ezamiah's deep voice floated across the air. "Calm your emotions. Allow yourself to enjoy this experience. I cannot tell you what you need to know when your Aura is tense and restricted."

Nigel took a deep breath. A feather tickled his nose. He sneezed.

"That is better," Padwick encouraged him. "Deep breaths clear the mind. You do want to know what is expected of us, do you not?"

Nigel nodded, concentrating on breathing. Breathe in, count two, breathe out, count two. He shifted his weight slightly. Nothing terrible happened; he didn't plummet to the ground, and the swan didn't break a wing.

"Wow," Nigel breathed out. "I'm really doing this. I'm riding a giant swan hundreds of feet above the nearest land."

"You are a born adventurer," praised Padwick.

"Indeed," Ezamiah said. "Now, listen. You have traveled far; you have further still to go. To be successful in the future, you must have knowledge of the past. Ezamiah took a deep breath. He flew his bird closer to Nigel, leaned over and touched the back of Nigel's right hand with his forefinger.

Nigel flinched, but felt no pain, only a stillness, an expectant calm.

"Look at me," Ezamiah commanded.

Nigel looked at Ezamiah. The blue eyes seemed larger, deeper and he felt drawn into them, surrounded by their color: sapphire blue, endless blue, deeper than the deepest ocean.

Hear me, Nigel. Ezamiah's voice was in Nigel's head. *Watch with me and learn.*

Nigel blinked rapidly. He had the feeling he was passing through curtains of time: days, years, centuries. The impression faded and a landscape solidified: green grass, tall trees with heart-shaped leaves tickling multicolored skies. Atla.

Nigel saw two children, a boy and a girl, both with black hair and dark eyes. They were playing together and yet they were fighting, too.

Through Ezamiah's *zinahday*, Nigel knew they were twins, brother and sister. And they were not playing, they were practicing. Practicing their Magics. The brother was losing.

"I win, Fahgerdahl!" shouted the girl as she stabbed at the air in front of her. From the tip of her index finger, a thin beam of purple light shot at her brother.

"Only for now, Fahdra," said her brother.

Fahdra and Fahgerdahl, thought Nigel. *Unique names because they were special people*; Nigel remembered Padwick's teaching. They were to be honored.

Attention, Nigel, said Ezamiah's voice. *Look and learn.*

Nigel saw the boy's face. It was angry. It even looked dangerous. He felt something was very wrong with the boy.

The curtains of time moved forward and the siblings were older, perhaps grown. They were arguing, but Nigel could not hear their words. The brother, Fahgerdahl, touched his sister's shoulder and she flinched. A moment later, someone came to take him away.

Where? Nigel wondered.

He saw the fields and inns of Atla grow smaller; a green ocean stretched before him and then a new landscape appeared. It was an island, small and dark. Barren and cold. Karn.

Nigel shivered. He saw Fahgerdahl walk beside an older man. A tutor. But Fahgerdahl was not listening. Nigel could see it in his face: the black eyes were remote, the features impassive.

What happened to Fahdra? Nigel asked in his mind.

Like a picture being developed, he saw a young woman laughing and dancing. No. She was practicing Magic. Her movements were deliberate, and purple light often shone from her hair like fireworks. Her tutor was pleased. It was Ezamiah.

Before Nigel could speak, the scene changed. It was dawn. Fahdra was standing before a council of Atlan Elders. She was about to *zinahday* with the Eras Magic of their world.

Then he saw Fahgerdahl.

Tall and confident, exuding power. Pale skin, black eyes, and alone. Fahgerdahl strode to where his sister stood, arms ready to embrace him, and he smiled. A smile bereft of light and love. A smile so sinister it paled the moons.

He challenged Fahdra to a duel.

No, thought Nigel, not understanding his concern. He was experiencing history. Why was he afraid?

Fahdra was speaking. She was accepting the challenge. It would be a duel to the death. A duel for the right to *zinahday* with Atla's Eras Magic.

The picture broke apart like a kaleidoscope. Nigel jerked back to the present. He was gripping the shoulders of his swan and holding his breath.

"I will speak now," said Ezamiah. "You are caught in the story and are unaccustomed to the intensity of Atlan emotions."

"I'm sorry," said Nigel. "I'm trying."

"I know. Now, listen. The two Vengers dueled and the moment Fahgerdahl struck his first blow it was obvious why he was so confident."

"Why obvious?"

"His Magic was colored with Siskis: blue instead of purple. Somehow, while on Karn, Fahgerdahl had sought out the Siskis Magic and learned to manipulate it. Perhaps he killed his tutor as a test of his power. We watched, helpless, as he attacked his sister.

"Fahdra had not yet made the *zinahday* with Atla. She could not draw upon the Eras of the land and had only her Agenta Magic to parry Fahgerdahl's blows.

"Fahgerdahl tore at her with the Siskis. Striking Fahdra again and again, battering her until she faltered then fell. He was ruthless. His power seemed unending. At dawn, Fahgerdahl overpowered Fahdra's defense. She perished."

Ezamiah bowed his head for a moment, then continued. "Fahgerdahl turned in triumph to face the people, ready to attempt the *zinahday*. I think he expected praise, even adulation. But we felt only anger and revulsion.

"The people surged together. Projecting their Auras into the land, they created a vast wall of fire to prevent Fahgerdahl from consummating his Siskis Magic with the Eras.

"Fahgerdahl repelled the fire briefly, but he was weakened from his battle. In fear, he fled from us. Careful, but determined, several of us tracked him. To our horror, his trail led to the Hall of Doors."

"And he escaped and that is why we dare no longer use the Hall," Padwick broke in, too excited to remain silent.

"Padwick." Ezamiah's voice was patient. "Be still."

"Yes, Ezamiah."

"The Hall of Doors, Nigel," explained Ezamiah, "is a bridge between Atla and all other worlds. It is a citadel wherein we have harnessed an elusive combination of Magics, creating spells and fashioning enchantments to hold the Magics in place forever.

"Fahgerdahl escaped through one of the doors in the Hall. By the time we arrived, the trail was cold and none could discern which door he had used.

"We had much to fear now. For, while we had prevented Fahgerdahl from creating a *zinahday* with Atla, who would stop him from doing so with another world? If he could lay claim to Eras Magic, he would be invincible. Our only solace was that he had traveled alone and could not, therefore, return."

Nigel risked a glance down, forgetting he was hundreds of feet in the air. Through wisps of clouds, he saw waves of bottle green: Atla's ocean. Feeling dizzy, Nigel looked at Ezamiah again.

"Why can't Fahgerdahl return alone?" asked Nigel.

"Few can travel from world to world alone and unassisted as you have, Nigel. Atlans have ever had to travel in threes, balancing the Magics of the doors with the Magics and Gifts of the trio.

"Many times in the past we have tried to imprint a talisman with the energies and Magics of a successful journey. If we could do so, we could *fairow* it a thousand times and then any one of us might travel alone and return safely.

"But none have yet had a Gift true enough for such a spell to take. Until you."

"Me?" Nigel didn't like the implications of this. "Hey, I came here by accident."

"Do you think so still, Nigel Nessel? Have you not yet realized that your name is one of honor? Your ancestors, Nigel, were Atlans."

"What? How? You said you couldn't use your special hall."

"Long before the coming of Fahgerdahl, three of our people journeyed to your world using the Hall of Doors. They found beauty and happiness there and they never returned to Atla. The Seers often saw their descendants in visions. Great artists, musicians, adventurers all. As are you."

"Me? I'm not an adventurer. I'm just a seascape artist. I'm completely unqualified for heroic duties. No offense, but I think you've made a mistake."

"Your lineage is in your eyes, Nigel, your name, the very core of your being. All Atlans have a love for the ocean, whether it is the ocean of Atla or the ocean between worlds."

"Unbelievable," Nigel muttered.

Ezamiah raised his hand for silence. "Yours is the truest Gift in many years, Nigel. Not since Breegan has anyone held such a concentration of potential Magic. You may believe me or not as you choose, but your Gift is essential to our endeavor. Keep your doubts inside you, do not let them surface. They will only hinder you and your companions."

"What companions?" Nigel felt like he was being drafted.

Ezamiah did not answer. They were nearing their destination and he had more to tell. "And now to your task," he said. "Fahgerdahl has been a peril so great that we have forbidden the use of our Hall of Doors, waiting for a new Venger to create a *zinahday* with Atla."

"That is Breegan," Padwick said to Nigel.

"A new Venger," Ezamiah repeated, "who can challenge Fahgerdahl and destroy him.

"We realized too late, all those many years ago, that Fahgerdahl had no soul. Bent and twisted inside, he had siphoned his sister's Aura like a leech. We believe he did the same with the Aura of his tutor.

"The false Aura Magic allowed him to use the Siskis. Without a soul of his own, however, Fahgerdahl could not sustain the connection. He could not maintain his power."

"If he's powerless, then what's the big deal?" asked Nigel. "Why are we afraid?" *Why am I afraid?*

"Because somehow Fahgerdahl has manipulated the Siskis Magic and is using it as a surrogate for the absence of his Aura Magic. The Siskis is now both an anchor and a catalyst. Even as we speak, Fahgerdahl is draining the Eras Magic from another world. When he is done, he will have the power to return to Atla. In his anger and his vengeance, he will destroy us."

"Isn't he a little too old to be fighting duels?"

"The Siskis Magic has sustained him in his Prime," Ezamiah answered.

"Oh, great. So, what's the plan?"

"You must seek him out and annihilate him."

"What?"

"Padwick is the Tool, Breegan is the Weapon, and you, Nigel Nessel, are the Key."

Chapter Four

Breegan looked across the field at the Hall of Doors. She had no wish to leave her home. Even here, on the Isle of the Hall, she could be content. Breegan watched as green waves capped with foam rushed against the beach of the tiny island. The Hall of Doors was the only structure here. It stood alone against the prismatic sky, surrounded by turquoise grass and white flowers that stopped abruptly at the narrow beach.

And yet it is not alone, thought Breegan. *Like me, it is connected to everything.*

Not for the first time in her life, she wished she did not have the Gift of Agenta.

As a child, it had prevented her from joining other children when they played games. Her ability to channel the Magics of others was instinctive and Breegan's Aura Magic was too strong for the other children to tolerate her presence for more than an afternoon. Breegan had to spend her time learning not just how to use her Magics, but how to control them.

When she grew older, the Council sent an examiner to assess the trueness of her Gift. They needed to determine if Breegan had the potential to achieve a *zinahday* with Atla. If she did, Breegan would have to be properly instructed and closely supervised.

To her dismay, it was determined Breegan was a born Venger. A tutor was assigned to help her purify and perfect her Gift: Ezamiah.

At sixteen, Breegan's life was no longer her own. Long days of teaching and tests were followed by late nights of study and practice. Learning to wield the Magic of Agenta demanded all of her time and attention.

Breegan was close to her Prime when the Council contemplated changing her name. She resisted, arguing that her Gift had not been tested enough. Breegan insisted she first prove her strength and establish the *zinahday* with Atla before accepting such an honor as a special name.

Secretly, Breegan wanted to keep her birth name. She wanted that small part of herself to remain when she was bound to Atla forever, without the solace of a soul mate.

Ezamiah had been immovable on that issue, but he had agreed to let Breegan keep her birth name. He believed retaining a small portion of her own identity would add to Breegan's strength and, therefore, the strength of Atla. He assured the Council that Breegan would remain loyal to her duty as Atla's protector.

And I remained loyal, Breegan insisted to herself. *I made the zinahday with Atla and survived. I was strong enough. But now? Will I still be strong enough now? Will I find what I seek and fear? Will I be triumphant?*

Breegan had knelt beside a Well of Thoughts in Jeraj, part of a *zinahday* with Ezamiah and the Seer, Dalyse as they stood at a Well in Hardisty.

"What do you see as my challenge, this time, Dalyse?" Breegan said carefully.

"You must fulfill your duty as a Venger and protect Atla. You must destroy Fahgerdahl, thus keeping the Siskis imprisoned in Karn."

"How will I accomplish such a feat?" Breegan asked, already knowing the answer, but feigning ignorance and using her Agenta Magic to protect her mind from the Seer.

"No doubt the combinations of Magics aroused by Fahgerdahl will aid you," Dalyse answered. She separated from the zinahday.

"No doubt," Breegan scoffed. She focused on Ezamiah. "I will need a Tool, Ezamiah."

"I will find you one, Breegan. Be strong. You are a Venger. Prepare!"

And what have I done instead? By the Light! Breegan clenched her hands into fists. *What have I done?*

She straightened her shoulders. *Enough! I have done what I had to do, for the sake of my own sanity and my strength.*

"And here I am," Breegan murmured.

"And here am I." A warm voice wrapped around Breegan.

Breegan turned to her soul mate, Judson. He had refused to stay at their home in Jeraj. "You need me near," he insisted.

"You cannot follow where this task will take me," said Breegan.

"I know," Judson answered, "but we have made the Pledge. Our Auras are one now. My heart follows yours, remember?"

Breegan smiled. "My heart follows yours."

"And if your heart should stop, mine will beat for you."

Breegan reached out to brush a strand of hair from his forehead and Judson caught her hand, kissing its palm. Their Auras intermingled. She felt what he felt. He knew what she knew. They kissed.

"I want you," Breegan whispered. "I need you. I love you. Share yourself with me."

Judson drew her down to the grass. "I will."

An anguished gentleness and desperate fierceness permeated the couple. Since they had made the Pledge, creating a permanent *zinahday* between them, they had never been apart. Now they did not know if they would ever be together again.

The colors in the sky faded and Atla's two moons became visible. Breegan slid from Judson's embrace and began to dress. In her mind, she could still feel his arms about her body, warm, loving. Concerned.

Concerned? Breegan looked up, sensing another presence.

"Someone is coming," she said, her voice somber. *It is beginning,* she thought.

Dressing, Judson followed Breegan's gaze. "Ezamiah?"

"Yes. And Padwick." She paused, concentrating. "And someone else, as well. Someone with a great Gift. I sense it in his Aura. Come."

Together, the two crossed the field to wait at the steps of the Hall. White feathers fluttered down upon them followed by a cry of dismay. Overhead, three elegant birds circled. Two descended gracefully. The third seemed hampered by its rider, who was clutching its neck and cursing loudly. The bird landed and shook its rider loose with a disdainful flourish.

"Ow!" Nigel landed with a thump.

Ezamiah dismounted. He patted the bird he had ridden.

"You did well, Nigel," Ezamiah congratulated him.

"I did? Thank you." Nigel glared at his swan. "It was my first bird ride."

His bird called to its companions and Nigel imagined it was complaining about him. Mouths full of flowers, the other two stretched and flapped their wings. A few seconds later, the trio took off, heading south for Eshref.

Padwick waved to them as they flew away. "Are they not beautiful?" he asked Nigel.

Nigel swatted at the feathers covering his jeans. "Oh, yeah," he answered, not looking up.

Ezamiah strode toward Breegan, stopping three feet in front of her so as not to intrude on her Aura.

"Greetings, Breegan." Ezamiah bowed his head. "And to you, Judson."

"Old friend." Breegan smiled, taking a step forward with her right arm extended, hand palm up. They stood facing each other, Ezamiah's palm above Breegan's palm. Neither spoke.

Nigel watched, fascinated. It was one of the variations of a *zinahday* that Padwick had told him about. Knowledge was exchanged, as much or as little as the occasion required. It could be anything from a simple introduction to an entire history of a person or event.

At last, Breegan nodded. She clenched her palm into a fist and the *zinahday* was broken.

"Padwick?" Breegan called.

Padwick stepped quickly forward. "Yes, Breegan."

"Your student has certainly kept you busy." She glanced at Nigel.

"He is more my friend than my student, Breegan. He teaches me as much as I teach him."

"In four days you call him friend and say it with sincerity?" Breegan arched an eyebrow.

"I do," said Padwick.

"You have always been too charitable, Padwick," chided Breegan.

"And I have always been well rewarded for it."

A brief smile flirted with Breegan's mouth. "Then let us meet this remarkable person."

Nigel had been listening appreciatively to the gentle, singsong syllables. He started as Padwick gestured him forward.

"Come, Nigel. I will introduce you."

Feeling nervous, Nigel joined Padwick. His artist's eyes soaked up every extraordinary detail of Breegan..

She was taller than Nigel, perhaps six feet, with wide shoulders and a long torso. Her body was lean and muscled, clothed in knee-high boots, pants that clung to her like leotards, and a long-sleeved tunic in a rich amethyst color. Her hair was a cascade of Macintosh apple red. Emerald green eyes studied Nigel as he admired her high cheekbones and long neck. She was not beautiful, but she exuded beauty.

"Nigel," said Padwick, "I introduce the Venger, Breegan."

Nigel bowed his head.

"Breegan," Padwick continued, "I ask to present Nigel Nessel. My friend."

Breegan did not bow her head. "Welcome." Breegan's voice was low. Firm, but not unkind. She nodded to the man at her side. "I introduce Judson. My *casielle*."

Nigel bowed his head again, not catching Ezamiah's frown at the introduction.

Judson stood about an inch shorter than Breegan. He was dressed all in white and was strikingly handsome.

Like some fierce Nordic god, thought Nigel, fidgeting under the piercing blue gaze.

"It's an honor to meet both of you," Nigel said, hoping he was passing Judson's inspection. Or at least Breegan's.

"You did not tell me you had made the Pledge, Breegan." Anger weighted Ezamiah's words.

"It is done," Breegan said. "It will not interfere."

"And if it does?"

Defiance turned Breegan's eyes cold and remote. "It will not interfere," she repeated.

There was an angry silence.

"No," Ezamiah said at last, "it cannot." He turned away from Breegan. "Nigel!"

Nigel jumped, startled at being singled out. "What? I mean, yes?"

"What did you bring with you from your world?"

"What? What did I bring with me?"

With the patience of age and experience, Ezamiah nodded. "We must select a talisman, Nigel. Something of yours which we can *fairow* for others to use if your journey is completed."

"If?" Nigel repeated.

A small smile creased Ezamiah's face. "Come, Nigel. You are a born adventurer. You will be in good company. Put aside your fears.

"What possession of yours would prove a good talisman? It must be something that has your Aura firmly imprinted on it. Something you have used each day."

"Each day. Hmmm." Nigel considered his options. "My bicycle; I don't have that with me. My handkerchief; not very prepossessing. Hey! My keys!"

Nigel foraged in the right front pocket of his jeans and pulled out his key ring. It had several keys of varying ages and sizes on it. He held them up.

"Excellent," Ezamiah announced. "Keep them safe. I will pray for their return and yours."

"Great. I mean, thank you. Very much. Glad to help." Nigel tried to squelch his doubt and anxiety. It was all so dramatic and he was just Nigel Nessel.

As Ezamiah spoke to Breegan, Nigel whispered to Padwick. "What the hell are we up to?"

Padwick leaned toward Nigel and whispered back.

"It is simple, my friend. You and I have the privilege of assisting Breegan. With your Gift of Colors, she will be able to find Fahgerdahl and prevent his return to Atla. Perhaps we will even create a successful talisman." Padwick's excitement shone from his eyes.

Nigel didn't have the heart to discourage him.

"Sounds simple enough," said Nigel, feigning calm.

"You have already traveled unassisted from your world to Atla," said Padwick, not fooled by Nigel's outward demeanor. "The next step is but further."

Ezamiah interrupted. "You know enough for the moment, Nigel. Too much instruction will hinder your valuable intuition. As your Aura develops, Breegan and Padwick will answer your questions. Soon you will answer them for yourself. Now, come."

The company started up the steps that led to the Hall. Ezamiah first, then Breegan with Judson close by her side. Padwick followed and Nigel brought up the rear.

Nigel studied the steps, counting them as he climbed in an effort to distract himself from his anxiety. The stones were gray, cracked—*five*—with moss and flowers growing between them. The steps—*eleven*—were long and wide. Their texture was rough—*fifteen*—like granite. Pieces were missing in places—*twenty-three*.

They came to a halt before an enormous archway. Despite the brilliant light from the two moons, beyond the arch it was dark and deathly quiet.

"Now we shall see," said Ezamiah. "Are you prepared, Breegan?"

Breegan turned to Judson for a moment, holding his eyes with hers, touching his Aura, memorizing his face. He smiled at her and placed his hand over his heart.

"Yes," Breegan said. "I am prepared."

"And you, Padwick?"

"By the Light! I am prepared indeed." He patted a few of his pockets.

Ezamiah turned to Nigel. "Are you prepared, Nigel Nessel?"

Nigel fingered his keys and glanced at the archway. "Well, I don't think I'll be much of a dragon slayer, but I guess I'm as ready as I'll ever be."

"Good." Ezamiah nodded. He stepped back and faced the trio. "Once you step under the archway, you will be apart from Atla. There can be no turning back until your task is completed. Be swift. Be wary. Be strong."

Judson moved away from Breegan. She faced the archway, Nigel on her right, Padwick on her left.

"Let us go."

As one person, they took a step forward. Immediately beneath the archway, Nigel felt disoriented. Glancing back, he saw Ezamiah and Judson as if from a great distance.

"What's happening?" asked Nigel. "I feel strange."

"It is the Magic of the Hall of Doors, Nigel," said Padwick. "I feel strange, as well."

"Follow," said Breegan.

They passed under the archway into the darkness of the Hall, their footsteps echoing in the vastness of the interior.

"A light, Padwick," Breegan whispered. She had never been inside the Hall and the presence of the ancient spells and magics unsettled her.

"Kesla!" said Padwick.

A small torch snapped into existence. Padwick held it aloft in his right hand.

"There's a notch in the wall beside you," said Nigel, pointing.

Padwick tiptoed over and reached up to set the torch into the groove. Instantly the Hall was ablaze with light.

Nigel shaded his eyes. "That's a hell of a light."

"It is the magic here," Padwick explained. "It seized the energy of the torch and embellished it."

"Scary stuff," Nigel commented. He looked around at the architecture.

Unlike the granite stones of the steps and archway, the inside of the Hall was untouched by time and yet heavy with age. It was constructed of wood and marble, its floor made of luminescent stones of purple and blue that interconnected like a jigsaw puzzle.

The doors were set in either side of the Hall: tall rectangles of burnished wood, beautiful in their simplicity. Runes and inscriptions were carved above the doorframes and between each door stood a slim, white pillar.

Nigel tilted his head back. He couldn't see the ceiling. Like the archway, the ceiling was obscured in blackness.

Only five feet across, the Hall stretched endlessly into the distance until Nigel's eyes ached from trying to see its end.

"It has no end," said Breegan.

"No end?"

"The magic here is part of infinity. The first door was constructed with rare and ancient spells and enchantments. It multiplied on its own. There is one door for every world, every universe. We will start with the first door, there, on our left," Breegan announced.

"Start?" Nigel was dumbfounded. "Are you kidding me? We're talking infinity here. I mean …"

Breegan's face darkened. One brow arched imperiously over an icy green eye.

Nigel scrunched his objections under his sense of self-preservation.

There was something threatening about Breegan. He walked up to the first door.

"Hey! It's got a keyhole," said Nigel. "And a big one, at that."

The door did indeed have a large keyhole. No handle, no latch or doorknob, only the keyhole, just about eye level, in the centre of the door.

"Odd place for a keyhole," Nigel remarked.

"It is so one may look upon the world before entering," Padwick explained. "But it is too high for me."

"No matter," said Breegan. "It is Nigel who must look. Only he can tell through which door Fahgerdahl passed, and it is only Nigel who will perceive if anything is wrong with a world."

"Wait a minute," Nigel protested. "I'm just providing the talisman, maybe a little artistic input. You're the Venger. You have the *zinahday* with Atla."

Breegan tapped her foot, restless and uneasy. She had faced challenges before, but never had she risked so much: her *zinahday* with Atla, the safety of her two companions, the welfare of all Atlans and her Pledge with Judson. She held onto her façade of calm.

"I do have a *zinahday* with Atla, Nigel. But I do not possess the Gift of Colors. You are the one whose Gift can ally you with the Eras of any world. I am bound to Atla. Your Gift of Colors will allow you to touch the Eras of each world. If the Eras is disturbed, you will feel it and we will know Fahgerdahl is there."

Breegan pointed at the first door's keyhole. "Now, look."

Nigel wanted to object to being treated like a child, but he didn't doubt that Breegan would haul off and smack him.

He walked slowly up to the first door. Taking a deep breath, Nigel closed one eye and leaned forward. He looked through the keyhole.

It was like observing something through the wrong end of a telescope. Everything looked small yet incredibly detailed. Nigel watched, astonished.

Volcanoes were erupting; tidal waves lunged forth to tear at the molten land. Then, as if someone was rotating the world, he saw windswept plains and snowy mountains. The scene changed again; a herd of horses thundered by.

Nigel stepped back from the door, dazed.

"This is fantastic!"

"Is it the one?" asked Breegan.

"What? Oh. I don't know. I don't think so. It all went by so fast. But it was exciting, alive. A new world just beginning."

Nigel paused. It had been a strong impression: the newness, the life beginning, the very start of a world. It had been dizzying. He had felt all that with a rare certainty.

"It's not the one," said Nigel.

"Then we try the next door."

Padwick looked at Nigel. "Are you well?"

Nigel nodded his head. "Yeah. I'm okay." Nigel looked at the door. "You should have seen it, Padwick. It was beautiful, electrifying. If I could paint something like that …"

Nigel looked over his shoulder at Breegan. She waited beside the next door, hands clasped behind her back. Her impatience was palpable.

"Okay." Nigel clapped his hands together. "Round two."

"Pardon?" Breegan managed to look puzzled and sound annoyed.

"Sorry." Nigel reminded himself that Breegan was a person of tremendous importance on Atla. She was the one who would save the day. Where were his manners? *Probably back on Earth*, he thought.

"There is need for haste," said Breegan.

"Right."

Nigel walked up to the next door. He didn't hesitate this time. He was excited. He looked through the keyhole.

Satyrs and nymphs frolicked in the moonlight. Dwarves mined gold and silver. A dragon circled low over a castle and a white knight came charging forth.

Nigel stepped back. "Just like a fairy tale."

He looked again.

The knight was no longer there. Nigel saw mermaids and pink whales, then a wall of mountains. Beyond the mountains were valleys and rivers. The scene changed and the satyrs were dancing with the nymphs again. Or was it still?

"It's like I'm circumnavigating the world."

"Nigel?" It was Padwick.

Nigel wrenched his eyes away from the alluring world beyond that door.

"It's definitely not that one," he said.

They went on. And on. Nigel lost count of how may doors, how many worlds. The images began to blur in his mind. *We're gonna be here forever,* he thought.

At the next door, Nigel felt a prickle of apprehension.

Breegan sensed it at once. "This may be the one," she said. "Be wary."

Nigel edged up to the door and once again stepped up to the keyhole. He looked in upon the world beyond the door.

An exquisite lake of royal blue spread out before him. A mountain sloped up from its shores. A bird flew past. Then he was beyond the mountain and the land became a meadow, covered in flowers and dotted with bushes and green trees.

Small, furry animals scurried within tall grasses while birds soared and butterflies flitted. The sky was pale blue with soft, fluffy clouds grazing it like sheep. A gold sun shone upon the land.

Nigel was about to step away when something caught the corner of his eye. The flowers, hadn't they been brighter? And where were the butterflies? Was this a different meadow?

No. It was the same meadow. But now it was turning brown at its edges. Brown, then gray, now completely colorless.

The scene changed. There were more hills and valleys brimming with flowers and animals, birds and butterflies.

Wait! There it was again. A gradual paling in texture and color. A tinge of bleakness that definitely did not belong in such a paradise.

Nigel stepped back. He felt sick to his stomach.

"This is it."

Breegan tensed. "Are you certain?"

"Yes."

"Then take your key and fit it in the keyhole," Breegan said.

"And hold tightly to the key," Padwick added.

"Hold tightly to the key," Nigel repeated.

A terrible feeling of foreboding made Nigel want to turn and run.

Run where? Nigel gave himself a mental kick. *Back to Earth? Back to my furnished bachelor apartment and that damn hide-a-bed that's too small?*

Nigel heard the tapping of Breegan's foot behind him.

Come on, Nessel. They believe you can do this even if you don't. You wanted something extraordinary to happen. Well, here it is.

Groping in a pocket of his jeans, Nigel hauled out his key ring.

"Okay. Which key?" he asked Breegan.

"It does not matter," she answered. "Your energy will focus on whichever key you choose and it will become our talisman."

"My energy. You mean, my Gift?"

"Yes." Breegan didn't elaborate.

As close-mouthed as a clam, Nigel thought. *Of course, she did say my Gift would let me touch the Eras of other worlds and it did. This is just the next step, the extension of an ability I didn't even know I had.*

"I need a drink," Nigel decided.

"Water?" suggested Padwick.

"No. No. A drink." Nigel looked at Breegan. "Can you *fairow* Southern Comfort?"

Breegan yielded to the stress of the moment and Nigel had his drink and one for the road, as well. She lost her patience at three and returned Nigel's haversack to wallet size.

Nigel tucked it carefully away in his breast pocket. He cleared his throat. "As the official Key …" He leaned over to Padwick. "That's what Ezamiah called me, right?"

"That is correct." Padwick nodded.

"Okay." Nigel straightened and held up his mail key. "Well then, as the official Key, the one who can communicate with other worlds, et cetera, I hereby choose this key."

He waved the key back and forth. "This key will be the official talisman." *May it bring more luck than it did mail,* thought Nigel.

He approached the door and held the key to the keyhole. *One,* he counted to himself. *Two.* He tightened his grip on the key. *Three.* He pushed the key into the keyhole.

The door glowed. Nigel squinted against the brightness. His arm vibrated. A wind blew all around him.

He clenched his teeth. His fingers felt hot. The key jiggled in the lock. Nigel held onto it. The door swung open.

"Wow!" Nigel stepped back, amazed. "This is some Gift."

Just beyond the threshold was the perfect meadow: rich with tall grass, flowers blooming, trees providing shade and a stream trickling into a sunlit pond.

Nigel smiled. *I could get used to Magic.*

"You have done well."

Breegan's voice broke Nigel's trance. The unexpected praise embarrassed him. He shrugged. "Nothing to it, really."

Flexing his fingers, Nigel stuffed all the keys back into a pocket of his jeans. He bowed slightly and swept one hand toward the door. "Ladies first."

Breegan did not laugh. She crossed the threshold and walked into the meadow.

"Your Gift is true indeed, my friend," Padwick grinned, hurrying to catch up to Breegan.

"Hey! Hey, wait for me!" Nigel stepped across the threshold.

The door slammed shut.

Chapter Five

Nigel wheeled about as he heard the door slam. "It's gone! Padwick! The door's gone!"

Padwick turned. "So it is."

"How can you be so calm?"

Nigel searched the air where the door was supposed to be. "We could be stuck here forever. How do we get back?"

"I do not know." Padwick called to Breegan. "Breegan? How do we return?"

Breegan was scouting ahead, alert for any change in the Eras. She could not harmonize with it. She would have to rely on Nigel to lead her to Fahgerdahl. The prospect made Breegan uncomfortable.

Hearing Padwick's call, she paused beside the pond and looked back. "Yes?"

"The door has disappeared," said Padwick.

Breegan looked past him. "Good."

"Nigel and I are wondering how we return."

"Good?" Nigel was stunned. "What's so good about it? We can't get away. We're trapped. How the hell do we get out of here without a door?"

"The door is meant to disappear," Breegan said. "To protect the Hall of Doors."

"To protect the Hall of Doors," Nigel repeated. "What about us?"

"Breegan will protect us," Padwick said.

Breegan took a deep breath and exhaled slowly. "You have just arrived and already you wish to depart?" she asked Nigel.

"Well, no. Not exactly." Nigel shifted his feet, uncomfortable under Breegan's stare. "But I would appreciate knowing where the exit is. Just in case of an emergency."

"You draw a door," Breegan said. "You then insert your talisman into the keyhole, open the door, and walk through."

"That's it? Draw a door?" Nigel felt foolish and inadequate. Breegan made it sound obvious. She was so calm. And those eyes. They were beautiful and scary at the same time.

Nigel looked away, unnerved. "Fine. And by the way, I don't draw, I paint. In oil colors. I'm an artist, you know.

"I know of your abilities," Breegan replied. "Now, come. We will walk through the meadow until you have harmonized with the land. Then you can lead us to Fahgerdahl."

"I'll harmonize with the land?" Nigel shook his head. "You can't be serious. I can't even whistle. And I never said I could lead us anywhere, especially to your arch nemesis."

Breegan folded her arms across her chest and tapped her right foot, holding back her impatience before it manifested as a rush of Agenta Magic.

Padwick spoke up. "You must trust your Gift, Nigel. Did you not choose the right door and open it?"

"I think so. But ..."

"Did you not *fairow* water on your first day in Atla?" Padwick said.

"Okay, okay. I'll give it a try. How do I go about getting in harmony with the land?"

"Walk through the meadow, my friend," said Padwick. "The harmony will come to you as easily as the *fairowing* of water."

Like that was easy, thought Nigel. He surveyed the landscape. It was like an ocean of green waves rippling in the breeze. Flowers in myriad colors were the whitecaps. He wished he could sit and paint. Instead, he strode forth.

"Okay, harmony," Nigel said, "come and get me."

A butterfly flitted before him, catching the sunlight on its wings.

The world beckoned; Nigel followed. He could smell the colors, feel the scents. He wandered about for a long time.

A bird flew up from a copse of trees. It looked like a swallow.

Nigel watched its flight. For a moment, it soared on an updraft. Suddenly, it crumpled. Nigel felt as if someone had slapped his face. The bird plummeted to the ground and Nigel ran to find it.

He came to a halt. The swallow lay before him, dead. It was devoid of color, almost transparent, and the grass surrounding it was brown, the flowers wilted.

Nigel felt inexplicably grieved. A breeze blew a sweet scent across the long grasses. Beneath its touch, the grasses withered, becoming dry and brittle. The petals of the flowers curled as if burnt. Then the colors began to fade. Horror froze Nigel.

Like blood sucked from a vampire's victim, the colors were sucked from the dead vegetation leaving the land stark, like an artist's sketch. It stopped as suddenly as it had begun. But the colors did not return. The land did not revive.

Nigel knew it wouldn't. He also knew the terrible, calculating extraction of Eras would begin again. Perhaps was even now persisting in some place too far away for him to feel. A loathing welled up in Nigel.

"Damn you!"

Breegan came up behind him. She looked at the swallow and the perimeter of lifelessness that spread out from it.

"This is Fahgerdahl's doing." Her voice was low so Padwick would not hear.

"Yes," whispered Nigel.

He turned to Breegan, feeling devastated. He felt a flicker of hope as Breegan touched him with her Aura. His pain eased and Nigel took a deep breath.

"We'll get the bastard, right?"

"I will."

"Okay." Nigel held on to the promise of a happy ending. "Okay."

Breegan turned away. "We will spend the night by the pond. You are tired and can do no more today. We will rest. Tomorrow you will lead me to Fahgerdahl."

"How about if I just point in his general direction?" Nigel quipped.

Ignoring him, Breegan gazed at the cloud-speckled sky. "You are the Key," she said. "I am the Weapon. You will lead us to Fahgerdahl. I will destroy him."

Or he will destroy me, she thought.

"Padwick!" Breegan called. "A light meal, if you will."

"Yes, Breegan."

Padwick started toward them and Nigel stepped quickly forward, concealing the bitter spectacle. He remembered an evening during his trek with Padwick.

Nigel had been trying to *fairow* fire. "My dad always loved a good campfire," Nigel had said. "Roasting marshmallows and hotdogs, the works."

"You told me your parents are no longer living," said Padwick. "That may be why fire is difficult for you to *fairow*. It reminds you of their absence. You are distracted.

"I also have trouble fairowing sometimes," Padwick admitted. "Usually simple things that remind me of my mother and sister. They were attacked and killed by a pack of *carolaks*."

"*Carolaks?*"

"Creatures like wild dogs, vicious and deadly." The memory had silenced Padwick.

Nigel remembered clearly the whiteness of Padwick's face as, years after, he lived the nightmare again.

"Over there," Nigel pointed at a small tree by the pond. "We'll get a better view."

Padwick stopped. "A view of what?"

Appreciating Nigel's concern for Padwick, Breegan joined him in his distraction. "Yes. A view." She began walking toward the tree. "A view of …"

"The sunset?" Nigel offered.

"The sunset," said Breegan. Sitting beneath the tree, she looked east.

Pointedly, Nigel sat down facing west. Padwick glanced between the two and *fairowed* their meal.

They ate in silence, each watching and listening to the strange world around them. The sky blushed pink then red as the sun descended.

"How beautiful," Padwick murmured.

"It is nice," Nigel agreed.

"Is it always so?" asked Breegan. "On a world where there is no Aura Magic to fill the sky, does the sky only change colors at the end of day?"

"On my world it does," replied Nigel. "Morning, too. And here."

I wonder where "here" is, thought Nigel. *What's the name of this place? Nigel-Land.* He smiled. *Funny how, now I'm here, wherever that might be, I don't mind. Like Atla, I seem to fit into some predestined niche.*

Stretching, Nigel lay on his back and folded his arms behind his head. Yes, the sunset was nice. And dinner, like all the food Padwick prepared, had been delicious and filling. But he missed chocolate. He didn't want to ask Breegan to *fairow* the piece of chocolate Padwick had saved. She was once again remote and unapproachable.

Besides, thought Nigel, *if my Aura is so incredibly strong, I ought to be able to do it myself. But first, I have to master fire.*

He considered that. It was growing cool. Soon they'd need a fire to get them through the night. *A nice little fire just the right size for roasting marshmallows,* Nigel thought wistfully. Chocolate marshmallows, he decided.

"*Kesla,*" he said aloud.

A small circle of fire popped into existence not a foot away from him.

"What the hell?" Nigel scrambled to his feet. "Where did that come from?"

"Nigel! You *fairowed* fire." Padwick was delighted. "Well done."

Nigel eyed the orange and yellow flames. "I did that?"

Breegan had been waiting to see how long it would take Nigel to mix his Magics and realize a little of his potential. "You harmonized with this world's Eras," she said.

"I guess so," said Nigel. "Hey, Padwick. Do you still have that piece of chocolate I gave you?"

"I do." Padwick investigated a few pockets. "Here it is." He tossed it to Nigel.

Catching the small square of chocolate, Nigel placed it in the palm of his hand.

"The incantation?"

"*Tessa, katra, nook,*" said Padwick. "And concentrate," he added.

Nigel looked at the chocolate. He envisioned a huge block of it:

rich, dark and delicious. "Tessa," he said. "Katra." Nigel closed his eyes. "Nook."

A great weight made him stagger. He opened his eyes. A large block of chocolate rested on his hand a moment before toppling to the ground.

"Wow!" Nigel was ecstatic. "It must be ten pounds." He sat down beside the block and broke off a piece.

"This is great," he said, his mouth full. "Just the way I like it. Want some?" Nigel offered a chunk to Padwick, who accepted with enthusiasm.

Breegan declined. She watched as the two men stuffed themselves with the sweet. *Soon*, she thought, *the questions will begin.*

"Wait a minute." Nigel, having sated his craving for the moment, was realizing the implications of his ability to *fairow* a substance that Padwick could not. A substance which had little, if any, Eras in it. Not to mention his fire coup. "How did I do this?"

"You have achieved harmony with the Eras of this land," said Padwick, between mouthfuls. He decided he liked chocolate better than *lassenberries*.

"Yeah, but ..." Nigel looked across the fire to where green eyes watched him.

"That is so, Nigel." Breegan responded to his unasked question. "Through the Magic of your Gift you have attained a moderate *zinahday* with this world's Eras. It will grow stronger as your Aura advances.

"The combination of the Magic of your Aura, the Magic of your Gift, and the *zinahday* with this world's Eras is how you were able to *fairow* chocolate. Your Gift makes you especially sensitive, able to combine Magics as easily as you mix colors of paint."

"No kidding." Nigel waited, but Breegan offered nothing further. He tried another tack.

"What about your Gift? Will you tell me about it?"

Breegan leaned back against the tree, her face obscured in darkness. When she spoke, her voice seemed far away.

"My Gift, the Gift of Agenta." She sighed. "It keeps me forever separate and forever joined. It leads me down two paths that have the same destination. It is my joy and my burden. It demands all my energy and gives more than I may ever need.

"The Gift binds me in an unbreakable *zinahday* with Atla. That is why I cannot harmonize with this world. On Atla, I am in harmony with the Eras. I can sense every Magic as it is applied. I can perceive each individual's Aura.

"I am in unceasing communication with the Eras and whenever I need its power, it is mine to wield. It is a part of me, no less than my heart, and I am a part of it, like a tree, a river, even a mountain wind."

Breegan remembered when she first made the zinahday with Atla. The push and pull of power that surged through her body had been painful at first. The Eras interfaced with her Agenta Magic, overwhelming her Aura until she thought she would lose consciousness. But she remained strong, determined not to fail. Just as she was determined not to fail now.

Breegan spoke again, her voice a whisper.

"My *zinahday* with Atla is the most crucial ingredient in defeating Fahgerdahl."

"There's more?"

"My Gift of Agenta is a Magic of its own. The *zinahday* with Atla is another. And there is my own Magic, my Aura."

No wonder Breegan is intimidating, thought Nigel. *She's like a walking nuclear warhead. And, unlike what's-his-name, Breegan keeps all that power in check. She doesn't let it get the best of her.* "And you were born with this?"

"Yes." Breegan's voice was so low Nigel had to lean forward to hear her. "The welfare and protection of Atla is my responsibility. The care for the harmony of its Eras falls to me. All that I am is for this duty alone."

Breegan thought of Judson. She should have waited until the outcome of this challenge before making the Pledge with him. If their Pledge interfered with her Gift, she would have to break it. Once broken, it could never be regained.

"But you have a soul mate." Nigel interrupted Breegan's thoughts as if he were reading them. "You introduced Judson as your *casielle*. Padwick told me Atlans make a Pledge when they love someone, creating a permanent *zinahday* with that person."

"If my Aura is strong enough, my Pledge will not hinder my Gift."

"And if it isn't?"

Breegan said nothing.

Way to go, Nessel, Nigel chastised himself. *Why don't you put your other foot in your mouth while you're at it? This must have been what Breegan and Ezamiah had been angry about.*

Padwick broke the unpleasant silence. "Listen. Something is coming."

"Some *thing?*" Nigel repeated. He tried not to think about what kind of danger might lurk on such a beautiful world. Then he felt it, an evil presence.

"It's part of this world, but not part." Nigel spoke as if in a trance.

"Fahgerdahl has sensed us," said Breegan. "Whatever approaches is of his doing."

"What do we do now?" Nigel whispered to Padwick.

"We wait."

"Be still," Breegan commanded. "It is stalking us, seeking a weakness."

Nigel and Padwick sat motionless.

The hairs on the back of Nigel's neck tingled. His palms were sweaty. He could hear the beast as it circled them. He knew it was an animal. Some kind of creature Fahgerdahl had *fairowed* into existence, using his dark Siskis Magic and the Eras he was stealing.

A foul smell made his nose wrinkle. Nigel repressed a shudder.

The stench grew stronger, closer.

Breegan spoke in a low voice. "When it strikes, Padwick, set the tree alight."

Set the tree alight? Nigel wondered.

A throaty growl pierced the night.

Nigel held his breath. Nothing happened.

He looked at Breegan. She wasn't there.

A roar like a lion filled Nigel's ears. A huge wolf-like beast sprang at him. Nigel yelled, expecting to be torn limb from limb.

The creature never reached him.

As Nigel yelled, Padwick set the branches of the tree alight.

Standing behind Nigel, Breegan raised her right arm and pointed her index finger at the beast. The Eras flowed from the fire of the tree into Breegan's Aura. She fused the two Magics together and channeled them through her body. The lethal combination struck the creature like a bolt of lightning.

It fell without a cry upon Nigel's campfire. For an instant, its hideous shape was outlined in flame. Then it was gone.

"You did well, Padwick," said Breegan, striding around Nigel to stand in front of the glowing tree.

"It was an honor. And so exciting! Was it not, Nigel? Nigel?"

"Exciting?" Nigel couldn't believe he was still intact. "I'm nearly chopped liver for some maniacal super wolf and you're excited?"

He put his head down in his hands for a moment, his mind reeling, heart thumping.

Breegan felt a moment's sympathy. She turned to Padwick instead.

"Yes, Padwick," she said, "it was exciting. And there will be still more excitement before all is done. But for now, we must give your friend a lesson in *zinahdays* so we may be better prepared the next time."

Nigel lifted his head. "The next time?"

Breegan nodded and sat down beside him. "Fahgerdahl knows we are here. I do not think he suspects that I am a Venger, only that I am a threat. We all are. He will try to distract or eliminate us while he gathers Eras Magic."

"Oh, great."

Nigel noticed the tree. Its branches were still bright with flames. He had a harrowing vision of a big hairy beast with long fangs and red eyes leaping at him. Then Breegan making purple lightning snap from her fingertip.

"I think I missed something," said Nigel.

"Perhaps," said Padwick. "Do you recall Breegan instructing me to set the tree alight when the beast struck?"

"Yeah, I meant to ask you about that."

"Setting something alight is one step further than *fairowing* fire. You project your Aura into the land's Eras and maintain the connection, creating a well of energy. Breegan used part of the sustained Eras energy to destroy the beast."

"But I thought ..."

Padwick held up his hand. "Breegan cannot *zinahday* with the Eras of this world, but with her Gift of Agenta she can easily channel the combination of its Eras and her Aura Magic."

"Oh."

"All of us felt the Siskis in the beast," Breegan said. "I decided a combination of Magics would be more effective than a singular attack using my Aura."

"Better safe than sorry," said Nigel.

"I must preserve my Agenta Magic for confronting Fahgerdahl."

"Naturally."

"Now"—Breegan moved closer to Nigel—"we must teach you to *zinahday*."

She looked across the fire to Padwick. "Thank you for your assistance, Padwick. You may break the connection. I do not believe Fahgerdahl will try again this night. He has not yet gathered enough Eras."

"*Rion!*" Padwick clapped his hands together.

The tree blazed brighter for an instant then the flames disappeared. The branches were once again green with leaves.

Breegan snapped her fingers. At once Nigel's small fire grew larger and warmer.

"Hey, you didn't use a Key Word," Nigel objected.

"Breegan's Aura is far too strong to need Key Words," Padwick said.

"Must be nice," commented Nigel.

"We shall begin," Breegan announced. "Look at me, Nigel."

He looked into her glorious green eyes.

"Nigel, you are realizing only a small portion of the potential of your Aura. You are naturally receptive to Eras Magic because of your Gift of Colors. Now you must become receptive to Aura Magic. You must learn to hear me when I do not speak, touch me when I am not near, see me when I am invisible."

"Invisible?"

"Do not interrupt."

"Sorry."

"Give me your hand, Nigel. Your left hand. Place it on top of mine."

Breegan extended her right arm, palm up.

Nigel hesitated, remembering the electric jolt when he and Padwick had accidentally touched.

"Do not be afraid." Breegan's voice was suddenly soft, almost gentle.

Nigel placed his hand on hers.

"Close your eyes."

Nigel closed his eyes.

"I am blocking my Aura from yours, Nigel. Now I will release a portion. Feel it, see it, hear it."

Nigel's hand felt warm. He felt warm. He became aware of Breegan's thoughts: her concern for him and his safety, her deep love of someone, her need to find Fahgerdahl, her suspicion of … The thoughts faded, leaving Nigel with the impression of Breegan standing close beside him.

"Open your eyes, Nigel," Breegan ordered.

She was standing by the pond. Astonished, Nigel looked down at his hand. He could still feel Breegan's hand beneath his.

"Wow."

"You are a quick student," said Breegan. "Now extend this *zinahday* to Padwick without touching him."

"How do I do that?"

"Look at Padwick, not me. Make your thoughts heard, make your presence felt."

Nigel looked at his friend. "Here goes," he murmured.

Padwick? Nigel thought. *Padwick, can you hear me?*

Yes, Nigel, Padwick answered without speaking.

"Great stuff!"

"By the Light!"

"Enough," said Breegan.

The two stopped grinning and tried to look solemn.

"You have a question, Nigel," Breegan stated.

"Right. I was wondering why we can do this when you're not supposed to *zinahday* with anyone."

"There are many levels of a *zinahday*," Padwick answered. "I have told you of only a few of the variations."

"Okay. But why didn't I get a shock when I touched Breegan's hand?" Nigel turned his attention to Breegan. "I got a shock the first time Padwick touched me."

Padwick spoke up. "When I touched you it was accidental and not intended as a *zinahday*. It was only because of the strength of your Aura that I received an impression of you and your world.

"This time you were prepared and would have received a shock only if Breegan had so wished it or if she had been unprepared. Her Aura is advanced far beyond either of us."

"I see. Well, what do we do now that we're one big, happy family?"

"We rest." Breegan came back into the glow of the fire. "Each of us will be alert to danger according to our abilities. If any one of us senses danger, so will we all. It is a simple *zinahday*, but it will serve to protect us."

Stretching her arms above her head, Breegan sat down across from Padwick and Nigel.

"Padwick? It is late. I would like a soft blanket to sleep upon, if you please."

"Certainly." Padwick got the correct pocket on the first try. "A favorite color?"

"Blue," Breegan said, thinking of the color of Judson's eyes.

"Nigel?"

"Surprise me."

Padwick held three squares of cloth in his palm and recited the incantation. *"Tessa, katra, nook."*

He disappeared under an enormous pile of blankets. "I keep forgetting to think about size." Padwick's voice was muffled.

"When you use your incantation near me, Padwick," said Breegan, "you magnify its properties. The next time you *fairow*, say the incantation in your mind only."

"Why's that?" asked Nigel.

"Because of the strength of my Aura. It generates a halo of energy around me, like a magnetic field."

"Really." Nigel tried not to look impressed.

Padwick tossed a blanket on him, breaking Nigel's concentration.

Lying down, Nigel tucked the blanket around him and looked up at the night sky. It was black, with only a few faint stars. He missed the two moons of Atla.

I'll never be able to sleep, he thought.

Padwick chuckled as Nigel began to snore. Curling up beneath his big pink blanket, he closed his eyes and quickly fell asleep.

Breegan watched over the two men for a short time. She surveyed the meadow once more. It was quiet, at peace.

She missed Judson. On Atla, she could sense his Aura anywhere on the planet. Here, on this strange world, she had only her memories.

Lying down, Breegan closed her eyes, picturing Judson safe at their home in Jeraj.

I will keep it safe, she promised herself. *I will keep all of Atla safe.*

"My heart follows yours," Breegan whispered. She slept.

Chapter Six

Nigel rolled over. Above him, the sky was pale blue, the pink haze of dawn slipping away. He rubbed his eyes and reached for his glasses. A blur on the edge of his vision became Breegan. Nigel looked quickly away then slowly back.

Breegan was bathing in the pond, her back to Nigel, red hair floating on the water. She rose suddenly, stretching. Lean muscles rippled under porcelain skin; long legs and torso gave her a sleek, streamlined figure.

"Wow," thought Nigel, not realizing he said it aloud.

"Pardon?" Breegan turned in Nigel's direction.

"Oh, uh, good morning," Nigel sputtered, pretending to examine a blade of grass.

"Good morning."

As Breegan splashed out of the pond, Nigel couldn't resist another look.

Breegan was pulling on her pants, boots following with a quick tug. She paused, feeling Nigel's interest. "Is something wrong?"

"Wrong?" Nigel wanted to pull his blanket over his head. "No. Nothing's wrong. Just enjoying the weather." He looked around him. "Nice day, isn't it?"

Frowning at Nigel's prevarication, Breegan pulled her tunic over her head and wrung the water from her waist-length hair.

"Padwick!" Breegan walked toward the pink mound on the grass.

Padwick jerked awake. "Yes?" He sat up. "Yes?"

"It is time to prepare for the day ahead."

Padwick tossed his blanket off and hurried to the pond. "Come along, Nigel."

"Now?" Nigel knew Atlans weren't self-conscious about nudity, but he felt awkward with Breegan there.

Padwick divested himself of his clothing and plunged into the pond.

"Ah! Refreshing. Come, Nigel. No better way to prepare than with a bath."

Nigel crawled out from beneath his blanket. He unbuttoned his shirt, all too aware of his hairy chest, his nipples, and his scruffy beard. He felt every inch like the Huki that Padwick had said he resembled.

Expecting an editorial comment from Breegan, Nigel cringed mentally. Silence. He looked over his shoulder. Breegan wasn't watching. She was scanning the meadow. He could feel her impatience.

Stripping faster, Nigel waded into the pond.

"Do all humans look like you?" Breegan asked, now eyeing him critically.

"More or less."

"Hmmm," Breegan responded absently, looking again to the meadow.

Nigel splashed deeper into the water, annoyed with himself. True, he had always felt insecure around beautiful women. *Make that all women,* he amended. But that hadn't been much of a problem. His relationships, if they could be called that, were always eclipsed by his desire to paint.

So what's the problem here, Nessel? he asked himself. *This isn't a romantic relationship; it's a working one. She's got a job to do and I'm supposed to help. Somehow.*

It didn't seem to Nigel that Breegan needed much help. She had all the qualities he admired: beauty, physical strength, ability, talent and, most of all, confidence.

Yes, he had found the right door. *Maybe* he could paint a door to get them back to Atla, but beyond that, Nigel felt he was in over his head.

Nigel cupped some water in his hands and washed his face. He decided being a descendant of adventurers had some serious drawbacks.

The expectations of Breegan and Padwick were high and Nigel didn't want to disappoint either of them. Shaking water from his ears, he set a speed record for dressing when wet.

During breakfast, Padwick chattered happily about the weather, the flowers, the beauty of the mountains, and the variety of butterflies.

Nigel knew better than to interrupt the rambling. Breegan, too, knew better. She and Padwick had been friends for many years.

When they finished breakfast, Breegan looked at Nigel. "Which way?" she asked.

"Which way what?"

"In which direction do we proceed?"

Nigel opened his mouth to protest and then shut it. Breegan was asking for help. Nigel remembered the strange moment the night before when he had felt the creature nearing them. Apparently, he was in harmony with the land. He concentrated on Breegan's question. A tingling sensation raced up his back from the ground. Nigel felt like the needle of a compass.

"That way," he said, pointing to the mountains.

"Lead then," commanded Breegan.

The trio set off.

The grass that had been up to Nigel's knees gradually shortened then thinned. The flowering trees and bushes grew further and further apart. Several times small animals dashed in front of them. Furry and wide-eyed, looking like bear cubs with long tails.

The butterflies, however, were everywhere. Startled by the approaching trio, they rose up, forming rainbows of color as they fled into the sky.

Nowhere did they see signs of people. Breegan questioned Nigel briefly about the absence of Atlan-like life forms. "Do you not sense anyone?" she asked for what Nigel was sure had to be the millionth time.

"I'm telling you, no. Zip. Not a one. Nobody's home. If it's that Fahgerdahl guy you're worrying about, by all means, keep worrying. But he's not keeping company with any natives."

"Very well. If you are certain."

Nigel rolled his eyes and slowed his strides so he could fall behind. Way behind.

"Hey, Padwick. What do you think of this place?" asked Nigel.

"I think it is marvelous and beautiful. Perhaps we can visit it again when it is safe to do so. Though the Council may put a ban on it until the Eras has recovered from Fahgerdahl's interference."

"Oh, yeah? Well, we have conservation on Earth, too. But, listen, about this Council, who are they exactly? I mean, do they know I'm here? Is Ezamiah a member?"

"He is, but he is not a representative of a province like the other members," Padwick answered. "Ezamiah serves as Breegan's Advisor. The rest meet at the beginning and end of each season to discuss new architecture and landscaping. They exchange news and bring it to the people of their province. And so, yes, my friend, the Council knows you are here. Why do you ask?"

"I was just thinking how much I enjoyed our journey in Atla and wondering whose permission I had to get to spend more time there."

"You have to get Breegan's permission, Nigel."

"Ah."

They walked for hours without stopping. Nigel subsisted on his harmony with the land. Padwick and Breegan relied on their natural stamina. It was late afternoon when Nigel faltered.

They had walked in almost a straight line from the pond. The land had gradually quieted, becoming bare of life. Now, as they neared the foothills, the colors faded. Nigel's energy and sense of direction faded with them. He stopped.

"What is wrong?" Breegan asked.

"I don't know. I'm not sure of the way anymore. I guess I'm tired."

Breegan came up close to Nigel. Her green eyes caught and held his attention.

"Touch me," she said, "but do not feel me."

"What?" Nigel felt a bit dazed.

"Touch my Aura with yours," Breegan said slowly, "as I taught you last night."

Nigel looked away, shaking his head, feeling unreasonable and anxious. "I can't," he argued. "I'm too tired to practice magic right now."

Breegan took a deep breath, wishing she could inhale patience. "You are too close to the Eras of this world, Nigel. As Fahgerdahl drains it, he drains you also.

"Touch me. Feel me. Breathe as I breathe. Let my strength soothe and revive you. Do not succumb to Fahgerdahl's hold on the Eras. Let it slip through you, let it pass over you, let it slide by you. You remain whole, untouched and unharmed."

Nigel looked into Breegan's eyes. Bit by bit, he relaxed. Her strength seeped into his weary body and mind. It was heady, almost overpowering, like liquor drunk too fast.

Nigel swayed unsteadily, then sank to the ground.

Padwick knelt beside him, concerned.

"He will be fine," said Breegan.

She scanned ahead. They were close to the foothills. "We will take a short rest," Breegan decided. "Padwick, please prepare food and drink. Then we will continue."

Padwick nodded. "Nigel, you will be fine. We will rest now."

Nigel stretched his arms, tucking his head into his chest, breathing deeply. He didn't realize it, but he was drawing on Breegan's Aura and the Magic of the Light that she laid claim to. A great heaviness passed through him and was gone.

Feeling better, Nigel lifted his head slowly. He started to get up and stopped.

"What?" He stared. "I mean, who?"

Padwick followed his gaze, then Breegan.

"You said you did not sense Atlan life forms," said Breegan.

"She doesn't look Atlan to me," Nigel defended his prediction.

Several feet away stood a fairy-like creature. Petite and delicate, watching them with large violet eyes. Short white hair lay sculpted about her oval face. Twin antennae twitched atop her head.

Four colorful wings arched from her back, not feathered, but a collage of transparent scales like the wings of a butterfly. She was naked; her lithe body the color of honey.

"Wow," said Nigel, feeling revived.

Breegan frowned at him, annoyed. She was unable to touch the mind of the being that waited before them. Breegan closed her hands into fists, readying to fight.

"Hello," said Nigel. "Who are you?"

The being quivered. She did not speak, but Nigel felt a whisper in his ear.

Unrestricted by inexperience or vows, Padwick stretched his

thoughts out to the fragile looking creature. "Her name is Phaedra," he announced.

The being tensed a moment then relaxed and took a step forward.

"My … name … is … Phaedra," she said, her voice high and sweet, like a flute. She stood still and studied the trio.

"By the Light! She is a quick learner," said Padwick, impressed. He had been aware of her picking up information as their thoughts met, but this sudden verbalization surprised him. He had not sensed a strong intelligence.

"Who are you?" Phaedra asked.

"We are adventurers," said Breegan.

Phaedra shrank from the harshness of Breegan's voice.

"Don't be afraid," Nigel soothed her. "She won't hurt you." He looked up at Breegan, checking just to be sure. "Will you?"

"No," said Breegan, all icy eyes and stiff posture.

"Okay, then." He patted the ground beside him. "We were just about to eat. Would you like to join us?"

Phaedra hesitated, wary of Breegan. She took another step forward then, unfolding her wings, flew to a spot between Nigel and Padwick.

"Wow," Nigel said again, captivated.

"Enchanting," agreed Padwick. He, too, was caught in Phaedra's spell of beauty.

"Food and drink, Padwick?" prompted Breegan.

"Oh! Yes. What would you like to eat?" Padwick asked Phaedra.

Phaedra thought a moment, her antennae waving. "Perhaps some nectar of a *burginoise* flower?"

Padwick and Nigel exchanged a glance.

"Gee, fresh out," Nigel apologized. "Have you ever tried *lassenberry* jam?"

"I have never heard of it, therefore I do not think I have tried it."

"Please try some," Padwick urged. "Now let me think. Where did I put it last? Ah, here it is."

Phaedra clapped her hands, delighted, as Padwick *fairowed* jam, bread, fruit and water.

"Oh, how clever you are," she fawned.

Breegan watched the two men as they fussed over their visitor. Phaedra was coy and flirtatious, wrinkling her nose at the strange food, finally allowing them to persuade her to sample it. Nigel and Padwick were completely unaware of what a silly picture they made. They seemed to have forgotten Breegan altogether.

She walked toward the picnicking threesome.

Restricted though my Aura may be, Breegan thought, *I still harness the Magic of Agenta. If this creature is of Fahgerdahl's doing, I will snap her in two.*

"How do you like it?" Padwick was saying.

"Oh, very much." Phaedra smiled. "It is very nice. Thank you."

Breegan sat down across from Phaedra.

"How quickly you have mastered our language," she observed.

Forgetting her earlier fear of the woman with hair the color of the setting sun, Phaedra fanned her wings slowly and smiled, guileless.

"Remarkable, is it not?" said Padwick, his eyes upon the ethereal creature.

"Yes," Breegan mused. "Tell me, Phaedra, do you live on this world?"

Phaedra's laughter tickled the air. "What a strange question. Where else would I live? Do not you live here?"

She asked it innocently enough, but Breegan thought Phaedra's eyes narrowed at the question.

"Yes," Breegan answered.

"No," Nigel said at the same time.

Phaedra tilted her head to one side. "One says yes, the other no."

"He means," Breegan amended, "that we are from a distant corner of this world. We have traveled far to get here."

"How far?" Again the voice innocent, the eyes sly.

"Far enough," snapped Breegan before Nigel could speak.

"Tell me, Phaedra," Breegan asked, "are there others like you?"

"Others? Not quite like me. No. I do not think so. I have been sleeping. I sleep through the winters," she said to Nigel.

He nodded. "Of course. Who wouldn't? I mean, I would if I could sleep that long without somebody waking me up. What I mean to say is …"

"What you mean to say, you have said," Breegan interjected.

"I was asleep when a stranger woke me," Phaedra confided, oblivious to Nigel's babbling.

"A stranger?" Breegan prodded.

"Yes. Tall like you, with hair like a starless night. His eyes were full of promises and mystery." Phaedra thought a moment.

"He was very handsome," she added, this time to Padwick, "but not so handsome as you."

Padwick smiled, unaware of the flattery.

"He woke me as he passed," Phaedra continued. "He did not speak or do me harm. Only gazed at me with those eyes. As if he knew a secret and would not tell. I love secrets," she said to Padwick.

"No doubt you have many," suggested Breegan.

Ignoring her, Phaedra smiled at Nigel. "Are you truly adventurers from far away?"

Nigel smiled back. "Yes. Adventurers. All three of us."

Still smiling, Phaedra returned her attention to Padwick. "How did you get here? What is it you seek?"

"Well …" began Nigel, then closed his mouth at Breegan's warning look.

"We walked," Breegan said. "We seek the stranger who woke you. Do you know which way he went?"

"I cannot be certain," Phaedra answered, "but I thought I saw him disappear into the Crystal Mountains."

"How long ago?"

"I cannot say." Phaedra sighed, bored with the interrogation. She flicked her wings idly. "Perhaps a day, perhaps more. What is time to me? There is always too much and yet not enough."

"Then we must be swift," said Breegan, rising.

"Must you go?" Phaedra pouted.

"We must hurry," Padwick apologized, stuffing his pockets with Prime ingredients.

"Perhaps you could join us?" offered Nigel.

Breegan opened her mouth to object, then thought a moment. Nigel was so smitten with Phaedra he would not know if she was of the land or of the moons. Not yet, at least. To have her with them might be dangerous. *But,* Breegan reminded herself, *better to see the blade than to feel it.*

"You may journey with us," Breegan said, "if you do not slow our pace."

Phaedra clapped her hands together, pleased. "Oh, thank you. And I shall be no trouble. No trouble at all."

You already are, thought Breegan. She turned to Nigel.

"Are you rested now?"

"Oh, sure, sure." Nigel got up, dusting grass from the seat of his jeans. He stood still, concentrating. This time, the response was slower in coming, but it came. Like a telegraph signal.

"A little to the left. There's a river up ahead. Follow the river."

With those directions, Breegan took the lead, Padwick following a step behind and Nigel bringing up the rear.

Phaedra flitted back and forth between the two men, occasionally flying off to investigate a flower or a tree bearing enticing fruit. She grew less frolicsome as the sun set. By the time they reached the river, Phaedra was quiet.

Padwick immediately set about *fairowing* dinner and a fire. Phaedra sat near him, her eyes half closed, wings fanning slowly, too tired to applaud Padwick's efforts.

Breegan scouted ahead a hundred yards. Her keen eyes noted the waning color of the land even in the eerie half-light of the moon. She could not sense Fahgerdahl.

She turned her attention to the river. It was narrow, twisting like a snake around treacherous rocks. The current churned to an angry froth.

Breegan knew it would have been calm once. It was disturbed now by Fahgerdahl leeching the Eras.

Nigel watched the river, too. Despite the distraction of Phaedra, he had been aware of the land. It had become silent, barren of color and life. Even now, he could feel the trees on the far side of the river holding their branches aloft with effort. He could feel them gasping for life, for air.

Nigel gagged. His throat constricted. He choked, feeling as if someone was strangling him. He couldn't breathe. His heart pounded in his ears. He couldn't see.

A voice called from far away. "Nigel."

"Nigel." The voice penetrated the darkness again.

Nigel wheezed and coughed. He gulped great lungfuls of air. His heart stopped laboring, his breathing eased. He relaxed. Someone's arm was about his shoulders, supporting him.

He looked up. It was Breegan.

"Hi," Nigel croaked.

"Hello," she said, her voice gentle.

Nigel tried to step away and nearly fell. Catching him, Breegan held him close against her.

"Thanks," Nigel managed despite his sore throat.

"Padwick," Breegan said over her shoulder, "get a blanket ready for him."

Leading Nigel to the fire, Breegan helped him sit down. She withdrew her hands from him slowly, careful not to cause any sudden break in the *zinahday* she had created to save his life.

Padwick draped a blanket over Nigel's shoulders. "How do you feel?" he asked, worried.

Nigel waved a hand. "Never better," he rasped. "What happened?"

"Your harmony with the land intensified," said Breegan. "You must learn to control your Aura."

Nigel nodded, chastised. She was right. He had to develop his Aura. He couldn't keep relying on Padwick and Breegan. It wasn't fair and it wasn't safe.

You are right. It is not safe. Breegan's voice was inside his head.

Startled, Nigel absently accepted the bowl of soup Padwick offered.

"For now," Breegan said aloud, "the *zinahday* between you and I is stronger. It will fade by morning. Until then, I am a part of you."

Uh-oh, thought Nigel, trying to concentrate on his soup.

Breegan pointed at Phaedra, who had slept through the entire incident, curled into a tiny ball, her wings folded.

"Can you feel if she is of this world?" Breegan asked.

Nigel looked at Phaedra over the rim of his bowl.

"Well, sort of. I mean, when she first sat down next to me I felt very strongly that she was a natural part of this world. But now …"

"But now?" Breegan pushed for more. "What do you feel now?"

"I'm not sure," Nigel lifted his shoulders, feeling helpless. "She feels vague, out of focus. Maybe that's because she's asleep."

"She certainly sleeps deeply," Padwick remarked.

"Yes," Breegan agreed. "Too deeply." She walked over to where Phaedra lay. "What can you sense, Padwick?"

Padwick studied Phaedra. "I sense nothing from her, Breegan. Not even dreams. It is as if she is not here with us at all.

He looked at Breegan. "Shall I try to wake her?"

"No."

"You don't trust her," said Nigel.

"No."

"Why not?"

"It is enough that I do not," said Breegan. She went to the fire. "Be wary of her, both of you."

"Okay. We'll be wary." Nigel looked at Padwick. "Right?"

"Oh, yes. Wary."

Breegan frowned, questioning Nigel's influence on Padwick.

Nigel finished his soup. He was feeling much better. *All I need now,* he thought, *is a bit of...*

"Southern Comfort," Breegan finished the thought out loud.

Nigel started. He'd forgotten about the increased intensity of the *zinahday*.

"What is your preoccupation with this beverage?" asked Breegan.

"It's not a preoccupation," Nigel insisted, put out by the invasion of his privacy. "Alcohol is often used for medicinal purposes."

"Very well then." Breegan snapped her fingers and the flask floated out of Nigel's shirt pocket, reaching full size as Nigel grabbed it.

"Does chocolate also have medicinal purposes?" Padwick asked.

Breegan repressed a smile. She *fairowed* a small square of chocolate for each of the two, like a parent rationing cookies before a meal.

Nigel took a swig from the flask and offered it to Breegan.

"No."

"Padwick?"

Accepting the flask, Padwick took a sip. "By the Light! It is strong."

"But good," Nigel pointed out.

"If you are well enough," Breegan said to Nigel, "we will leave at dawn."

"Dawn it is," agreed Nigel amiably, the liquor creating a nice euphoria. He passed the flask back to Padwick, who took a bigger drink

"It goes down easier the second time," Padwick observed.

"Wait until you get to the third."

Chapter Seven

Breegan awoke with a brutal headache. Through the pounding in her skull, she recalled Nigel and Padwick sitting by the fire, passing the flask between them and giggling.

I should have put a stop to it, thought Breegan.

She had not told Nigel the *zinahday* was physical as well as mental. As Nigel imbibed, Breegan had felt little effect from the liquor; its aftereffect, however, was pronounced. She stood up slowly.

"How can he enjoy such a beverage?" Breegan winced. Her voice sounded unnaturally loud.

"Good morning," Phaedra trilled. She flew in a low circle then landed lightly.

The pounding in Breegan's head increased.

"Shall I wake the others?" asked Phaedra.

"Yes," Breegan gritted out between clenched teeth.

Choosing her steps with care, Breegan walked to the edge of the river. She knelt and splashed her face repeatedly with the ice-cold water, cupping some into her mouth.

The pounding subsided and Breegan became aware that the *zinahday* had dwindled to its initial thread.

"Nigel! Padwick!" Phaedra sang, half flying, half skipping across the ground. "It is time to wake. The day has begun."

Nigel mumbled sleepily. Padwick groaned.

Coming up behind them, Breegan stamped her foot, purposely causing a tremor that jarred the two awake.

"What? What?" Nigel shoved his glasses in place as Phaedra skipped by him.

"Time to wake!" she called in a singsong voice.

"Better than an alarm clock any day," Nigel said.

Padwick sat up slowly, holding his head with both hands. "Is it morning?" he asked, squinting his eyes against the daylight.

"It is," said Breegan. "And we have no time for ..."

Phaedra skipped by again.

"Foolishness," Breegan snapped.

"Right." Nigel stood up and stretched his arms wide. He was surprised he didn't have a headache. *Must be all this fresh air*, thought Nigel.

He turned to Padwick. "Are you okay?"

"I do not know. My tongue feels fuzzy and my head hurts."

"Give me your hand, Padwick," said Breegan. She helped him up, channeling his hangover through her as she did.

"Thank you, Breegan." Padwick sighed, feeling better.

"I think I had too much of your medicine, Nigel," said Padwick.

"Next time we'll mix it with something."

After breakfast, Breegan led them along the riverside. Her purposeful stride belied her uneasiness. On Atla, Breegan's *zinahday* with the Eras allowed her to sense any Aura she focused on and trust her Magics to find her way through any doubt or difficulty.

Here, she had to rely on Nigel for her information. It made her feel resentful. She was unaccustomed to dependence on anyone, except Judson.

Breegan had hoped that being a Venger would be enough to let her sense Fahgerdahl or the Siskis Magic that would surround him. It had not. He had caught her off guard with his beast, and again with the rapid drain of Eras. He could be watching them now.

Phaedra flew past, carelessly close, and Breegan almost swatted at her. As Phaedra disappeared into a copse of trees, Breegan stopped to speak with Nigel and Padwick.

"Can either of you sense anything odd? I feel we are being watched."

"No, Breegan," said Padwick.

"Not me," Nigel shrugged. "At least, not specifically."

"What are you saying?" Breegan asked Nigel.

"Well, this feeling I have about which way to go is just a feeling. I stop and take a step in this direction"—Nigel stepped toward the trees—"and I feel certain that's not the way to go. I step over here …"

Nigel moved toward Breegan, then a few steps past her. "And I feel different … "

He paused.

"What do you feel?" Breegan demanded.

"I feel anxious," Nigel answered, surprised. "In fact, now that you mention it, I do feel like we're being watched."

Phaedra swooped over their heads.

"That's probably why." Nigel pointed at Phaedra.

"She is distracting," Padwick agreed.

Breegan frowned. "Do you still feel we should follow the river?"

Nigel thought about it. "Yes."

"Very well. We shall continue to do so." Breegan looked along the river's channel. "Let me know if your anxiety increases," she instructed.

"You bet."

They walked silently for a time, interrupted only by Phaedra's aerobatics.

Stumbling on a rock, Nigel glared at it. Why couldn't the right way have a path? "Is it just my imagination," Nigel asked, "or is the right direction also the more difficult one?"

"It is more difficult because it is the right direction," Breegan spoke over her shoulder, concentrating on her footing. "The closer we get to Fahgerdahl, the nearer we are to the initial drain of Eras."

"It is less pleasant than when we first arrived," Padwick said. "The ground is uneven. The grass is sparse. Even the butterflies have gone away."

"Have they?" Nigel looked around. They were at the foot of the mountains. The landscape was soundless, empty. *Tired-looking*, thought Nigel. *Like a beach when the tide was out.*

Phaedra flew by again and Nigel envied her. His feet were sore.

My ancestors might have been great adventurers, thought Nigel, *but I bet they didn't have to walk all the way.*

As Phaedra zigzagged across the river for the eighth time, he called out to her. "Hey! Why don't you do some exploring while you're over there?"

Phaedra hovered over the river, heedless of its frenzied motion. "Exploring?"

"Yeah!" Nigel responded. "Have a look around. See if you can find anything interesting."

Like a path, he thought.

Phaedra smiled and waved. With a flick of her wings, she vanished behind the trees on the other side.

"An excellent suggestion," said Breegan. She was weary of Phaedra's chatter.

Watching their beautiful acquaintance fly away, Padwick asked, "Have you noticed that Phaedra always asks the same questions, but in different ways?"

"Yes," answered Breegan. "As if she is trying to break a code. She does not believe we are of this world. She repeatedly asks how far we have traveled and from where."

"And how," Padwick added.

"She's just curious." Nigel defended Phaedra even though he, too, was bored with her inanities.

Beautiful, he thought, *but feather-brained.*

The subject of their conversation appeared further upstream, wings fluttering in excitement.

"Oh, do hurry!" she called, her high voice carrying over the steady rush of the river.

The three quickened their pace. When they reached the bank opposite Phaedra, they saw the cause of her excitement.

Six broad flat rocks jutted from the water, like stepping-stones. The spray made them wet, but they looked navigable.

"Do we cross?" Breegan asked Nigel.

"I guess so."

"You guess?"

"I just know we have to follow the river," said Nigel, his sore feet making him feel disagreeable. "What difference does it make which side we're on?"

"It could make a great deal of difference."

"Okay, okay." Craning his neck, Nigel called to Phaedra. "Hey! What's on the other side?"

"Come and see!" she called back.

Breegan studied the rocks, mapping the safest footing in her mind.

"I will investigate whatever Phaedra has discovered," she said. "Padwick, you will come with me.

"Nigel, stay here," Breegan ordered.. "Concentrate on which side of the river we should follow. But do not concentrate too hard," she warned.

"Believe me, I won't." Nigel did not intend to let his *zinahday* with the Eras intensify again.

He watched as Breegan stepped onto the first rock, balancing skillfully. As she moved to the second, Padwick followed. Sure-footed as mountain goats, the two arrived on the far side safely, if wet.

Padwick waved to Nigel, then disappeared after Phaedra and Breegan into the trees.

Nigel looked around him. Beyond the rocks, the river turned sharply to the right and wound itself about the foot of the mountains. Even the bright noon sun could not lessen the bleakness of the landscape.

From a distance, the mountains had looked green, inviting. Now they rose up like walls of steel, with harsh angles and angry cliffs. The snow on their peaks looked like ice.

"Maybe that's why Phaedra called them the Crystal Mountains," Nigel said. "But they weren't like this when I first saw them from the meadow."

He walked alongside the river. The trees and foliage, which had once softened the contours of the land, now sharpened it with gnarled gray trunks and leafless branches. No animals or birds disturbed the silence.

Nigel moved away from the bank of the river and headed around a large rock. "He sure moves fast," he muttered, thinking of Fahgerdahl. "Two days ago this place was a paradise and now look at it."

"Yes. Look at it. Now it is mine."

Nigel whirled about.

"Fahgerdahl," he whispered. He would have recognized him even without Phaedra's description. What surprised Nigel was how handsome he was. Handsome and youthful. For some reason, he had expected Fahgerdahl to be ugly, shriveled with evil if not age.

Instead, Fahgerdahl was tall and straight. Ebony hair fell about his broad shoulders and his features were aristocratic. Only his eyes were strange. Deep set, they were black wells without light.

Without soul, remembered Nigel.

The eyes imprisoned him.

"Who are you?" Fahgerdahl's voice was quiet, but menacing. "How did you come to be here?"

"Me? I'm nobody. Just out for a walk. That's all. A walk."

Dark brows drew together. "Do not lie to me," hissed Fahgerdahl. "I have watched you, felt you from the moment you arrived. You have the Secret. Give it to me."

"Secret? What secret?"

"Give it to me now, fool, if you value your life." Fahgerdahl snapped the words like a wolf on the heels of its prey.

Nigel backed up a step.

"Look … Sir, I … I really don't know what you're talking about." *Where the hell is Breegan when you need her?* thought Nigel.

Phaedra flitted into view.

"Run!" Nigel cried, forgetting she could fly.

Fahgerdahl turned to Phaedra and beckoned her to him.

She came obediently, landing lightly, an adoring smile on her face.

"Did I do well?" she asked Fahgerdahl, unafraid.

"Yes."

"But she's of the land," Nigel protested.

"You did not recognize the variation of the name?" Fahgerdahl sneered. "I named her for my foolish sister, Fahdra. A simple demonstration of my power. Behold."

Fahgerdahl waved a hand at Phaedra.

"Oh," she sobbed, dismayed. "I was having such fun."

Nigel watched, horrified.

Phaedra's body blackened. Tiny hairs covered her as a second pair of arms appeared. Her breasts flattened and her limbs became thinner and thinner. The worst of the transformation was her face. Her violet eyes turned black and began to bulge. Her hair matted to her skull and her whole head became black and round.

With a snap like a branch breaking she all but vanished. A butterfly swayed on a single blade of grass in the place where Phaedra had stood.

"Come," Fahgerdahl commanded.

The butterfly flew to him, landing in the palm of his hand.

"You see, she is of this land. How easily you are deceived."

Nigel felt sick.

"She has been my eyes and my ears," Fahgerdahl continued. "She has told me you have the Secret. Give it to me!"

"I … I swear I don't have it."

Fahgerdahl crushed his fingers about the butterfly.

Nigel imagined her scream.

The butterfly's body dropped to the ground. As she hit the earth, she twisted and became transparent, like the swallow.

"Damn you," Nigel whispered.

"I can crush you as easily." Fahgerdahl's voice was threatening, like thunder in the distance. "Give me the Secret."

"I don't have the Secret. I don't know anything about a secret."

Fahgerdahl moved toward Nigel, slow, graceful: a cat stalking its mouse.

And I'm the mouse, thought Nigel. He couldn't even manage a squeak of fear.

A long, slender hand reached out to grip his throat.

Curtains for you, Nessel.

The black eyes held Nigel frozen.

No! His mind screamed it as the fingers slid about his neck.

"Breegan!" Nigel yelled at the top of his lungs.

Fahgerdahl snatched Nigel to him.

"Give me the Secret," he snarled.

Nigel struggled now, hands clawing at Fahgerdahl's grip.

"I … don't … have it," he choked.

Fahgerdahl hurled Nigel against a tree, catching him about the throat again as he slumped. This time his fingers burned Nigel's flesh.

"Let's talk," Nigel gurgled.

Fahgerdahl dropped him to the ground.

"Speak."

Nigel tried to avoid the eyes, but the voice dragged him into their cold emptiness. He fingered his throat gingerly.

Bluff your way out of this one, Nessel.

"Fahgerdahl!"

Fahgerdahl wheeled. A beam of purple light struck his chest. He staggered. The air crackled with electricity. His body glowed blue for an instant, then vanished. A blue slime oozed across the ground where he had stood.

Nigel stared.

"Nigel!" Padwick hurried over to Nigel. "Nigel, are you injured?"

"I think I'm okay," said Nigel, fingering his neck.

Breegan prowled the area. Satisfied that Fahgerdahl was gone she joined them. "Are you injured?" Breegan asked Nigel.

"Are you injured?" Padwick repeated.

Nigel rubbed the shoulder he'd landed on when Fahgerdahl dropped him. "Only parts of me," he said. "Did you kill Fahgerdahl?"

"No."

"No? But he vanished in a puff of smoke. Uh, slime."

"He retreated to his Well of Siskis. He is not yet strong enough to face me."

"He seemed strong enough to me," Nigel objected. "Where were you guys anyway?"

"Phaedra led us into the woods on the other side of the river," began Padwick.

"And left us there," Breegan finished.

"I felt your fear and pain through the *zinahday*," Padwick said. "We returned as quickly as we could." He looked around. "Where is Phaedra?"

"Over there." Nigel pointed to the crumpled butterfly.

Padwick's mouth formed a wordless "oh".

Breegan went to examine the remains.

"Was she like that thing that attacked us?" Nigel asked.

"No," said Breegan, returning to Nigel. "That was a fabrication from this land's Eras. Phaedra was, as you correctly sensed, completely of this world; transformed, yes, but not a beast out of Fahgerdahl's imagination made with Siskis and Eras Magics."

"But Fahgerdahl said she was part of him, too."

Breegan's eyes narrowed. "What else did he say?"

"That Phaedra had been his eyes and ears."

"Yes, of course. Mentally she was part of Fahgerdahl, like being hypnotized."

"That is why she had no thoughts," said Padwick. "Last night, as she slept, Phaedra was with Fahgerdahl in spirit."

"That's probably when she told him I have a secret," Nigel said.

"Secret?" Breegan pounced on the word.

"Yeah. That's why he was throttling me when you …" *Rescued me.* Nigel finished the sentence in his head, embarrassed. When was he going to be a benefit instead of a liability?

"What did you do?" Nigel asked Breegan. "I didn't see anything set alight."

"She called upon her Agenta Magic," Padwick whispered to him.

"What secret?" Breegan said sharply, casting an annoyed glance at Padwick.

"I don't know," answered Nigel. "He kept saying, 'Give me the Secret,' and I kept telling him I didn't have it. That I didn't even know what it was."

"Would you have told him if you had known?" Breegan knelt down, sitting on her heels, eyes focused on Nigel.

Nigel examined that possibility before he answered, aware of Breegan's consternation. He had never been so scared in his life, and yet he'd wanted to protect Padwick and Breegan. "No," he said at last.

Breegan nodded. "Then I will tell you the Secret. As you know, Fahgerdahl grows stronger as he drains the Eras from this world. It is his intention to combine the Magics and attempt to return to Atla." Breegan rose and turned away from Nigel, studying the rocks and cliffs of the mountainside. She folded her arms across her chest, feeling cold and very much alone.

"I say attempt," she continued, "for the leap between worlds is perilous. Atlans must always travel in threes to achieve the necessary intensity of Magic required to return home.

"Fahgerdahl knows we must be certain of our return or I would never have left Atla. The risk of permanent separation would have been too great."

"Would have been?"

Breegan turned to face Nigel. "Have you never wondered, Nigel, why you can paint with such ease and understanding? Never wondered why you are drawn to the colors and motion of the sea? Never wondered why you long for places you had never been or why you ache to belong to something you cannot name? Your Gift, Nigel, is more than the sum of this Trio. It is the Gift of effortless passage. You can travel anywhere in mind, spirit … or body."

Nigel felt a prickle of anxiety.

"The Secret," said Breegan, emphasizing each word, "is the Key."

"You mean me."

"Yes."

"You know, if I'm going to play such a damned important part in this escapade, I'd really appreciate being better informed."

"I tell you as you need to know and as much as your Aura can assimilate."

"Uh-huh." Nigel stood up slowly, beginning to hurt all over. He walked over to Breegan. "Look, I know Ezamiah said too much information too soon would stunt my growth or something, but I can't keep improvising this whole Key business. Please. You've gotta give me more to go on."

"Very well." Breegan started walking back the way they had come. "As of now, if you have a question, you have only to ask and Padwick will answer. He is far better with words than I. Now come."

So much for standing up for myself, thought Nigel.

"Come, Nigel," said Padwick. The two men followed Breegan back to the stepping stones. "Do you have any questions?"

"How about, why are we trying to cross this giant, man-eating river?"

"We found a path on the other side," said Padwick, stepping onto the first rock, "just before Phaedra abandoned us." He jumped to the second rock. "Be careful of your step."

Nigel wobbled on the first rock. "Believe me, I'm being careful."

"As I was saying," continued Padwick, leaping to the third rock, "we came across a path that would take us up a mountain, but in the same direction as the river, and … How are you doing?"

"Fine, just fine." Arms spread wide, Nigel balanced on the second rock and glanced at the torrent of water racing by him. He jumped quickly to the next rock and the next.

"Breegan thought you had best come and look at the path—" Padwick reached the far side—"and tell us if it would lead to Fahgerdahl."

He looked back at Nigel. "Nigel!"

Nigel had slipped on rock number four. Desperate, he clung to its side while the river tried to wrench him loose and swallow him whole.

"Breegan!" Padwick shouted in alarm. "Breegan! Come quickly.

Nigel is in danger!" Stumbling in his haste to help Nigel, Padwick fell down on the riverbank. A strong hand helped him up. It was Breegan.

Without a word, she spanned the rocks to Nigel, grabbed him under the arms and pulled. "Let go of the rock, Nigel," Breegan instructed. "I have you."

Nigel let go. As he sneezed and sputtered, Breegan hoisted Nigel's right arm over her shoulder, slung him onto her back, and returned to Padwick.

"Dry him off," Breegan said, dumping Nigel to the ground.

"Ow!"

"And then bring him to the path."

"I will," said Padwick.

Nigel sneezed.

"Give him some *chessit*, too," Breegan added. "The water has chilled him."

Padwick nodded and Breegan went on ahead.

Nigel sneezed again.

"Are you well, Nigel?" asked Padwick.

"Yeah. I'm okay."

Checking several pockets, Padwick found his small bottle of *chessit*.

"I understand why Breegan is easily irritated," said Padwick thoughtfully. "Her challenge is great and she is preoccupied. But why are you irritated, Nigel? Your Gift is maturing and your Aura is strengthening."

"It's not that I'm irritated, Padwick. I'm just accustomed to a quieter life. One where I have a semblance of control. For instance, when I'm painting and talking to myself, I always get the last word. Here, Breegan gets it. I'm not used to somebody else being in charge."

"Neither is she." Padwick *fairowed* a glass and offered the *chessit* to Nigel.

"What do you mean?"

"Breegan must rely on you to help her find Fahgerdahl."

Nigel sipped his drink. "Good point."

"You and Breegan are much alike, Nigel," said Padwick.

"No we're not."

"Yes. You are. You both bear great Gifts that carry unexpected responsibilities."

Nigel considered that.

Padwick stood up. "Now, my friend, I will dry your clothes. Pay attention, please. It is an important lesson and will help you develop your Aura."

Padwick squinted at Nigel. "*Kesla,*" he whispered.

"Hey!" Nigel jumped, expecting to be French-fried. Instead, he was warm and dry, right down to his sneakers. "How did you do that?"

"It is a simple variation of *fairowing* fire. I did it the night we first met. You were very wet then, too. You focus your Aura on being warm, and then project that feeling into whatever you wish to dry. And remember, the Key Word must be said very softly," Padwick warned, "or you will catch fire."

"Don't worry. I'll remember."

"Excellent. Shall we go?"

Nigel drained his glass, handed it back to Padwick, and stood up. "You bet. I'm ready for anything. Well, more or less."

They headed after Breegan. Padwick tried to ignore the bleak landscape. Several trees had twisted branches with only burnt tips where blossoms should have been. The dry ground threw dust at his boots and made him long for Atla.

"Padwick?"

"Yes, Nigel?"

"What's a Well of Siskis?"

Padwick thought a moment. "I have told you that Siskis is a Dark Magic. Fahgerdahl wields it as Breegan does her Agenta, but he can only take with him a portion of its power because he has no Soul. Breegan's Agenta Magic is at her command whenever she wishes and even though we are far from home, she still maintains her *zinahday* with Atla."

"I see," said Nigel. He looked up. Storm clouds circled the mountains like vultures and the rock seemed to be a paler gray. *Fahgerdahl,* thought Nigel. He stumbled as he avoided bumping into Padwick.

Padwick stood still. Not far ahead of him, a small rodent champed its teeth and fluffed its tail, glaring at Padwick and Nigel as if blaming them for the loss of its home.

"Hey! A squirrel!" said Nigel.

The squirrel stayed a moment longer then dashed into the sparse protection of the woods. The two men watched, grateful for the brief distraction and a sign of life, no matter how small. A breeze urged them forward.

Returning his thoughts to their task, Nigel asked, "Since Fahgerdahl can't create a *zinahday*, how does he access his Magic?"

"He must create a central place where the Siskis Magic can exist in a physical form outside of himself."

"Like the Well in Karn."

"Yes. Fahgerdahl must return to that Well frequently to perpetuate his power. Once he has Eras, however, he will not need a Well to store his power. He will be able to channel it through himself at his wish."

"So we've got to beat him soon, while he's still vulnerable."

"Precisely."

The trees thinned out. A short distance away, Breegan waited for them.

Nigel looked at the narrow path that streaked up the mountain's side. "I know, I know." He held up his hand before Breegan could speak. "I'm the Key. I'm the walking map." He stopped. An eerie wave of electricity passed over him.

"Further still and yet too close," Nigel spoke in a monotone. "Falling. Falling."

"Nigel." Breegan watched him closely, aware of his connection with the land's Eras, wary of his poor control.

Nigel shuddered. His eyes focused on the path. It followed the direction of the river and disappeared among the rocks and cliffs. He knew it would lead them to Fahgerdahl.

"Okay, this is definitely more than I was ready for," said Nigel.

Chapter Eight

Deep within the mountains, a small blue pool churned then quieted, releasing smoke and mist from its unnatural source: Siskis.

Fahgerdahl paced. The ground sizzled beneath his boots. With each step, the Siskis within him scorched the earth. It oozed from his pores, veiling him like a cloud.

What is he? Fahgerdahl asked himself again. *Phaedra said his name is Nigel. That is a name of honor. She said the other two followed him.*

His eyes are dark, like mine, yet when I held him in my grasp, I felt his Aura. It is almost as strong as the woman's. Is he a Venger like her?

Phaedra said they called the woman Breegan. No honor in that name. Yet she attacked me. And her Aura is strong. Too strong for now. I must wait a little longer before I attack again.

And what did Phaedra say about the smaller man? She called him pretty. Yes, pretty Padwick who made things out of air. It is easy to guess his purpose. A helper to ease the journey of the other two, allowing them to save their Agenta Magic to use against me. No doubt a guard, as well, so that they may rest under the illusion of safety.

Perhaps the two are Pledged to each other to match my strength. Or could they be twins as I once was?

Fahgerdahl stopped by his Well of Siskis, remembering his sister. When he had killed her, he had felt an enormous hollow within him, emptier than his lack of soul had ever left him. Then the Siskis had poured into the empty space.

Now, when he looked at himself, he no longer saw his twin, only the Siskis.

It had been too long since he had been corporeal. When he fled Atla, the Siskis had spread his being apart, sustaining him as a formless creature, until the world he had escaped to was vulnerable, ripe and ready for consumption.

Silent and deadly, the Siskis had coiled itself about the new world. It manifested as a whispered word, an errant correspondence. A broken treaty. An ineffective vaccine. A bomb.

The Siskis Magic permeated the people of the world, twisting their minds until they destroyed themselves. It had gorged on the horrors of war, the atoms of destruction. And when the land recovered, Fahgerdahl was waiting.

Now he was himself again, as much as he had ever been and more. The Siskis was his sister, his blood, his soul. As he combined it with the Eras Magic, he realized he would soon have enough power to journey between worlds unassisted.

The power and the Magic, yes, but without an incantation to harness the energies he could lose his way. He could fail, die in the abyss between worlds. Having the Secret would secure his success.

Turning away from the dark cloud in the pool, Fahgerdahl inhaled the bittersweet fragrance of the Siskis Magic. Again he brooded.

One of the two leaders has the Secret to the Hall of Doors, thought Fahgerdahl. *It must be the one named with honor: Nigel.*

His Aura is strong. As a bearer of the Secret, he could not dare to battle me lest he be injured. Separate him from the other two and the Secret is mine. But how? They are already too close.

Fahgerdahl stopped pacing. A cold smile lifted his lips back from his teeth.

The bridge, he thought. *Take him from the bridge. Isolate him and he will yield the Secret.*

And if Nigel does not yield the Secret? Fahgerdahl looked up at the darkening sky. *Then I will kill them all.*

***

Nigel paused to catch his breath. The path lurched upward, his stomach with it. The river seesawed far below, increasing his vertigo.

Steady, steady, he said to himself.

"Nigel."

Padwick's voice prodded Nigel and he continued following Breegan's lead. Anxious from the increasing height, Nigel wondered what sort of animal could have made the path they climbed. The possibilities increased his uneasiness.

Calm down, Nessel. You can do this. In fact, you are doing this.

Ten feet ahead of him, Breegan scanned the path. Though scattered with rocks and gravel, the narrow path was well-worn, pounded smooth by much use and great weight. It dropped away on their right to the river a hundred feet below.

A dangerous route for anyone, thought Breegan. *Or anything.*

She looked up. The tips of the mountains were obscured by ominous clouds. It would rain soon.

Breegan glanced back to where Nigel edged his way along the path, encouraged by Padwick. His slow pace made her impatient, but she said nothing.

Through the protective *zinahday*, Breegan could feel Nigel's fear. She scuffed a small stone out of her way, glad Nigel and Padwick were preoccupied with the climb. They could not be aware of her anxiety.

She did not fear whatever creature the path might belong to, but the confrontation with Fahgerdahl had unsettled her. It had been a minor victory. She had drawn on her Agenta and it had answered, but would it be enough?

As she had struck him, she had felt Fahgerdahl's strength. He was bold to have attacked them so soon. Bold and powerful. His use of Phaedra was particularly clever.

I should have realized she was a spy, Breegan admonished herself. I have pined for what was, resented what is and been afraid of what is to come. Afraid I may have to break my Pledge. Afraid I may fail to protect Atla.

I might have killed Fahgerdahl if I had only tried harder, if I had not been afraid.

My fears made me hesitate; my hesitation may be my undoing ... and theirs.

Breegan clenched her hands into fists. The safety of Nigel and

Padwick is my responsibility. Equal to the safety of Atla. I have chosen my path. I am a Venger. And I will prevail.

She remembered Judson's warm voice. *My heart follows yours,* he had promised.

Some of the tension eased from Breegan. She stopped. The path swooped down and to the left, away from the river.

Nigel, intent on putting one foot in front of the other without throwing up or falling down, bumped into Breegan.

The unexpected contact gave him a small electric shock. "Ow! I mean, uh, sorry." Needing to keep moving, Nigel pushed for a response. "What's wrong?"

Not answering, Breegan studied the terrain. The river angled away to the right. It had narrowed as they climbed until they were scaling the side of a deep ravine. To continue following the river further would involve precarious climbing, but the path disappeared into the guts of the mountain.

Breegan frowned. "Which way?"

"You can't be serious." Nigel said. "We have to follow the path."

"You said to follow the river."

"I know, but …"

"Concentrate. In which direction do we travel?"

Nigel grappled with his vertigo, trying to feel the Eras, afraid that Breegan might force him to climb the jumble of rocks and precipices ahead. All he could feel was the mountain as he pressed his back against it.

"I can't tell for sure." Nigel swallowed a yell. "Let's follow the path."

"You must be certain," Breegan insisted. *And so must I,* she thought.

"I can't tell."

"You must."

"Can't you help?" Nigel's fear of heights started up his throat.

Breegan felt again her own trepidation and she spared a moment to calm herself, projecting that calm into Nigel through the *zinahday*.

Steadied, Nigel took a deep breath. He was about to continue protesting, when it came to him: the telegraph signal. He stood still. "Follow the path," he said tonelessly.

"Nigel?" Padwick stepped nearer to his friend. "Nigel?"

Nigel jerked as if coming out of a light sleep. He looked at Padwick, then Breegan. "We can follow the path," he reported, relieved.

Breegan felt his certainty. "You did well, Nigel. You are developing your Aura."

"Oh, yippee," Nigel said, "my new goal in life."

Sensing Nigel's fatigue and Breegan's impatience, Padwick spoke. "Perhaps we should think about a place to stop for the night. It is almost dusk. I am tired and hungry. Perhaps you, too, are tired and hungry?"

The thought of food distracted Nigel from his fear.

"Yeah. I think I felt a valley."

"You 'felt' a valley," Breegan repeated.

"That's right," said Nigel defiantly. "And I'd appreciate it if we could get the hell off this ledge and find some place to have dinner."

He pointed at the split in the mountain's side. "Thataway," Nigel announced. His conviction made him brave and he started down the path.

Fairowing a torch, Padwick hurried after him. Breegan brought up the rear. A wind whistled through the ravine as they left it behind. The rain began.

They walked for another hour. The path leveled after a mile and the torch threw strange shadows on the walls of the mountain.

"You don't suppose there are bats around here, do you?" Nigel's question bounced along the fissure, loud against his ears. He glanced over his shoulder at Padwick.

"I do not suppose so." Padwick lifted his torch higher.

"Yeah, you're right. Bats live in caves. What would they be doing out here in the rain? What am I doing out here in the rain?"

"What are bats?" asked Padwick.

Nigel shook his head. "Never mind."

The fissure slowly widened and Padwick came abreast of Nigel. They walked side by side. Breegan followed. After a short distance, Nigel slowed.

Padwick shone his torch into the yawning blackness before them. "The valley?"

"You bet," answered Nigel, turning right without thinking.

They felt along the valley's edge until they came to a small cleft in the mountain's side. An overhang of rock protected it from the rain's steady drizzle.

"Here's a cheery spot to spend the night," Nigel remarked, trying to shake the feeling of doom the valley gave him.

"Any bats?" asked Padwick.

"I don't think so."

"What are bats?" asked Breegan, coming up behind them.

"Fur with wings," Nigel remarked. "And teeth."

They camped there, huddling about a small fire, silent with fatigue and the weight of the darkness.

"I think there's something out there," said Nigel, peering into the ink beyond the flames.

"Yes," Breegan said, "there is."

"Well? What is it?" Nigel was certain he wasn't going to like the answer.

"A user of the path we have followed." Breegan's voice was calm, almost uninterested.

"Uh-huh." Nigel fidgeted, pulling his blanket up under his chin. He waited. "So? What are we going to do about it?"

Breegan glanced at him then back out at the night, oily with rain and an almost tangible gloom. "Nothing."

"Nothing?" Nigel was indignant.

Undisturbed, Breegan stretched out, ready for sleep. "It is not of Fahgerdahl," she replied, as if that explained everything.

"That doesn't mean it's not dangerous."

"Perhaps. But it makes it less so. And," she added, her voice tinged with irritation, "it is afraid of us. You would feel that if you paid attention to your *zinahday* with the Eras."

"It is afraid," Padwick whispered. "Nigel, I feel it through you. Concentrate."

Taking a deep breath, Nigel focused on the Eras. He was rewarded with a tremor of anxiety. It wasn't his.

"Finally, something that's afraid of us."

Breegan did not comment. She slept. Beside him, Padwick was nodding off.

Nigel listened to the rain. He thought of the toothsome beast that had attacked him before and decided to keep watch, just in case their anxious spy got brave in the middle of the night.

The rain drizzled on. Nigel dozed. He dreamt he was in a pit. It was dark and wet. He was trying to climb out, but the sides of the pit were muddy and he kept sliding back to the bottom. Again and again he tried to escape, clawing at the rain-soaked earth. It oozed between his fingers and sucked at his legs. He struggled harder, struggled out of sleep.

Dawn breached the overcast sky. Nigel was soaked with rain and sweat, his blanket twisted about his legs.

"So much for standing guard," he muttered. He started to unravel the blanket and stopped. The hairs on the back of his neck were setting off an alarm. Nigel looked up slowly.

Two large eyes stared at him. They were attached to something that was swathed in the fog and mist. Nigel stared. The eyes stared back.

"Do not move," said Breegan.

"Who's moving?" Nigel retorted, his voice a strained whispered.

The eyes blinked and drew closer. A long nose like an anteater's came into view. It snuffled at Nigel.

"Do something," Nigel urged. He cringed, hoping Breegan would zap the thing before it had him for breakfast. The nose poked him in the ribs.

Breegan watched. "What would you have me do? It is only curious."

"I think its curiosity is based on how edible I might be."

The thing stepped forward.

"A giant raccoon!" yelled Nigel.

The animal stood six feet high at its rounded shoulders, supported by four sturdy legs. Wiry gray and black fur ruffled about a thick neck and white whiskers drooped from a long face. Rabbit-like ears flicked forward. A long black tail twitched. A stubby paw prodded Nigel carefully.

"Chukkkkkkah-chukkkkkkah," it husked.

"It does not feel dangerous," Padwick said.

"Oh, yeah?" But even as he spoke, Nigel could feel the animal's curiosity through its touch. He could feel it wasn't dangerous through the Eras. His fear had blocked his reception.

Nigel tried to relax under the animal's scrutiny. *Always wise to be friendly to the natives,* he thought.

"Uh, hi," Nigel offered.

"Chukkkkkkah-chukkkkkkah," it responded.

The animal waddled past Nigel to where Padwick sat.

Padwick extended a hand, which was sniffed, poked, then licked. He laughed. "I wonder what it is?"

"Beats me." Nigel scrambled up, relieved to be in one piece.

Whatever it was, it seemed to like Padwick's laugh and nudged him with its nose, *chukking* amiably.

Padwick stroked it behind its ears. "It is female," he said as he touched the animal's dim thoughts. "A simple creature, much like our rabbits on Atla. Perhaps a little more intelligent. She does not eat flesh."

"Good news at last," said Nigel.

Padwick patted the animal gently. "What shall we call her?"

"You want to name it?"

At Padwick's hurt expression, Nigel quickly amended his question. "I mean her. You want to name her, of course. Good idea."

Breegan was inspecting their visitor, now and then running a hand through the gray fur and giving her a pat. "It is possible she made the path we have followed."

"How can you tell?" asked Padwick, interested.

"Only possible?" Nigel tried to see through the thick fog, wondering if it hid any more surprises.

"She is two-toed," Breegan answered Padwick. "Her size and structure suggest great weight. She is quite fat, however, and does not appear agile. It is only a possibility she made the path. Perhaps there are others like her."

Breegan looked at Nigel. "Or perhaps there is something else that lives in this valley?"

"I was afraid you were going to say that." Nigel closed his eyes, trying to leave his mind blank, a receiver for the land's Eras. "Nothing."

"So we have a mystery, still. What made the path?" *Or who?* Breegan added to herself.

She turned away from the animal. "Nigel, where do we go from here?"

Nigel hesitated then pointed. "Across the valley. The path continues there."

"Very well. We will eat and rest. When this fog lessens, we will follow the path again." Sitting down, Breegan ran her fingers through the length of her hair.

"Name our visitor if you wish," she said to Padwick, "and make a fire, please."

Padwick named the animal Chukka and she stayed with them while they waited for the fog to disperse. She would not eat, but rested the tip of her long nose on Padwick's lap, content apparently just to have company.

"I think she has been lonely," said Padwick.

"Uh-huh." Nigel barely acknowledged the statement, thinking about his dream. Had it been a dream or part of his *zinahday* with the Eras?

"Padwick." Nigel voiced his thoughts reluctantly. "If Fahgerdahl can zip around from place to place, why are we able to track him down?"

Padwick glanced at Breegan. She remained silent.

"It is the Well of Siskis that you feel, Nigel," Padwick answered. "As I have told you, he must return to it until he commands all the Eras of this world."

"Okay. So, what's this well like?"

"I do not know."

"It is a pool," said Breegan, looking at the fire. "Small, deep, with a seductively sweet scent, or so it is on Atla. It is easy to overlook, difficult to avoid.

"We believed once, as you do, that what is good must be light and beautiful, and what is evil must be dark and ugly. We underestimated the Siskis, knowing it was dangerous and yet not recognizing how much so … until Fahgerdahl."

Breegan glanced across the fire at Nigel. "Why do you ask?"

"Last night I had a dream," Nigel said, feeling foolish, but determined. "It felt so real. It still feels real. Like a premonition. I feel like I'm getting mixed signals."

"Tell me."

"In the dream, I was in a pit: deep, circular. It was dark and muddy. I couldn't climb out. I was trapped.

"Before the dream, I felt the path was leading us to Fahgerdahl. Now, I'm almost certain it leads to the pit in my dream. But it doesn't sound like this Well of Siskis."

Breegan was silent for so long Nigel thought she wouldn't respond at all.

"It is possible," she said at last, "that as Fahgerdahl's power escalates, he is able to interfere with your *zinahday* with the land. The Eras here is weak and contaminated with Siskis. Perhaps Fahgerdahl is influencing you and misdirecting us."

"You mean, Fahgerdahl's in my dreams?" Nigel felt queasy all over, remembering his encounter with Fahgerdahl.

"I did not say that," Breegan snapped, "but it is a possibility we must examine."

Padwick had listened carefully. "Perhaps Nigel's *zinahday* with the land has extended to his dreams. As the Key, he is sensitive to what lies ahead. And he has the Gift of Colors. I do not believe he could be influenced by Fahgerdahl in any way."

"Thanks for the vote of confidence, Padwick," said Nigel, "but how can we be sure? Maybe Fahgerdahl's leading us on a wild goose chase."

"A chase for a goose?"

"What I mean is, Fahgerdahl might be making us look for him in the wrong place until he's got all the Eras. Besides, where the hell did the path come from? This world is uninhabited by people. Of that much, I'm positive."

"Uninhabited now," said Padwick, "but perhaps, long ago, it was not."

"Long ago," Nigel mused. "I suppose it's possible."

"Information in a *zinahday* is fleeting," Padwick pointed out, "unless you concentrate. As to Fahgerdahl's influence, Breegan would have felt it in your Aura."

Nigel looked at Breegan.

"It is true I should have sensed if Nigel were being deceived by Fahgerdahl," Breegan spoke slowly, "but it is possible I could not. Fahgerdahl is strong and I … I am uncertain of my strength."

"I am certain of it," said Padwick. "You have the strength and the power. You have shared *zinahdays* with Nigel three times on our journey. Each time you have remained steadfast. Not once did you sense Fahgerdahl. *Zinahday* once more," Padwick encouraged her, "then you will be certain."

"But I thought Breegan wasn't supposed to *zinahday* with anyone," Nigel objected. "I thought she was going through you."

Padwick shook his head. "There are many variations of a *zinahday*, my friend, just as there are variations of *fairowing* fire or projecting one's Aura."

"The Pledge I made with Judson is a deep *zinahday*," Breegan explained reluctantly, "second only to that which I have with Atla. The *zinahday* among us three is a simple one. It does not touch my Agenta Magic. The one I used to strengthen you when you faltered and that which I used to loosen your own *zinahday* with the Eras of this land touched my Agenta, but only lightly."

Breegan straightened. "To determine if Fahgerdahl is influencing you, however, would require a more complex *zinahday*: deeper, more personal and intense. It will be diffuclt for you. But we must be certain."

"Yes," Padwick agreed.

"Go for it," said Nigel.

Breegan bowed her head for a moment. When she looked up, her gaze lanced Nigel like a spear. She held out her right hand, palm up.

"Place your left hand above mine," said Breegan.

Nigel obeyed. A current of energy invaded him. It stabbed at his heart, burned into his brain. Breegan clasped his hand and the intensity increased. He felt panicky.

Do not be afraid, Breegan's low voice spoke inside Nigel's head. The burning sensation diminished. He felt light-headed, almost giddy. Gradually, he calmed, breathing in rhythm with Breegan. Then thoughts and feelings permeated him.

He saw Atla, veiled in the muted colors of dawn: *lork* trees and purple rabbits, the marshes of Deselber and the deserts of Jeraj. The perpetual motion of the Emerald Sea lapped at his mind and the wings of *seniyas* beat in his ears as they flew to the Isle.

People Nigel had never seen, he now felt familiar with; their ways no longer strange, their faces smiling, welcoming. Peace filtered through him. Peace and tolerance, where all were understanding and understood.

He felt an ache in his chest of love for that land, those people, and for the Venger with the bewitching eyes and the elusive smile.

Nigel was acutely aware of Breegan now. Her dreams and her passions swept him up and carried him beyond the strongest emotion he had ever known. Then his own world spread before them.

Through Nigel's eyes, Breegan saw smog lying heavy over a polluted ocean. She saw the petty delays and snags of Nigel's everyday existence: the strikes, the red tape, the traffic jams. Together they felt the pressure, the anxiety, the despair and the desperation.

Nigel tensed and tried to pull away.

Breegan held him close. They watched the sun set and counted stars. They saw dolphins breach oceans bright with dawn and listened as whales sang.

Together they experienced the small joys of humanity, cheered its desperate hope for tomorrow, and cried silent tears at its anguish.

They stood silent now, bathed in purple light. Breegan was smiling. Nigel thought a thousand suns could not equal the brilliance of her smile.

A longing to belong to that smile, that endless love and warmth, welled up in him. The intimacy became unbearable. He reached for her. His hand was empty.

"Nigel?" Breegan's voice was outside him now and Nigel missed her.

"Yes?" He did not look at her.

"I am certain, Nigel."

Is she as tired as I am? Nigel wondered.

"Certain?"

"Yes."

Her voice sounds tired, thought Nigel.

"Yes," Breegan said again. "I am certain. Certain of you and of myself. You are not under Fahgerdahl's influence." Her voice softened. "I do not think you could ever be."

"And the path?" His voice sounded strange to him, weary and a little sad.

"The path is old. Very old. Yet it will lead us to Fahgerdahl."

"Will it?"

Breegan touched Nigel's hand lightly and he smiled.

"Yes, Nigel. It will lead us both to Fahgerdahl."

Chapter Nine

An icy wind brushed the clouds aside and lifted Breegan's hair from her neck. She stretched, still tired from the *zinahday* with Nigel. Knowing he would need rest, Breegan had told him to sleep for a time. Padwick, too, had dozed off, no doubt tired from the constant need to *fairow* for them.

She studied the valley. It was a small, colorless basin, emptying itself into a rift in the east side of the mountain.

Chukka stirred and raised her long snout from Padwick's lap. Smelling change in the air, she trundled over to Breegan.

Breegan pulled gently at Chukka's left ear. "So, I am certain," she whispered. "Certain of my strength at last. I have maintained my zinahday with Atla and kept my Pledge to Judson, and I have had a deep *zinahday* with another being."

Breegan looked at Nigel. "A very strange and fragile being."

I hope he does not suffer much, she thought. *I was as gentle as possible, but his mind is unaccustomed to the spectrum of emotions and their intensities. And he is so vulnerable.*

"Nigel." Breegan spoke aloud.

Nigel blinked at the late afternoon sun. He ached all over. Images from the *zinahday* with Breegan tugged at his memory. He tried to focus on them and they disappeared like dreams. Someone was talking to him. "What'd you say?" he asked.

"How do you feel?"

"Like I was hit by a truck. A big one."

The corners of Breegan's mouth lifted as she recalled what a truck was. She would always retain Nigel's memories, but as she pulled away from his Aura, Breegan made Nigel forget the closeness they had exchanged. She had felt his longing for it.

"What do you remember?"

Nigel sat up, every muscle screeching, his head pounding.

"That we're certain," he answered, and again images teased his thoughts. His head hurt more when he concentrated on them. Reluctantly, Nigel let them go.

"Good." Breegan nodded at Padwick's sleeping form. "Wake him. It is time to go."

"Hey, Padwick! Time to hit the dusty trail."

Padwick sat up and yawned. "The furry trail it would seem," he said, pulling clumps of Chukka's fur from his jumpsuit.

Nigel laughed. He felt better. Sunshine, clear sky—maybe they would even see the sunset.

Chukka followed them to the end of the valley. Few of her kind were left. They had died out slowly over the years, sick from the diseases the war spread upon the winds.

Instinctively, Chukka wanted to stay with the two-legged creatures. She remembered their kind from long ago, before the valley died and the world changed.

Unhappy at being left alone again, she watched as first Nigel then Breegan entered the fissure in the mountain's side. Padwick was last. He patted her good-bye. Chukka waited until the sunshine hurt her eyes, then turned away.

A tremor ran through the ground. Chukka jumped aside as electric waves reached for her, but she was too slow. Fahgerdahl's Siskis snatched at the warmth of her body. She staggered then fell heavily. The wind moaned through the valley, across the pallid ground and Chukka's lifeless form.

"Chukka!" Nigel cried, feeling the change in the Eras.

"Do not stop," Breegan said.

"Is she …?" Padwick began.

"Dead," Nigel said, depression sapping his good mood.

"Move on!" ordered Breegan, knowing they could not spare time for sorrow.

They continued walking, Breegan resolute, Padwick grieving.

Nigel swayed between grief and anger. *Anger's better,* he told himself. *It'll keep me on my toes.*

His toes grew cold as the path led them higher. He shivered, rubbing his hands together and stamping his feet. Nigel knew it wasn't the chill of the altitude he felt. It was the coldness of death; the land was dying, fading as rapidly as the setting sun. The wind wailed as if in mourning.

Keep angry, thought Nigel. *Keep damning that son of a bitch. It's the only thing that will keep you going.*

They climbed long into the starless night. Although the fissure led them higher, the mountain's walls reached higher still.

Nigel was thinking vertigo might be preferable to claustrophobia when the path suddenly widened. Breegan grabbed his arm. The physical connection made him gasp.

"What's wrong?" asked Nigel.

"Look."

Breegan stepped up close beside him, then Padwick. The light from Padwick's torch jumped from the fissure's sides into nothingness. Nigel didn't need to see it; he could feel it. The path spanned a canyon.

"Oh, I definitely prefer claustrophobia."

Breegan crouched to the ground, examining where the path became a stone bridge only two feet wide.

"Padwick, can you set this bridge alight?"

"I will try."

Passing his torch to Nigel, Padwick extended his Aura. He reached for the Eras. A feeble thread of energy responded and he held on to the connection.

Brow furrowed, Padwick concentrated. There was a loud pop. Abruptly two sparks lit the edges of the bridge and streaked across it. It looked as if a thousand matches had been ignited.

"It will not last long," warned Padwick. "The Eras is weak and I am not strong enough to maintain the light alone."

"Understood," said Breegan. "We will cross at once."

Nigel hadn't moved. He still held Padwick's torch.

"How far a drop is it?" he managed to ask, thinking about how high they had climbed.

Breegan rose. She gave Padwick a meaningful glance as she freed the torch from Nigel's grip.

"Far enough," she said. "Imagine you are still within the embrace of the mountain. That will make the crossing of the bridge easier."

I doubt it, thought Nigel.

"Step forward," Breegan instructed. "Move slowly. Focus on staying between the lights. We will rest when we reach the other side."

"No!" Rigid with fear, Nigel stared at the bridge.

I won't reach the other side, he thought. The idea careened through his mind and made his heart pound in his ears. This was more than his fear of heights.

"I can't," Nigel protested, shaking his head. "I'm not a high-wire act. There must be another way to get to the Well."

"There is not time enough, Nigel," Padwick said. "Remember?"

"Yeah, but …"

"This is the way you chose, Nigel." Breegan had to reach for a reasonable tone. "You will be safe. I will go before you. Padwick will come after. The protective *zinahday* will act like a brace. Now, follow."

Breegan walked onto the bridge. It was straight and smooth.

"Follow!" Her voice was like a whip.

Nigel jumped, stepping onto the bridge before he realized it. Padwick was instantly behind him. Nigel couldn't back up if he tried.

"You can do this," Padwick encouraged Nigel. "I am right behind you, my friend. Stay between the lights."

Nigel took a deep breath, trying to feel the *zinahday*. It was as if Padwick had put a reassuring hand on his shoulder. Nigel steadied a bit and took a tentative step forward.

If only the path were wider, his mind screamed. About a mile wider.

"Okay, Nessel," Nigel spoke out loud. "You've already been through a lot worse than this. Get a grip on yourself. You're on solid ground. All you've got to do is stay between the lights and you'll be fine."

Stay between the lights, keep moving and don't fall, he thought.

Nigel walked with short, jerky steps, eyes glued to the toes of his sneakers, arms spread out as if he were on a balance beam. But he was moving.

They were halfway across when Padwick's lights dimmed.

Nigel stopped. "What do we do now?"

"Keep moving," Padwick urged.

"We are almost there," Breegan said.

Almost there, thought Nigel.

The Eras trickled through his fear. Nigel saw a pale blue pool next to a tree. The tree's branches shifted in the wind.

"We're almost there," said Nigel, astonished.

"Yes," Breegan nodded. "We are almost at the end of the bridge."

"No, no. I mean we're almost there. At the Well."

Nigel looked at Breegan, his fear momentarily forgotten in his excitement. "I can see it in my mind. A small pool by a tree. It's somewhere up ahead."

"Then hurry." Breegan moved quickly forward and just as quickly stopped.

"Now what?" Nigel asked.

"Fahgerdahl," whispered Breegan.

A cold wind howled down the canyon, emphasizing her words.

"Oh, great."

Padwick's lights braved the wind for an instant, then vanished.

Breegan lunged forward, brandishing the torch in front of her, fighting back someone Nigel could only feel.

A blue light shot out of the darkness. Breegan leapt to intercept it and missed. It struck Nigel squarely in the chest, knocking him off the bridge.

Nigel was so surprised he didn't even scream. Head over heels, he fell.

This is it, he thought. *I'm falling to certain death.*

But, shouldn't I be falling faster? I seem to be falling in slow motion. Maybe I've lost consciousness and I just think I'm slowing down. No. If I were unconscious, I wouldn't be having this conversation with myself. Funny, but I don't feel scared. I should be scared.

His body stopped cartwheeling. He was on his back now, unable to move, floating gently but definitely down.

Like a really big feather, thought Nigel.

There was a roar in his ears. He started picking up speed.

Okay, now I'm scared.

***

On the bridge, Breegan stood still, bitter and angry. Once again, Fahgerdahl had caught her unaware. Once again, he had escaped her.

And now I have failed to protect Nigel, Breegan berated herself.

"Can you sense Nigel?" she asked Padwick.

Tense and frightened, Padwick shook his head. "No."

"Then he is dead." Breegan turned away. Long strides brought her quickly to the other side of the canyon.

Padwick followed. At the end of the bridge, he stopped. "I would feel it, if Nigel were dead. I know I would feel it. I have been with him the longest. He is my friend."

Breegan did not comment. She lifted the torch high. The sides of the mountain sloped gently away from the bridge and the path became a trail of small white flowers.

"Let us go." She began to walk down the trail.

"I would like to wait until dawn," Padwick announced. He sat down, staring into the canyon's darkness.

Surprised by Padwick's obstinacy, Breegan paused. "Why?"

"The Eras will be strongest at dawn. Perhaps then I may sense Nigel's Aura."

Breegan understood. Yes, the Eras would be strongest at dawn and it would make a great difference if Nigel were alive. They could not return to Atla without him. He was the Key. But more than that, he was their friend.

Breegan sat down next to Padwick. "We will wait together."

***

Nigel groped about in the darkness. The last few feet of his fall had been swift and painful. He had landed on his buttocks and slid down a long incline into something that smelled truly disgusting.

"I guess this is the pit from my dream."

He fumbled about to be sure. Wherever he was, it seemed to be shaped like a funnel and he was at its bottom. The sides were slick with mud and slime, defying Nigel's attempts to climb out of his prison.

"What's the good of a premonition if you can't prevent it from happening?" Nigel complained.

After stumbling around for several minutes, Nigel gave up. Maybe Breegan and Padwick were already looking for him. He pulled out a corner of his shirt and tried to clean his glasses.

"I can't believe I need to be rescued again. Of course, I can't believe I'm alive and in one reasonably undamaged piece."

"Fortunate, is it not?" said a voice above him and a little to the left.

Nigel paused. He knew that voice. Fumbling, Nigel replaced his glasses, trying to see through the mud-smeared lenses.

Nigel looked up. "Hello?"

"Will you not thank me for saving your miserable existence?" the voice snarled.

"Thank you, Mr. Fahgerdahl."

I don't know why I should have to thank him, thought Nigel. *He's the jerk who knocked me off the bridge in the first place.*

"Now," Fahgerdahl continued, "you will return the favor. You will give me the Secret. Tell me how you will return to Atla unharmed. What is the incantation?"

"Here we go again." Nigel raised his arms in exasperation and dropped them to his sides. *Evil geniuses can be so dumb,* he thought.

"Why don't you just reach into my mind and pick it out yourself?" Nigel said aloud.

I can't believe I said that. Nigel wanted to kick himself.

"Enough of your insolence," Fahgerdahl raged. "Speak the Secret now. I know you have it."

Speak the Secret? Nigel's thoughts stumbled over one another in his effort to grasp the impact of what Fahgerdahl had said. Speak the Secret.

Of course! He can't zinahday with me. Fahgerdahl doesn't have a real Aura. Only the Siskis Magic.

Nigel almost cheered aloud. He clamped his hand over his mouth. *Think, Nessel. Stall for time. Maybe Breegan is around here somewhere.*

"Okay. First, you get a large cauldron, some eye of newt, a rabbit's foot. No, I think it's a whole rabbit."

"What do you know of me?" Fahgerdahl interrupted.

Nigel tilted his head, listening to a hiss, like fire against water, as Fahgerdahl circled the top of the pit.

"Well, I, uh. Not much really. You're well-traveled. A spiffy dresser. You'd probably make one hell of a dictator."

"I see you must learn to take me seriously."

"What? I take you seriously, really."

Nigel tried to hang on to the hope that Breegan was coming. He didn't care how embarrassing it was to be rescued; he just wanted it to happen. Now.

"Pain!"

"Wait a minute!"

***

As sunlight spread over the horizon, Padwick heard Nigel's scream of pain through the *zinahday*.

"He is alive!"

Breegan was on her feet. "Where is he?"

"I do not know." Padwick concentrated. "He is in terrible pain." Padwick's eyes widened. "Fahgerdahl has him."

"Quickly then. We must find the Well." Breegan was moving. "If we can reach the Well of Siskis while Nigel lives, I may be able to save him."

***

Nigel doubled over in agony. He writhed in the mud.

"All right," he moaned, "all right, damn you. I'll tell you. I'll tell you the Secret."

The pain ceased, but its memory lingered. Nigel pulled himself to his knees, gasping.

What do I do now? he thought.

Touch Fahgerdahl.

What? Nigel sat still, listening.

Touch Fahgerdahl. The voice inside his head was unmistakably Padwick's.

"Speak!" Fahgerdahl demanded.

"Okay, okay."

Nigel shivered. He no longer heard Padwick.

Cold, wet, covered in slime and mud, Nigel had to search hard for the bravado to obey Padwick's message. "Ah, I've, ah, got to tell you face to face. It's part of the Secret."

Invisible hands yanked Nigel to his feet and jerked him up. Black turned to gray as he was lifted from the pit. The cold dawn blinded him.

He was dropped abruptly and he sprawled, stunned. Fahgerdahl loomed over him. "Now," spat Fahgerdahl, "tell me."

Nigel extended a shaky, slime-covered hand. "We have to touch," he explained.

A white hand snatched Nigel's wrist, the grip so cold it burned.

"Speak the Secret now," Fahgerdahl's voice rasped near Nigel's ear. "It will be the last secret you share."

***

"Did you reach him?" Breegan threw the question over her shoulder as she ran along the trail.

"Yes!" Padwick's short legs kept him some distance behind.

"Did you tell him?"

"I tried!" Padwick had to shout. "The *zinahday* is fading. I only touched him briefly."

"It will have to be enough."

They hurried on. Far ahead of Padwick, Breegan finally stopped. "Padwick! I see it."

Padwick panted up behind her. The Well lay in the center of a grassy hollow before them: a small, blue pool flanked by a tall willow tree.

"Wait here, Padwick." Breegan's voice was grim. "I know what to do."

"But where is Fahgerdahl?" asked Padwick, anxious for Nigel's safety.

Breegan approached the Well cautiously. "He is here," she answered. "He is the Well; the Well is Fahgerdahl. Does he master the Siskis? Or is the Siskis his master? We shall know."

She stopped opposite the tree. "Now, Fahgerdahl. Now I will have you."

Breegan pointed at the Well. A purple beam of light leapt from her fingertip. The beam penetrated the Well's surface.

The sticky substance churned. There was a low rumble. The ground trembled. Nigel's scream shook the silence of the hollow. Before the echo died, he appeared.

Fahgerdahl was with him.

Chapter Ten

Breegan cursed. Fahgerdahl held Nigel's left wrist captive. If she attacked while they were physically connected, Nigel might die.

Fahgerdahl sneered at Breegan, aware of her handicap.

Nigel, too, realized Breegan's predicament. He pried at Fahgerdahl's steely fingers, using the mire as a lubricant.

Calming herself, Breegan smiled. She began to stalk Fahgerdahl, moving slowly around the Well.

"So kind of you to come, Fahgerdahl." Breegan tightened her right hand into a fist.

"Your invitation was difficult to resist."

Breegan's eyes narrowed. She continued closing in on Fahgerdahl, drawing her clenched fist back like a boxer aiming a punch.

"Strike me," Fahgerdahl warned, "and he will suffer for it."

Nigel swatted at Fahgerdahl's hand. Receiving no response, he tried again to twist free of his captor.

"He is nothing to me," Breegan shrugged. "A traveling companion, nothing more. A storyteller, to pass the time."

"You lie," Fahgerdahl snarled. "He is the Secret. You need him."

"I need only your death," Breegan replied. She moved closer. "You have sensed my power, Fahgerdahl. Did it not occur to you that my *zinahday* with Atla has allowed me to use the Hall of Doors unassisted?"

Fahgerdahl took a step back, pulling Nigel with him. "Another lie," he said, denying the small doubt that entered his mind. What if Breegan told the truth? Was he strong enough to win a duel?

"I have found your Well," said Breegan. "How deep is your connection, I wonder?" Kneeling, eyes still locked with Fahgerdahl, Breegan waved one hand over the pool. It glittered and foamed as her Agenta Magic stung its surface.

Pain sliced through Fahgerdahl. He thrust Nigel aside and flung a lance of Siskis Magic at Breegan.

"Run, Nigel!" Breegan dodged the Siskis even as she punched the air in front of her. The energy of Breegan's Aura combined with her Magic of Agenta; a ball of purple fire knocked Fahgerdahl off his feet.

"Over here!" Padwick shouted. Nigel ran to join him.

Fahgerdahl retaliated even as he fell; a blue ray of Siskis just missed Breegan's shoulder. She sprang aside and launched another attack, this time slicing the air with a karate-chop motion. A wide spread of purple light slapped at Fahgerdahl.

He staggered to his feet. His outstretched arm flung tiny barbs of blue at Breegan. Several pierced her like arrows. She stumbled, winded.

There was a moment's silence in the hollow. Both Vengers squared off like gunfighters, the Well between them. Neon purple and blue outlined them as they drew upon their Magics.

Now, Breegan said to herself. She inhaled deeply, tapping her *zinahday* with Atla. *Now, now, now!* The power pulsed through her with the rhythm of her chant.

Breegan drew her right arm back slowly, fist unclenched. Suddenly she swung it forward with a violent push. The purple flame focused on its target in a single concentrated beam.

Fahgerdahl cried out in pain and rage. He jabbed at the air angrily. Spears of blue fire stabbed Breegan. She clenched her teeth as the Siskis pierced her Aura.

Focus and project, her mind shouted. Breegan thrust the force of her combined Magics at Fahgerdahl again.

He faltered under Breegan's relentless attack. His shroud of blue paled. Once more, he struck back. A bolt of Siskis seared Breegan's heart.

Her *zinahday* with Atla wavered. She staved off another blow. The Siskis battered her. She reeled. With her Agenta, Breegan grasped the thread of her *zinahday* and flung it at Fahgerdahl with all her strength.

The beam lanced his solar plexus. It pushed him up against the tree then forced him to his knees. Fahgerdahl shrieked. The beam did not let up.

Pinned to the ground, Fahgerdahl pointed an unsteady finger at Breegan. He speared her with a final bolt of Siskis then, with a hiss and crackle of electricity, he vanished.

The last blow knocked Breegan over. She laid where she fell, her breath coming in short, wracking gasps. The force of the Siskis had ravaged her Aura and depleted her strength. Pain and shock added to her stupor. Breegan made one tremendous effort to rise then collapsed into unconsciousness.

Nigel and Padwick rushed to her side.

Padwick knelt beside Breegan, feeling helpless. He looked up at Nigel. "I am not a Healer," he said. "I am not allowed to touch her."

"Yeah? Well, I have the Gift of Colors and I say that makes me as close to a Healer as she's going to get in this place."

Ignoring the mud and slime that still covered him, Nigel lifted Breegan into his arms. He carried her up the slope and lay her down among the flowers.

"Make a pillow," Nigel told Padwick, "and a bucket of water."

Padwick started patting his pockets. "What is the water for?"

"My face and her forehead. I'll need a cloth, too."

Nigel smoothed Breegan's hair back from her face. She was pale and her skin was cold. He accidentally smeared slime against her cheek.

Nigel lifted Breegan's wrist. Did Atlans have a pulse in their wrists? He waited. Yes.

Padwick knelt down with a pillow, cloth, and a large pail of water. "How is she?"

"Her pulse is faint, but steady."

"What does that mean?" asked Padwick, his voice thin with worry.

"She's alive."

Putting the pillow under Breegan's head, Nigel soaked the cloth with water and gently wiped the dirt from her face. She didn't look intimidating now. She looked frail.

"I can't be sure, but I don't think anything's broken," said Nigel.

Padwick held out a blanket. "I think we should keep her warm," he suggested.

"Good idea."

Drawing the blanket over Breegan's still form, Nigel sat back and, pulling off his glasses, sluiced some water over his face and neck. He washed his hands and emptied the now filthy water onto the ground. Padwick refilled it.

Nigel wet the cloth again and placed it on Breegan's forehead. She didn't move.

"I think we should hold her hands, Padwick."

Padwick looked doubtful.

"It might strengthen the protective *zinahday* and help Breegan regain consciousness. We don't know how long we have before Fahgerdahl comes back."

"You are right."

Feeling like a trespasser, Padwick clasped Breegan's right hand with his. Nigel did the same with her left hand. They waited.

"Feel anything?" Nigel asked.

"No. Do you?'

"I think she feels a bit warmer."

Sunlight neglected the hollow. Nigel stretched his neck to ease a cramp. It was cold and he wondered if they should make a fire.

Padwick sat still. In all his daydreams of adventures, Padwick had never imagined an unhappy outcome. Defeat and death were not possible.

You will be all right, Breegan, he thought. *You must be.*

Breegan gasped. Her body jerked away from the ground. She wrenched her hands free, thrashing wildly, then lay still.

Nigel looked at Padwick. "I guess that's a start. She's still out cold. We'd better try something else. Got any smelling salts?"

At Padwick's look of confusion, Nigel wondered what he had with him that would substitute. "I've got it."

He fumbled with his breast pocket and pulled out his haversack. Opening it, he pinched a metal bottle from the contents. Nigel squinted through his glasses, just able to see the plastic cap. "I should have cleaned my glasses," he muttered.

"I can do that." Padwick waved his hand before Nigel's glasses. "*Pencha*," he said. The lenses cleared.

"Thank you!" Nigel twisted the cap off the bottle.

"Is that smelling salts?" asked Padwick.

"Close enough. Now, I'll wave it under her nose, you talk to her."

Sliding an arm under Breegan's shoulders, Nigel lifted her up a little and waved the bottle back and forth under her nose.

"Padwick, start talking," Nigel said.

"Breegan? Breegan, wake up. It is Padwick. Breegan, can you hear me?"

Breegan opened her eyes. She felt Nigel before she saw him. He smelled awful.

"What is that terrible smell?" Breegan whispered.

"Turpentine."

"Take it away."

"She must be okay." Nigel smiled at Padwick. "She's bossing me around again."

Breegan grimaced and pulled herself away from Nigel. She straightened her shoulders. "Fahgerdahl?" she said to Padwick.

"He disappeared as before. I fear he will return soon."

Breegan closed her eyes, concentrating. She could sense Fahgerdahl's presence now. He was not far, but he was spent, as she was.

She opened her eyes and looked around. Fahgerdahl would not return until dusk, perhaps later, but he would return. He had no choice.

Nor do I, thought Breegan. *I have no choice now.*

Pulling off the blanket, she stood up slowly, carefully stretching each muscle.

"We must all prepare," Breegan said. "Padwick?"

"Yes, Breegan."

"A meal, if you please."

"Yes, Breegan."

"Nigel?" Breegan looked at him.

"Yes?"

"It is time for you to draw the door."

"But you haven't finished off Fahgerdahl."

Padwick stopped searching his pockets. "Yes. Why not wait until the battle is done? You will surely best him next time."

"No." A touch of sorrow colored Breegan's voice. "I will not."

She ran a hand through the tangled mass of her hair and looked away. "I am not strong enough."

"I thought you were great," said Nigel.

"Indeed," Padwick agreed. "And you will be greater still."

Spreading a cloth upon the grass, Padwick began *fairowing* their meal. He was upset and the proportions were coming out all wrong.

"Listen," Breegan commanded, facing them. "I must break my Pledge with Judson."

Padwick gasped. "No, Breegan," he pleaded.

"It is interfering with my ability to focus my power. I must break it."

"Are you sure?" Nigel asked. "Maybe you just need to rest, you know, build up your strength a bit." He took a glass of *chessit* from Padwick. "Have a drink."

Breegan shook her head. "I felt the strength of my *zinahday* with Atla, but I could not realize its potential. I must break my Pledge with Judson and I cannot do that from this world. I must stand in the door, bridging both worlds at once.

"You will draw the door," she ordered Nigel. "We must guard it well. Fahgerdahl is close and he is very strong."

"Maybe just opening the door will be enough to strengthen your *zinahday*," said Nigel. "It could be distance that's causing the interference."

Breegan could not let herself hope. Her duty was to Atla and its people. Judson knew this when they had made the Pledge. She had known it since she was sixteen. She was a Venger.

Breegan took a deep breath. When she spoke, her voice was calm and steady. "You will need your paints, Nigel."

Nigel, clean and dry thanks to Padwick, held out his haversack.

Breegan snapped her fingers. Full size, the sack plunked into Nigel's lap.

"You've gotta teach me that sometime."

"You will teach yourself," said Breegan, "as your Aura develops. Remember when you *fairowed* chocolate?"

"You bet I do."

"So it will be with everything else when you want or need it most. Now, if you can eat and listen, I will tell you how to draw the door."

***

Fahgerdahl hunched over a rock. He was furious. He had overestimated his power. Now he was injured and far from the Well of Siskis. He could use it, but not protect it.

He would have to wait, letting the Siskis gather inside him, before he could confront Breegan again.

Pelladanseusk, Fahgerdahl chanted in his head. *Restore.*

Sparks appeared like fireflies, popping in and out of existence with each breath.

Fahgerdahl stood up, took one step, another. Billows of Siskis Magic swathed him like a hive of bees. He looked at his fingers. They were transparent. The battle had weakened his physical form.

Opening and closing his hands again and again, Fahgerdahl drew his arms alternately toward him, pulling the Eras through the Siskis Magic and into his body. He solidified, but he knew he was still vulnerable.

Attacking the Well had given Breegan the advantage over him. He had not expected it. Or her power.

Was it true, what she said? Had she journeyed unaided? She had pierced his false Aura with her Agenta Magic; now she would have a sense of his whereabouts.

I must kill them all, he thought. *I must chance the journey back to Atla on my own.*

I will wait until nightfall then beckon a mist from the Well to cloak my return. Then I will strike. First, the one called Nigel. I will drag him into the Well and let him drown, consuming his Aura as he dies.

Fahgerdahl smiled, feeling better at the idea, knowing every ounce of energy would be needed to kill Breegan.

"And the little one?" he said aloud, his voice raspy. His words foamed at the corners of his mouth. He silenced himself.

Pelladanseusk: restore, restore.

I will break his back, Fahgerdahl decided. *And let his Aura seep into the Eras. The Siskis will take it.*

He took a deep breath. A patch of ground near him paled, withered, died.

Fahgerdahl's lips pulled back from his teeth in a satisfied sneer. Tonight he would kill the Venger Breegan.

***

Late afternoon sunlight briefly touched Nigel's palette of paints. He knelt, brush poised. Breegan had said he must draw the outline of the door from the bottom left-hand corner up, across and down again. He was not to color it in. The door could be any color, size, and shape as long as the keyhole was pronounced. Nigel was to think of Atla while he painted.

"A canvas of air." Nigel hesitated, afraid he would botch the important assignment.

"Pardon?" Padwick stood nearby, Nigel's watchdog should Fahgerdahl return.

Breegan stood guard by the willow tree.

"I was just wondering," said Nigel, stalling, "why this place doesn't look as dreary as it feels."

"It is the Well," Padwick said. "On Atla, the land of Karn struggles to live until it nears the Well. There the land softens and blooms. At first, it appeared that the Siskis was nurturing the land and that all of Karn would flourish. Then we learned it was the reverse. The Siskis draws all the Eras near to it, leaving Karn and its Mountains barren except for the *seniyas* and their nests."

"You mean, the way Fahgerdahl is drawing all the Eras of this world to him?"

"Yes. But is it Fahgerdahl? Ezamiah warned Breegan that the Siskis might be using Fahgerdahl as much as he is using it."

Nigel glanced over his shoulder at the innocuous-looking pool. Now he could appreciate Padwick's uneasiness. "Are you saying the Siskis might be alive?"

"Ezamiah believes it is possible. Agenta Magic is one of the most powerful energies in the Universes. So much power requires a balance. The Dark Magic, the Siskis, seems to seek complete power. That is the sign of a living entity, not a Magic."

"Oh, that's just great," Nigel muttered. "Not only do we have a vengeful bad guy, we've got a power-hungry super monster as well."

Fifteen feet away, Breegan called to them. "What are you waiting for?"

Nigel dabbed his brush into green paint and swabbed at the air in front of him. A green smear hung in the air, as if he were painting on glass. "Great stuff!"

Distracted from Padwick's discourse, Nigel began to paint. He used long, decisive strokes. First the left side, then the arch, then the right side and the bottom.

Night poured over the hollow. It inked out the blades of grass one by one and swallowed up the tiny, star-shaped flowers. A half-moon highlighted the sky.

Nigel stepped back to survey his work. "Not bad, considering I've never painted on air before. I've never painted a door before."

Glancing at his paint palette, Nigel noticed he was out of green. "Does the keyhole have to be the same color?" He turned around.

The hollow was filled with mist. A few feet away, Padwick was holding a torch for him. Preoccupied with painting, Nigel hadn't been aware of time passing.

"It can be any color you please." Breegan's impatient whisper came from somewhere behind him. "Now hurry."

Nigel jabbed his paintbrush into his palette and began painting in electric pink. Paying no attention to the color, he concentrated on the details of the keyhole.

Neck and shoulders aching, Nigel looked at his work. *It's very pink*, he thought.

"Do I have time to do it over?" Nigel asked.

Breegan didn't answer.

"Look out!" Padwick's warning made Nigel spin about just in time to dodge Fahgerdahl's lunge.

Fahgerdahl recoiled instantly, but Breegan tackled him like a football player. The two Vengers wrestled, sparks flying as their Auras impacted against each other.

Padwick watched in dismay. He knew the physical combat meant their powers were faltering. Both Vengers were desperate to gain an advantage.

"Nigel!" Padwick ran to the door. "Get your talisman! Open the door!"

Nigel dropped his paintbrush and groped in the pockets of his jeans. His fingers curled about the key ring. Clutching his palette to his chest, Nigel fumbled with the keys.

Padwick extinguished his torch and grabbed Nigel's haversack. "Hurry, Nigel."

"I'm hurrying."

Nigel singled out his mail key and thrust it into the keyhole. The door glowed and swung wide taking Nigel with it. He lost his balance and fell headfirst over the threshold.

Holding on to the haversack, Padwick missed the first step and tumbled after Nigel.

Breegan grappled with Fahgerdahl. The moment the door opened, her *zinahday* with Atla flowed swifter, stronger.

Fahgerdahl felt the change in the balance of power. He drew more deeply on the Siskis in the Well, inhaling it like a drug until he felt dizzy with the rush of power.

Breegan jerked a knee upward into Fahgerdahl's stomach. He doubled over and released her.

Leaping up, Breegan sprinted for the door.

Fahgerdahl caught her as she reached it and the two Vengers struggled in the doorway, straining against one another.

Breegan grabbed one side of the doorway for leverage and pummeled Fahgerdahl's body with her free hand.

He clawed at Breegan's neck, cold fingers seeking a stranglehold

Breegan tried to twist away as Fahgerdahl's icy hands squeezed her throat. He pushed against her, all the energy of the Siskis spearheaded in him.

Breegan closed her eyes. She reached inside herself, seeking the core of her Pledge to Judson. As her thoughts brushed it, she felt something snap.

She was hurled backward, Fahgerdahl on top of her. They rolled one over the other down a steep incline.

Breegan hit the bottom first, jarred, stunned. Fahgerdahl had not relinquished his grip and his weight pinned her to the ground.

Breegan swung at him with her left hand. Pain seared her arm. Her wrist was broken. That was the snap she had felt.

Breegan struggled to breathe as the Siskis smothered her Aura.

Focus and project; the teaching trickled through Breegan's muddied thoughts.

She went limp, allowing her *zinahday* with Atla to gather within her. It surged up with dazzling speed and force.

Breegan grabbed at Fahgerdahl's fingers, breaking them as she plucked them from her neck. He fell away from her and Breegan struggled to her feet.

Fahgerdahl crouched, wary, feeling the renewal of Breegan's strength.

Breegan felt it, too. It flooded her body and mind. It revived and exhilarated her. She stabbed her right forefinger accusingly at Fahgerdahl.

The Eras Magic of Atla combined with Breegan's Aura and Agenta. She focused it as she had been born to do, channeled it through her and propelled it at Fahgerdahl.

At first, Fahgerdahl stood his ground, but he was unable to retaliate. He backed up a step. His face contorted in pain as the purple beam of energy continued to assault him.

Fahgerdahl strained against it, shielding himself with the Siskis.

"No!" he roared at Breegan. "You shall not win."

Breegan stepped forward and Fahgerdahl backed away. One step, then another.

He stumbled suddenly, fell sideways into a churning pool. A pool of Siskis.

Fahgerdahl's scream was swallowed by the sticky substance. He was no more.

Chapter Eleven

Nigel lay on his side, not moving. The silence after Fahgerdahl's scream scared him. What had happened? Was Breegan okay?

Feeling woozy, he sat up, wrinkling his nose at the cloying smell coming from the pool beside him, like hard candy left in the sun. Siskis.

Not another one, thought Nigel, too nauseated to panic. He searched the grass with his fingers, peering at the fuzzy green until he touched his glasses. Putting them on, Nigel stood up and took a few unsteady steps away from the pool's edge, still feeling dizzy.

I opened the door, he remembered. *I lost my balance. I think I tripped on something. I definitely fell down.*

Nigel glanced up. His door was at the top of a small incline, about two inches above the ground. *Well, that explains the fall,* he thought. *What about the scream?*

Looking around, Nigel noticed Breegan standing several feet away. "Is it over?"

"It is over," said Breegan, unaware she had answered Nigel. She felt dissatisfied and somehow detached from herself. No shout of triumph came to her lips.

"If it's over, why do I feel so terrible?"

Nigel's bitter tone penetrated Breegan's daze. It was over, but it was not yet finished. She moved to help Nigel. Being so close to the Siskis would have an ill effect on any person; on someone with the Gift of Colors, it could be devastating.

Keeping her injured wrist next to her ribs, Breegan slipped an arm about Nigel's waist and helped him move further away from the pool's edge. She sat him down at the bottom of the incline directly below his door.

The nausea vanished. "Thanks." Nigel took a deep breath. "Where's Fahgerdahl?"

"Dead."

"Great stuff! So, where's Padwick?"

Breegan scanned the area. "I do not see him."

"Padwick!" Nigel called. "Hey, Padwick!"

There was a thrashing in a clump of bushes beside them. Padwick's scratched and dirty face appeared between some branches. "I am here."

Extracting himself from the bushes, Padwick joined Nigel and Breegan. He dragged Nigel's haversack behind him.

"Are you okay?" asked Nigel, standing up.

"Are you injured?" asked Breegan, concerned.

"Just a bump on my head. I will be fine." Padwick noticed her wrist. "But you are injured, Breegan. How can I help?"

"I will be fine, too, Padwick," Breegan said. "Do not worry for me."

Nodding, Padwick looked about. "By the Light! We have returned to Atla. But I do not recognize the province."

"We are in Karn," said Breegan.

Padwick's joy turned to alarm. "Karn! Where is Fahgerdahl?"

Breegan pointed at the pool of Siskis; it was bubbling and gurgling. Suddenly it vomited something out of its depths. A charred skeleton rolled and broke apart on the ground beside the pool. "That is all that remains of Fahgerdahl," she said.

"It ate him?" asked Nigel.

"That is one way to describe the incident."

"Incident! The guy just got spat up like a fur ball." Nigel folded his arms, feeling well enough to be testy. "I admit falling through a door and down a hill makes a guy miss a lot, but I thought Fahgerdahl was Siskis incarnate. And a Venger, to boot.

"How did falling into a pool of Siskis do that"—Nigel pointed to the skeleton—"instead of making him stronger?"

"It is true that Fahgerdahl was a Venger," said Breegan. "He channeled much of the other world's Eras Magic into the Well, believing, as we did, that he would be able to harness the combination of Magics.

"But Fahgerdahl was only a vessel for the Siskis," she continued. "The Siskis preserved Fahgerdahl's strength and youth by keeping him incorporeal. When it recreated his body, it had to use the Eras of the other world.

"When Fahgerdahl stumbled into the Well, the Siskis merely consumed the Eras Magic and incorporated Fahgerdahl's small amount of Siskis Magic back into itself, leaving"—Breegan emphasized Nigel's choice of words—"only that."

Almost as one, the trio took a step back. Fahgerdahl's skeleton stuck out against the delicate green grass and the flowering shrubs, a stark reminder that the beauty of the pool was only a ruse, like Fahgerdahl's false Aura. All around them flowers beckoned to be touched and the moss-covered incline they had tumbled down looked soft and inviting. If it weren't for the scent of the Siskis, the landscape would be perfect for picnics and afternoon naps.

Nigel tilted his head, frowning at the skeleton.

"He's looked better," said Nigel.

Encouraged by Fahgerdahl's demise, Padwick asked, "What more have you learned about the Siskis, Breegan?"

"I sensed many things during my battle with Fahgerdahl," Breegan said. "Especially during the physical contact. I was aware not only of Fahgerdahl's thoughts, but of the Siskis itself, as a separate entity. A self-aware, thinking being."

Nigel rubbed the back of his neck. "Padwick mentioned that you and Ezamiah suspected the Siskis Magic might be alive."

"Yes. It is alive and it feeds on Eras Magic. It was the Siskis that forced Fahgerdahl to risk using the Hall of Doors alone. It chose the door, too, because it recognized the presence of its kind, lesser and malleable, like Fahgerdahl.

"The Siskis then gave Fahgerdahl just enough power to create a Well and drain the Eras Magic. Once he was successful, Fahgerdahl would then be the connector, like a living *zinahday*, between the Siskis here and the Eras Magic of the other world."

Breegan sat down. She felt tired and discouraged. She wanted only to return home, not to continue struggling against an incomprehensible enemy. She swept her hair over one shoulder and studied the pool.

"And all the while Fahgerdahl believed he was the master of Siskis," said Padwick.

"Yes." Breegan nodded. "And we believed Fahgerdahl was our only enemy."

"Well, what do we do now?" asked Nigel.

Breegan frowned. "I have not yet decided."

Nigel didn't like the worry in Breegan's voice or her indecision. He was used to a Breegan who knew what to do and did it. Uncomfortable, Nigel clapped his hands together. "Okay. I think that's enough Magic for me. Let's get out of here."

He started looking for his paint palette.

"I wish I could have seen you push Fahgerdahl into the Well," Padwick said to Breegan.

Breegan rose and looked up at Nigel's door. "I did not push Fahgerdahl into the Well, Padwick," she said. "He was backing away from my attack and he tripped over Nigel."

Padwick turned to Nigel. "Nigel! You tripped Fahgerdahl."

"I did?" Nigel found his palette. "When?"

Breegan sighed. "When you were lying on the ground by the Well, Fahgerdahl stumbled over you," Breegan explained. "He lost his balance and fell into the Siskis."

"No kidding." Nigel rubbed his right leg where it felt like someone had kicked him. "Well, glad to be of help."

"Ezamiah will be impressed," said Padwick.

"Hey, all I did was fall down and stay put until it was safe. Breegan did all the scary stuff."

Padwick turned back to Breegan, ready to praise her, but she held up her hand. "It is enough that Fahgerdahl is dead, Padwick. Is it not?"

Padwick nodded.

"Then let us say we did it together and be content."

"Yes, Breegan."

Pulling her sash from her waist, Breegan clenched her teeth and bound her broken wrist. She started up the incline. "Come, Nigel. I wish to inspect your door."

"My door?" Nigel looked up. "I thought it would disappear."

"I think that only happens to a door from the Hall of Doors." said Padwick.

The two men climbed after Breegan and joined her at the door. It was shut tight. The pink keyhole glistened, its paint thick and wet.

Breegan examined the door's frame. "It should have appeared in Atla, at whatever destination you were concentrating upon," she said to Nigel.

"I was concentrating on the door. It's my first one, you know," Nigel said defensively. "I was under a lot of pressure."

Breegan faced him. "Look through the keyhole, Nigel," she instructed. "The Well on the other world should have died when Fahgerdahl died. He was still connected to it when the Siskis here destroyed him."

"Technically it did appear in Atla," muttered Nigel.

"Look!"

Nigel looked through the keyhole. On the other side of the door, it was night. Moonlight shivered among the stars. He could see the hollow clearly.

The Well of Siskis was gone. The willow tree's branches swayed gracefully in a breeze and the hollow no longer had a ghostly cast to it. Now it looked enchanted.

What was that? Nigel started. Something was moving. "There's something happening," he reported.

Breegan was instantly alert. "What is it?"

"I don't know. It's … it's … it's pink!"

"What did you say?" asked Breegan.

"I said it's pink. The hollow is turning bright pink. Look for yourself."

Breegan looked. "I cannot see as clearly as you, but it should not be like that," she said, stepping back. "It is like the rebirth of the Eras. It should take a thousand years for the Eras to recover from Fahgerdahl's assault."

Standing on tiptoe, Padwick looked, too. "Everything is vague, yet what I can see is just the color of Nigel's keyhole," he observed. "A lovely shade."

Breegan scrutinized Nigel. "What was the last thing you did in that world?"

"I painted the door."

"And?"

"And then I opened it and fell through."

"Did you leave anything behind?"

"I don't think so. I have my palette." Nigel lifted it. "My tubes of paint are in my haversack. Padwick's got that."

"I have," Padwick nodded.

"I do not understand this." Breegan frowned.

"My paintbrush." Nigel spoke half to himself. "I must have dropped it."

Breegan arched an eyebrow. "Pardon?"

"Mind if I have another look?" Nigel pressed up close to the keyhole. He searched the long grass, now a lovely rose hue. Then he spotted it. His paintbrush.

"We were in a hurry," Nigel explained. "Padwick and I. We knew you wanted the door open. And Fahgerdahl was right there … Anyway, I was trying to get my key, I mean, talisman." Nigel held up his key ring.

"Put it safely away," Breegan ordered. She considered Nigel. "What did you drop?"

"My paintbrush. It was covered with pink paint. I'd just finished painting the keyhole when Fahgerdahl jumped out of nowhere. I ducked. Then I opened the door and, well, I dropped my paintbrush."

They all looked again in turn. The brush lay on the grass. Bright pink paint seeped from it into the soil. It glazed the hollow and then the sides of the mountain in varying shades of pink, moving steadily, reviving everything it touched. In pink.

"By the Light!" Padwick said, awed. "Your Gift of Colors is true indeed."

Nigel was bewildered. "I don't get it."

"Your Gift of Colors is restoring the Eras to the land, Nigel," said Breegan "Your Aura and your Gift were concentrated in the brush you used to paint the door and the keyhole. Your *zinahday* with the land allowed the Magic of that harmony to remain."

"Great stuff! But, uh, shouldn't we go back and paint it a more realistic color?"

"We cannot go back," Breegan said. "Not through this door. It opens from the far side into Atla. You must erase it so nothing can come to Atla, especially here, near the Well of Siskis."

"Now wait a minute. Let me get this straight. I've just created a pink world and you say, 'lovely shade' and would I please erase an entire door to prevent trespassers."

"Yes," Breegan said.

Nigel opened his mouth to object and changed his mind. After all he'd been through, why should this surprise him? "Okay," he shrugged. "I'll need my—"

Padwick handed Nigel his haversack.

"Thanks." Poking through the contents, Nigel added, "And thanks very much for looking after it, Padwick."

"It was my privilege," said Padwick.

Nigel shoved his key ring into the right front pocket of his jeans and armed himself with a rag and the bottle of turpentine.

Breegan stood silent, watching, until Nigel opened the solvent. She grimaced and backed away. "That smell!"

"Nice, isn't it?" Nigel teased. "The smell of second chances."

Smiling, Nigel faced his demolition project. Since he could paint on air, he would assume he could also correct and erase. Besides, he had the Gift of Colors. Apparently, nothing was now beyond his artistic abilities.

"When you have finished," Breegan said, "you will paint a boat and then we will return to Atla."

"A boat," Nigel repeated. "Uh-huh. Just paint a boat in the air, launch it from dry land, and sail it into the sunset."

"You will paint it upon a piece of paper." Breegan spoke as if that much was obvious. "You do have another paintbrush?"

"Sure. Lots of them."

"Then you can paint a boat and I will breathe life into it. For now, remove the door. Quickly."

Bossy doesn't begin to describe her accurately enough, thought Nigel.

Kneeling, he soaked the rag with turpentine and dabbed at a corner of the door. The green paint faded easily. Nigel rubbed at the door's frame, too worried about what Breegan had said to be impressed by his Magic.

A boat, thought Nigel. *I'm going to paint a boat and then we'll sail home.*

Where is home? Nigel asked himself. *Earth?* It hadn't felt like home since he came to Atla. No. Even before then.

In fact, he couldn't remember when Earth had ever felt like home. It was more like it reminded him of someplace familiar and welcoming. On warm days, when the ocean and the sky met in colors almost impossible to paint, he had felt welcome and at home.

That's probably because of my ancestry, Nigel mused.

He looked up a moment. Pastel blues merged with iridescent violets. Soft pink etched itself into pale shades of cornflower blue and blue into meadow green. The skies of Atla. Was this home? Should he stay here?

What if he didn't have a say in the matter? Padwick had said it was up to Breegan whether or not he could stay in Atla. What if she said he had to go back to Earth?

Well, I won't go. Nigel clenched his teeth stubbornly. *She can't make me. I'm not a citizen. I'll just paint a door of my own and hop through. At least, I think that's how it works. I'll have to ask Padwick.*

He returned to his cleanup job. The bright pink keyhole hung alone in the air. Nigel had saved it for last.

He stopped before it and leaned close, gazing once more upon that nameless world where he had such an awful, wonderful time.

The hollow was a myriad of pinks and reds. Every blade of grass was a variation on a theme of pink. The white flowers were now cinnabar, one side of the mountain was a pale vermilion, the other side a soft maroon.

Nigel smiled. It was beautiful. He stood back and wiped the keyhole out of existence. *Good-bye, Nigel-land*, he thought.

He packed away his cleaning supplies and pulled out his brushes, wondering how detailed the boat had to be.

Breegan and Padwick were sitting a little way off. They were looking down the incline at the pool of Siskis. Its sweet smell wafted up to them.

"Can you destroy it?" Padwick asked. Even sitting next to Breegan, a good distance from the pool, he felt uneasy.

Breegan kept her voice calm. "I do not know, Padwick. The Siskis is not what the Council expected or what the Seers predicted. I must heal my injury and consider what is to be done. If it is within my power to destroy the Siskis, I will."

A cry of mourning came from far over their heads. They looked up.

A *seniya* sailed on an updraft, circling higher and higher. The bird wailed again, flying aimlessly without its mate, bereft of purpose. A stab of pain stalled the bird in flight. For an instant it fell, then, buoyed by what felt like an air current, the *seniya* circled once above the Well of Siskis then flew away toward the northern mountain peaks.

"He has lost his mate," said Padwick, watching the *seniya.*

"Yes." Breegan eyes narrowed. *But why had it been so close to the Well?*

"Breegan?"

"Yes, Padwick."

"Since the Siskis is alive,"—he dropped his voice to a whisper—"can it hear us? Do you think it is listening?"

"It is possible."

Disquieted, Padwick sat closer to Breegan. "Can it possess us, as it did Fahgerdahl?"

"I do not know, Padwick. Fahgerdahl was willing and empty. We are not. I hope that is enough."

Nigel joined them, paint palette in one hand, brush in the other. He bowed like a courtier. "Anyone for a boat?"

Holding her injured wrist against her body, Breegan stood up carefully. She turned her back on the Siskis and began walking toward the low mountain range. "Wait until we are close to the shore," she said as she passed Nigel.

"Sure, no problem. Makes sense to me. Uh, where's the shore?" he called after Breegan.

"Come, Nigel," said Padwick. He picked up Nigel's haversack.

"Isn't she going to downsize it?" asked Nigel.

Padwick shook his head. "Breegan is injured, my friend. She must conserve her energy for the journey back to Atla's shores."

"Oh." Nigel nodded. "Right." Nigel gave himself a mental kick in the backside for being self-centered.

"Sorry, Padwick. I didn't mean to whine. I guess I got spoiled without realizing it. Just give me a minute to pack up properly."

"Certainly."

"Will she be okay?" Nigel asked as he wrapped his palette in a piece of tarp.

"Yes. Once we are on the ocean, Breegan will create a *donaderas*. It is a healing *zinahday* with the Eras. It will mend her wrist and cure her injuries."

Nigel took his haversack from Padwick and slung it on his right shoulder. "You haven't taught me about that one."

"Only Healers and Vengers can create a *donaderas*," Padwick said. He looked at Breegan's distant figure. "We must hurry."

"You bet."

They hastened after Breegan, relieved to get away from the Well of Siskis.

Nigel looked around at the land. It was rapidly transforming from lush to barren. The grass was beige, the ground was taupe, even a narrow stream had a sepia hue to it. No animals moved about the rock strewn, muddy landscape.

Not even a dandelion, observed Nigel.

"How long a trip is it?" he asked Padwick.

"It will take three days to walk to the coastline," Padwick answered. "There is a route that passes between the mountains. We will not have to climb them."

"That's a relief."

"If we are very fortunate," said Padwick, a trace of excitement in his voice, "we may find some *seniyas* to help us. Swans," he explained at Nigel's questioning look. "Breegan and I saw one flying toward the mountains."

"Oh, no. No more swans. Uh-uh. No way. I'll walk."

Padwick smiled. He looked about at the bleak landscape, missing the forests of his home province of Penkas. "We must walk faster, Nigel. It will be dark soon."

Nigel lengthened his stride. "Does Karn have anything spookier than swans?"

"No. But it will get very cold."

"It already is." Nigel turned up the collar of his shirt.

They weren't far behind Breegan now. A wind lifted her hair and it blew like a flag behind her. Ahead of them, a low mountain range darkened the horizon.

"Hey, Padwick. Why would the swans come to a desolate place like this anyway?"

"They migrate to the mountains to mate."

"Ah."

They had almost caught up to Breegan when Nigel paused. He felt a chill race down his back, like something clawing at him. He looked back at the trail of muddy footprints they were leaving. The land was as uninteresting as before.

Was he only imagining it looked menacing?

Padwick stopped. "What is it, Nigel?"

"I don't know. For a moment, I had this scary feeling that we were being followed. Or watched. It's gone now."

Nigel gestured to the desolate land. "Do you sense anything? You know, anything nasty that might be hiding out there. Maybe under a rock?"

Padwick closed his eyes, reaching out to the land's meager Eras. "No. I sense no danger. Not even a *seniya*."

Nigel squinted at the darkening horizon. "Not even a *seniya*," Nigel repeated. "Well, then it's nothing. Just nerves."

"What did you feel, Nigel?" It was Breegan.

Nigel jumped. *Somebody ought to put a bell on her,* he thought. Aloud, he answered, "For a moment I felt we were being followed. Now it's gone."

Breegan scanned the horizon. This was Karn, true, but the Eras was still of Atla. Hers to touch, to hold, to protect.

She sensed nothing amiss. Could her injury and fatigue be hindering her *zinahday* with Atla? Or was the Siskis blocking her?

Stretching out the fingers of her right hand, Breegan intensified the contact with the Eras. The Siskis was too close. She felt it writhing, as if it were trying to escape. Breegan dropped her arm to her side.

"I think you feel the nearness of the Well, as do I."

Padwick looked back in the direction they had traveled. "Breegan?"

"Yes, Padwick?"

"Why did we arrive in Karn?"

Breegan turned her gaze to the mountains. "I am not certain. Perhaps the violent exchange of Siskis and Agenta Magics interfered with Nigel's Gift of Colors."

"I resent that," said Nigel.

Breegan ignored him. "For now, Fahgerdahl is dead. He can no longer spread the Siskis Magic."

"Yes, Breegan." Padwick took comfort in her calm.

"You make the Siskis sound like a disease," Nigel said.

"In some ways it is similar. A being that perpetuates its existence by infecting others."

"What about the Well here in Karn?" asked Nigel. "Is it spreading?"

Yes, thought Breegan. Aloud, she said, "The Siskis here in Atla has always been confined to Karn. The Seers believe my *zinahday* with Atla prevents the Siskis from spreading."

"Because a Venger's *zinahday* helps maintain a balance in the Eras Magic," interjected Padwick. "Breegan can do more than evoke the Eras, she can control it."

"I see."

The trio walked side by side. Nigel broke the silence. "Okay, I can understand that the Seers missed the fact that the Siskis is alive. They were concentrating on Fahgerdahl. But how did they find Fahgerdahl in the first place?"

"Yes, Breegan," said Padwick. "How was Fahgerdahl discovered?"

"You need not concern yourself with such things, Padwick," Breegan answered.

"What about me?" Nigel said. "I'm concerned."

Breegan kept her eyes on the distant mountains. Finally, she spoke. "When the Seers searched for Fahderdahl, they did so by leaving their dreams open to their perceptions of Siskis as a Magic and to their theories of what it would be like on other worlds where it could spread.

"They watched for disruptions of Eras Magic: storms that became catastrophic, unnatural levels of violence, disasters, wars. And desolation, as you have seen here in Karn. It is what you recognized in the pink world.

"And it is how the Seers found Fahgerdahl. They thought he was causing the disturbances in the Eras of the pink world. They did not suspect that Siskis might already exist there. Nor did they think it was alive."

"So, the plan to eliminate Fahgerdahl was based on the assumption that the Siskis here in Atla was a Magic and therefore harmless without Fahgerdahl," said Nigel.

"Yes," said Breegan.

"Is it harmless now?" Nigel asked. "You fought Fahgerdahl. You said you sensed the Siskis as a separate entity. Are we safe? Were the Seers right?"

"I do not yet know."

Nigel knew that was all he was going to get for the moment.

Breegan looked at the Mountains of Karn. They were draped in rain clouds and still too far away to give her confidence, but she was tired; she had to rest.

"Padwick, make a tent there, please." Breegan pointed. "We will stay the night on this moor and walk on at daybreak."

"At once." Padwick began *fairowing*, glad of the distraction. *What if the Siskis were following them?*

Nigel concentrated on fairowing fire. *Where was their happy ending?*

They had no appetite for food or conversation. The night hung close about them. Nigel's fire did little to lift the gloom. A slow drizzle of rain would have put it out entirely if not for help from Padwick.

They sat together, alone in their thoughts.

This is ridiculous, Nigel decided. *My ancestors were adventurers. I'm not going down without a fight. Or at least a lot of complaining.*

"Maybe we should get in touch with the swans after all," said Nigel. "You know, get the hell out of here as fast as we can?" Given a choice, Nigel decided he would much rather ride a swan than sit around waiting to be attacked by an invisible enemy.

Padwick shook his head. "Not everyone can call the *seniyas*, Nigel. Breegan's Aura is strong enough, but she is injured. You and I must protect her and get her to the ocean."

"I could give it a try if you tell me what to do," Nigel volunteered. "I mean, I do have the Gift of Colors. I might be able to call a few birds."

Padwick looked to Breegan. She nodded.

"Very well, Nigel," said Padwick. "You must stand away from the fire and face the mountains. The *seniyas* build their nests among the peaks."

Nigel didn't like moving away from the fire. Reluctant but determined, he stood up.

"Uh, that way?" Nigel pointed into the dark.

"Yes, Nigel," Padwick answered.

"You must raise your arms to the sky," Breegan instructed, "and call: *Bethen-yah, bethen-yah. Ah-divesh, ah-divesh.* Come to me. I am in need."

Nigel repeated the words several times, making certain he could pronounce them correctly. He didn't want to piss off a giant swan because of his accent.

"Okay. I think I've got it."

Lifting his arms to the night sky, Nigel began to call to the *seniyas*. "Bethen-yah, bethen-yah. Ah-divesh, ah-divesh."

He looked at Padwick. "What do they do? Call back?"

Padwick raised a finger to his lips.

"Again," said Breegan.

Feeling silly, Nigel kept his arms high and repeated the chant several times.

"Anything?" he asked Padwick.

"No. But they may not hear your words until dawn."

"Heavy sleepers?"

"The Eras is strongest at dawn, Nigel."

"So, I try again then?"

"No," Breegan said sharply. "Your words are on the wind. If they have evoked the Eras Magic, it will find the *seniyas* and bring them to us."

"Great stuff." Nigel plunked down by his haversack. "Anyone for chocolate?"

Chapter Twelve

The wind was howling, closer, heavier, like a living thing struggling to breathe. Nigel pulled his blanket tighter about his shoulders. Someone poked him.

"What?"

"Nigel." Padwick's voice was a frightened whisper. "Nigel, wake up."

"I'm awake, I'm awake." Nigel reached for his glasses. "What's going on?"

"The wind has put out your fire."

"So? We'll make another one."

Breegan spoke from the darkness. "It is a wind created by the Siskis. We cannot fight it. We must escape. Creatures of Siskis are approaching."

Nigel had to squint to make out Breegan's silhouette. Dark clouds streaked across the moons, making their light shift across the uneven landscape. "What creatures? Padwick said there are only swans here. I mean, *seniyas*."

"They were *seniyas*," Padwick said. "Now they are transformed."

"Into what?"

"Breegan suspects they are *carolaks*."

Breegan stepped close to Nigel. "Paint a door," she said. "Quickly."

"A door? In this light?"

"Do not argue." Snatching up Nigel's haversack, Breegan thrust it at him.

"Imagine a door; mark the keyhole with a circle. Take any color of paint, use your fingers if you must, but do it now."

"Right. Okay." Nigel groped in his haversack. The noise he had thought was wind now had a distinct, growling undertone.

"What is that?" he asked Padwick.

"*Carolaks,*" Padwick whispered.

Nigel grabbed a tube of paint, fumbling as he opened it. "Don't tell me how many, just make a light."

"I cannot. The Siskis is too strong."

Nigel squeezed the tube, squirting the contents into his palm. Kneeling, he swiped two fingers in the paint and made a quick arch in the air.

"It's a little small," Nigel warned.

He drew a circle for a keyhole. "Damn, I need a key."

"Use your finger," Breegan hissed.

"Really?"

The sound of many feet circling made Nigel shut up. He poked his finger in the circle. The small wood door he had imagined glowed for a second then swung open.

"Nothing to it," Nigel said.

"Where will it take us?" asked Padwick, looking all around him. Dark shapes were scuttling closer with red eyes flashing in the dim moonlight.

"It does not matter," Breegan snapped. "Get in!"

A loud baying began. Padwick slipped through the door and disappeared.

Nigel saw a giant dog leap at Breegan. Shouting, he swung at it with his haversack. It yelped and ran back to its companions.

Grabbing Breegan's sleeve, Nigel shoved her at the door, ducking in after her. His haversack stuck in the doorway. Growling filled his head as he yanked at the sack.

Red eyes glared. White teeth snarled.

Nigel hauled on the haversack. Padwick joined him. Together, they pulled it free.

The *carolak* lunged. Nigel kicked the door shut on its nose.

"Son of a bitch!" Nigel flopped back on the ground, breathing hard. "Helluva way to wake up."

"Thank you, Nigel." Breegan stood up and brushed snow off the sleeves of her tunic. "You did well."

"Yes. Yes, Nigel," Padwick agreed. "You did very well indeed. Thank you."

Nigel waved a hand. "No problem. Anytime."

He sat up. Painfully bright sunlight made him shield his eyes with one hand.

"Where are we?" Nigel asked.

The sun sparkled on snow. Snow. In every direction. No mountains, no lakes, no trees, not even a polar bear. Snow.

"Let me guess." Nigel stood up, already feeling cold. His breath swirled around him. "The North Pole."

Breegan looked around. "We will not be staying to find out if you are right. Please paint another door."

Nigel rubbed his hands together and stamped his feet. "Can I have a fire this time? Oh, yeah, and an explanation?"

Padwick *fairowed* a torch to avoid melting the snow. "I could not *fairow* fire with so much Siskis in the air," he apologized. "And Nigel?"

"What?"

"Your hands are blue."

Nigel looked at his paint-covered hands. "I forgot I was finger painting." He raised his hands toward Padwick. "Would you mind, please, Padwick?"

Padwick nodded. *"Pencha!"*

"Thank you. I've definitely got to learn that one."

Padwick quickly *fairowed* a cloak for Breegan and offered it to her. "The Eras is strong here, Breegan. This will keep you warm while we wait."

Breegan nodded, uncomfortable with being looked after. Stooping, she picked up Nigel's tube of blue paint. The cap was missing.

Nigel produced the paint tube's cap from the cuff of his sleeve. "I've got it," he said. "I tossed the paint tube after Padwick. I wasn't expecting a hasty exit."

Breegan nodded and handed Nigel the tube of paint as she scanned the landscape.

Feeling shaky but annoyed, Nigel replaced the cap. He shoved his freezing arms into a jacket provided by Padwick.

"So." Nigel tried to jump-start an explanation. "What happened?"

Breegan did not answer. *Not what*, she thought, *but how?*

"Listen," said Nigel, as stubborn as the cold, "I don't understand what happened back there and I'm going to stand around in this frozen wilderness until I do."

He glowered at Breegan. "How did *seniyas* transform into *carolaks*?" he demanded, blowing on his fingers. "Who sent them and what the hell is going on now?"

Breegan raged inside, feeling helpless. Now that she was apart from Atla, her broken wrist hurt. She needed to reach Atla's ocean and create a *donaderas*. Only then would she be strong enough to use her Magics to their full extent.

The cold air stung Breegan's cheeks, reminding her of Biachin in an unpleasant way. She felt the same loneliness she had experienced when her Gift was first recognized by the Council. To be the protector of all Atla was a daunting challenge. Yet she had succeeded. Until now.

Nothing she had been taught, nothing she had learned and practiced had prepared her for what she now faced: a being more powerful than herself. *How am I to overcome this evil?*

The answers to Nigel's questions were unsettling, but Breegan knew her conclusion was correct. With effort, Breegan forced herself to appear calm. When she spoke, her voice was steady. "The Siskis sent the carolaks, Nigel."

"What?"

"Yes," said Breegan. "I think the Siskis did more than consume Fahgerdahl's body when he fell into the Well. It consumed his mind, incorporating everything he knew or suspected of us."

"So?" Nigel shrugged, trying to stave off anxiety. "So the Siskis is what now? Paranoid?"

"Do you not understand?" Breegan frowned. "Nigel, the Siskis wants you as a replacement for Fahgerdahl."

"Me?" Nigel glared at his blue door. "What for? I'm a nice guy. I have a soul. What could the Siskis possibly gain from kidnapping me? What? Make me paint really bad portraits?"

Breegan pointed at the door. "It knows you are the Key. Fahgerdahl saw you paint a door. He recognized your Gift of Colors. And now the

Siskis does as well. If the Siskis could insinuate itself into a hollow place within you it would have unlimited access to Eras Magic.

"You can travel anywhere and, by manipulating your Gift, the Siskis could consume Eras wherever you journeyed."

"But I don't have any hollow places. You said so yourself."

"Not while you are alive."

Dumbfounded, Nigel stood still, barely breathing.

"Nigel's Gift would perish with him if he died, would it not?" asked Padwick, worried for his friend.

Nigel was worried, too. He didn't like being the center of attention when the subject was dying.

"Not if the Siskis kept Nigel at the edge of death."

Edge of death? Nigel felt sick to his stomach.

Breegan began to pace, like a detective solving a crime.

"The Siskis decided to avail itself of what it had already poisoned in order to capture you as a replacement for Fahgerdahl."

"The *seniyas,*" Nigel said.

The word seemed to hang frozen in the air. "The Siskis waited, it listened ..." Breegan stopped pacing and looked at Padwick.

"Remember the *seniya* we observed, Padwick?" Breegan's voice was gentle. "It had lost its mate. I think the Siskis possessed it."

Breegan turned back to Nigel. "The incantation I gave you provided the Siskis with enough Eras Magic to transform the *seniyas* you summoned from peaceable beings of light and air into predators."

"*Carolaks,*" whispered Padwick.

Breegan nodded, feeling Padwick's distress. "I believe they were sent to isolate Nigel."

"Isolate me? How?"

"By killing us," said Breegan. "Padwick and me."

"But the *seniyas* have always migrated to the Mountains of Karn," Padwick protested. He looked at Nigel's small door, absurdly blue against the pristine snow. He could not bear the thought of the beautiful creatures he admired being twisted into hideous beasts of violence.

"What hollow place could they ever have to make them vulnerable to the Siskis Magic?" Sadness lowered Padwick's voice to a whisper.

"Loneliness," said Breegan. "*Seniyas* mate for life. Not all survive the migration. Storms swallow some, *fekinats* kill others. Those without mates are lonely. The loneliness of a long life span spent in sorrow. We hear it in their bird song: a great longing and pain. The Siskis must have tainted them in their grief, curling deep inside them, too deep for me to sense. And then it waited."

Restless, Breegan started pacing again. "Patience is a powerful weapon. Whenever a pair of *seniyas* was separated, the Siskis could infect the survivor. It could lie dormant within the *seniyas*, traveling with them, altering their appearance and their instincts only when they were weak with despair. That would explain the increased numbers of *Carolaks* in Atla. The unprovoked attacks. Even some of the predators in our ocean may be Siskis aberrations. They, too, are more numerous."

Breegan stopped in front of Nigel. "I never sensed the Siskis as a living thing because it was cloaked within the *seniyas*. I thought I knew my enemy, I thought I knew my goal, but all the while the true nature of the Siskis went unnoticed because I focused on Fahgerdahl."

"Classic decoy," Nigel said. "Make your opponent look in one direction so you can attack in the other."

Padwick looked down at the snow on the toes of his boots. He had forgotten to *fairow* a cloak for himself. Was it the cold that made him shiver or the sadness? His beloved birds had been turned against him.

Noticing his friend's unhappiness, Nigel created a distraction. "We should give it a name," he said, forcing a cheerful demeanor.

Padwick looked up. "Pardon?"

"The pink world. We can't keep calling it that. Who knows how many doors I'll have to paint? Think of a name, would you, Padwick?"

"And make a cloak for yourself," said Breegan.

"Yes. Yes, Breegan. How careless of me."

"Do not speak of carelessness," Breegan murmured. She turned her back to Padwick and Nigel, wishing she were with Judson. She could confide in him, confess her fears and failure.

Breegan straightened her shoulders. "I should have realized we were not yet safe. I should have recognized the Siskis for what it has become, perhaps always was: a living entity."

"You can't think of everything," Nigel said.

"Perhaps not. But it is my duty to try. When we returned to Atla, I allowed my sense of caution to lapse. We would not be here if I had remained focused on my goal."

"You're right," said Nigel. "We wouldn't be here. We'd be dinner for *carolaks*."

Quest for Evil

Breegan did not respond. Taking the torch, she walked away from the two and headed across the snow.

"Hey, wait!" Nigel took a step after her.

Padwick held up his hand to stop him. "No, Nigel. Breegan needs to be alone. She wants to plan her next move."

Feeling like a chessman, Nigel huddled into his jacket.

Padwick quickly *fairowed* another torch and a big, puffy jacket like the one he had made for Nigel.

He felt inside several pockets. "Poor Breegan," Padwick said, feeling sad for his friend. "It must have been very hard on her to be so close to returning to Judson. And now, she is further away from him than ever."

"Yeah." Nigel nodded. "But she's tough. She'll be okay." He looked at Padwick. "Won't she?"

"Her physical injury impairs all her Magics. I am certain it is frustrating for her, but yes, she will recover. She is the Venger, Breegan."

Padwick *fairowed* a rug and a footstool. "This is for you. To sit on as you paint," he explained. "I do not think Breegan wants us to stay here long."

"Neither do I, but I'm not really keen on heading back to Karn and I don't know what to imagine while I'm painting."

"What were you imagining when we escaped the *carolaks*?"

"Getting the hell out of there in a big hurry."

Padwick considered this. "You could think of someplace warm," he suggested. Looking at the snow-covered landscape, he added, "Someplace green."

Nigel placed his haversack on the rug, sat down on the footstool, and poked through his haversack. "Now we have two worlds without names," he grumbled.

"Indeed," said Padwick. "You asked what I might call the pink world. I think something that describes renewal. Does your language have such a word?"

Nigel decided he'd stick with the Azure Blue paint, only this time he'd use brush and palette. "Springtime," he said absently.

"That is nice," Padwick nodded. "Springtime. Yes. That is very nice."

Nigel didn't comment. He started painting on air: big, bold strokes far enough apart to facilitate a crowd of three.

Padwick watched for a moment then looked to see how far Breegan had gone. She had stopped walking and was looking back at them. Smiling, Padwick waved.

Breegan raised her hand in response then turned away. She pulled up the hood on her cloak. It had been a long time since she had felt the icy air of a winter landscape.

I will go to Biachin when we return to Atla, she thought. *Judson has never seen it and I have been away too long.*

Narrowing her eyes, Breegan scanned the horizon. The sunlight glazed the snow making it look like it was on fire.

Where has Nigel's Magic brought us? Breegan wondered. *And where will it take us next? His Gift is true indeed, as Padwick said. I should have protected him better.*

Breegan kicked at the snow.

The Siskis is more dangerous, more powerful, then any of us imagined. Not only is it intelligent, it is cunning. I must stop it. But how?

A wind blew snow in Breegan's face and whipped the cloak about her legs. The torch blazed brighter against its adversary.

Lifting the torch to the sky, she swung it down in an arc and up again, watching the flames sizzle and snap.

Padwick is right, thought Breegan. *The Eras of this world is strong. The Eras.*

Breegan's heartbeat quickened. *No matter what the Siskis has tainted, physically it is still confined to Karn. Karn is part of Atla. And the Eras of Atla is mine. I know what to do.*

Returning to Padwick and Nigel, Breegan suppressed a smile. The two were sitting on a woven rug with a ring of torches melting the snow around them. They were sipping something that steamed and smelled of chocolate.

"Look, Breegan!" Padwick held a mug up to her. "Chocolate can be a liquid."

"Wonderful," she said. "Is the door ready, Nigel?"

"You bet," Nigel answered, standing up. "But I was wondering what I should do about the other one." He pointed at the smaller blue door.

"Erase it."

"See," Nigel turned to Padwick. "I told you she'd want it erased."

Picking up his haversack, he trudged to the door, feeling like a doctor making a house call.

"But we know it will return us to Karn," said Padwick.

"Yes," Breegan acknowledged. "And to the *carolaks*. They are patient killers. They will be waiting."

Nigel, now kneeling beside the first door, peered through the circular keyhole. An eye peered back.

"Geez!" Nigel fell back into the snow. He scrambled away from the door.

Breegan tensed. "What is it?"

"My guess is *carolaks*," said Nigel. "They must be waiting, like you said."

Nigel frowned, annoyance replacing his fright. He always resented being interrupted when he was working. Nigel tried to view the door as a bad piece of art instead of a flimsy barrier between himself and several sets of fangs with tails.

"Can the *carolaks* get through that door?" he asked, dousing a cloth with turpentine.

"Not if you are quick," said Breegan.

"Okay. I'll be quick." Nigel edged toward the door and paused. "Padwick? Would you stand by with a torch? You know, just in case I'm not quick enough."

"I will, my friend, and do not worry. Worrying will spoil your concentration." Taking a torch from the circle, Padwick joined Nigel by the smaller blue door.

Breegan held her torch higher, poised to strike if needed. She was still a Venger and the protector of Atla.

Nigel squatted and slapped the paint with the cloth, pouring some of the turpentine directly on the lines of the door.

"Do not use it all," Breegan cautioned.

"Right, right," Nigel muttered. Capping the bottle, he handed it to Breegan and continued working.

Nigel imagined he heard growling on the other side of the door. The ground even seemed to shake. There was an inarticulate shout.

Nigel looked up. "What the hell?"

An army of fur-clad horsemen was galloping toward them.

"Hurry!" Breegan tossed Nigel's haversack to Padwick. "Run to the other door."

Padwick ran. "Hurry, Nigel!" he called.

"I'm hurrying!" Nigel rubbed out the keyhole and staggered to his feet. Wobbling, knees stiff, he headed toward the large blue door.

Breegan was close beside him. "Do not push me this time," she warned.

"Right. No pushing."

They reached the door.

"Do I have to use my finger?" Nigel protested.

"Yes!" Breegan shouted over the approaching din.

Nigel pushed his finger into the keyhole. The door glowed. It swung open. Warm air hit them like a wave.

"Go! Go!" Breegan commanded.

Padwick obeyed. Nigel thought he heard him yell.

"What?" was all Nigel had time to yell. Breegan pushed him through the doorway and jumped after him.

Nigel felt a rush of wind just before he hit water. Instinctively, he kicked his legs and flailed his arms, surfacing in seconds, coughing and spitting, struggling to swim against a strong current.

Water pushed and pulled at him. He thought he heard Padwick, but a rushing noise dulled the words. Nigel dog-paddled through the waves, concentrating on keeping his head above water.

Water! Please don't let this be an ocean, Nigel thought, trying not to think of sharks or sea monsters. *Where the hell am I? Where's Padwick? And Breegan?*

"Nigel!"

Nigel paddled harder in what he hoped was the direction of Padwick's voice. He peered through the lenses of his water-fogged glasses and saw Padwick wading toward him. Heartened, Nigel stood up. The water reached his waist.

"Nigel!" Worried, Padwick looked him over. "Are you injured?"

"I don't think so." Nigel stretched his arms out and wriggled his fingers. "Drenched, but no blood. I guess I'm okay. How about you?"

"I am fine," Padwick answered. "Where is Breegan?"

"Here." Breegan dragged herself from the water. Her tunic hung down to her knees and her hair was plastered against her face and neck. She peeled a matted lock away from her mouth.

"Before you paint another door," Breegan said to Nigel, "I will explain more about focusing your energy."

"More?" Nigel's relief at seeing Breegan was washed away by his indignation. "You haven't explained anything about focusing my energy. I'm just winging this whole 'paint a door at the snap of your fingers' thing."

Breegan stalked past him. Still fuming, Nigel glanced around him, trying to spot his door. "Where's my door?" he asked Padwick.

Padwick pointed. Nigel's door stood fifteen feet above a small lake, just to one side of a large waterfall.

"What were you imagining when you painted it?" asked Padwick.

"Just what you told me to. Someplace warm and green."

The two of them surveyed their surroundings. Sunshine splashed a rainbow through the waterfall. Tall trees dropped green leaves in the lake. The day was warm and a sandy shoreline gave way to pale green grass and yellow flowers.

"It is warm," Padwick said. He splashed through the shallows to the narrow strip of beach. Nigel followed and they joined Breegan. She was studying Nigel's door.

Nigel and Padwick turned to look at it again.

"What do we do about them?" asked Nigel.

A crowd of natives from the previous world peered through the doorway with furrowed brows and grunts of consternation.

"Shut the door, Nigel, and lock it," Breegan ordered. "See it in your mind then make it happen."

"I can do that?" In his excitement, Nigel forgot to be annoyed.

"You should be able to by now," Breegan answered. "It is part of your Gift, imagining the possibility and then creating the reality."

"No kidding? I mean, sure. No problem."

Folding his arms, Nigel stared hard at his door. In his mind, he saw it close firmly against their unwelcome voyeurs. The door shuddered on its hinges, moved a little then swung violently shut.

"Do I have talent or what?" Nigel shouted.

"Now lock it," Breegan said quietly.

"Right, right."

Feeling giddy with power, Nigel had to take a deep breath. He visualized the keyhole turning just enough to lock. "I think I got it," he said. "It's hard to know for sure."

"It will have to be enough," said Breegan, speaking almost to herself. She moved to the grass and sat down, holding her injured wrist against her chest.

"Padwick?" Breegan drew his attention from Nigel's door.

"Yes, Breegan?"

"How strong is the Eras in this place?"

Padwick's eyes lost their focus for a moment as he concentrated on touching the Eras Magic. "It is only fair, but I can manage. Shall I dry us off and make a breakfast?"

"Do you feel the presence of Siskis?" Breegan asked. "In any form?"

"No, Breegan. It is more like the Eras is sluggish, almost lazy."

"Very well. Wake it, please. Just long enough for our needs."

Padwick began drying and *fairowing*, happy to be warm and safe for a little while.

Nigel sat down near Breegan. He regarded his door. *Good shape, nice texture, the color goes well with its surroundings,* Nigel thought.

"Why did my door materialize above the ground?" he asked Breegan. "My first door did that, too." Nigel thought a moment. "So did the second one."

"It is because you did not have a clear enough image of your destination," said Breegan. She pointed at the door.

"You wanted someplace warm and green. We were leaving a barren landscape of snow. I suspect in your mind you turned the snow into water, bringing us to a waterfall. No doubt you wanted trees, hillsides …"

"And I got the side of a cliff and a forest," said Nigel, beginning to understand.

"Yes. When you think of a destination, you must concentrate on where you want to be when you get there. You must focus not just on the journey, but the arrival."

Breegan shifted her weight off her bruised thigh, irritated by her injuries. "You must not let yourself be distracted." The chastisement was intended for herself as well as Nigel.

"That's easy for you to say. All this 'be quick' and 'hurry up' is very distracting. That probably helped the Siskis move my first door to Karn."

A sadness clouded Breegan's eyes. "No. The Siskis is strong enough to despoil the best of plans. But we will do better next time."

"Sure. I'll use the key."

Breegan shook her head. "You are the Key, Nigel. Your heart, soul, mind, and body. The talisman is for others to employ. It has been imprinted with a successful journey."

"Successful?" Nigel scoffed.

"We departed Atla and returned. You are the Key. Use your finger."

"How about a handprint?" Nigel suggested. "You know, for a swinging door?"

Breegan looked at Nigel skeptically. "Why?"

"It hurts!" Nigel held up his right index finger. "All that energy centered in one push. I'm surprised I don't have a blister."

Breegan looked away, biting back a smile. "You cannot lock a swinging door."

"True, but I can erase it."

"Very well. You may try a handprint on the next trip. After we eat and rest, you will stand by the water and think of a beautiful place. It should be rich in Eras Magic and devoid of Siskis. Someplace quiet and calm with all the things you love in its embrace."

"I don't think I know of any place like that."

"Imagine one," Breegan said. "Anything you can imagine exists somewhere. You have only to see it in your mind and the door you paint will take us there."

Nigel rested in the beauty of Breegan's eyes. "Okay."

Chapter Thirteen

Nigel swept his paintbrush up. The last stroke. The finishing touch. The perfect door. *Maybe I should sign it,* he thought.

Padwick joined him. "It is beautiful," he said, admiring the rich purple color. "Where is the keyhole?"

"There isn't one." Setting aside his brush and palette, Nigel gave the door a small push. It moved inward, like a single kitchen door in a restaurant.

"By the Light!"

"Does our destination have a name?" asked Breegan, coming to stand between the two men.

"I don't know," said Nigel. "I imagined a paradise, someplace safe, untouched, undiscovered. Until we get there.

"And look"—Nigel pointed—"no keyhole. I just push." Nigel pushed. "Whoa!"

Nigel stumbled through the doorway. He staggered forward, arms flailing. Regaining his balance, he looked around. "Hey! This is great!"

Nigel turned, expecting to see Breegan and Padwick. The door was shut.

Uh-oh, he thought. *I'm in trouble now. I'm the only one who can open the door and I just left an injured Venger on the other side.*

He imagined *carolaks* would be nicer to face than an angry Breegan. Returning to the door, Nigel opened it a little.

"Hi!" he said. "The door works great."

Padwick looked worried. Breegan looked furious.

"It's level with the ground and everything," Nigel said quickly. Holding the door open, he stepped back into the waterfall world. "Want to see?"

Breegan said nothing, but Padwick spoke up. "Never do that again, Nigel. We must not be separated by a door. You could have been injured or killed and Breegan and I would have been unable to help you."

"You're right. I'm sorry. I'll be more careful. I promise."

Under Breegan's scowling scrutiny, Nigel packed up his supplies and hoisted his haversack onto his left shoulder.

"Here," he offered, still apologetic, "let me get the door for you." He opened it slowly, watching Breegan.

Without acknowledging Nigel, Breegan strode through the doorway.

Padwick stepped forward, pausing on the threshold. "It looks very nice," he said. He followed Breegan into the world beyond.

"Thanks." Nigel brought up the rear.

The trio walked through long sea grass to a wide beach littered with tide pools. Whitecaps surfed on an incoming tide. Beyond them, green mountains held fluffy clouds against a warm, blue sky.

"I've always liked walking on the beach when the tide is out," said Nigel, pulling off his sneakers and socks. "And this time"—he curled his toes into the wet sand—"no rocks."

Observing Nigel, Padwick removed his boots and rolled up the legs of his pants, delighted to feel warm sand against his feet again. He, too, enjoyed the seaside.

Unable to relax, Breegan looked behind them at the purple door.

We will leave it for now, she thought, *in case this world does not have enough Eras.*

"Do you like it?" Nigel waved an arm at the seaside.

Breegan spoke to Padwick instead of answering Nigel. "Is the Eras strong, Padwick?"

Padwick stopped splashing in a shallow pool. He inhaled deeply, releasing a happy sigh. "The Eras is very strong, Breegan. Refreshing and young."

"Excellent." Surveying the landscape, Breegan pointed to a small knoll just above tidelevel. "We will spend the night there. At moonrise, I will create a *baskaray*."

"A *baskaray*?" Padwick's brow furrowed in an uncharacteristic frown. "With your injury, Breegan, will you be strong enough?"

"I will be strong enough," Breegan declared. "I need only to rest."

Padwick nodded. "Yes, Breegan. It is your decision."

"What's a *baskaray*?" asked Nigel.

"It is a special kind of *fairowing* used to center Eras Magic in one place," said Padwick. "It can only be created by a Venger."

Alarmed, Nigel looked at Breegan. "You mean, like Fahgerdahl's Well of Siskis?"

Breegan shook her head. "Explain to him, Padwick," she said, her voice tired. The pain in her wrist had increased.

Padwick turned to Nigel. "A *baskaray* does not drain Eras Magic, Nigel; it gathers energies from the Eras and combines them temporarily."

"What kind of energies?" asked Nigel, feeling uneasy. "How many? And why?"

"Light and motion. They must be indirect at first so they can increase in power gradually. The quantity of energies varies."

"So, you mix a few energies and get what? What do they become?"

"Padwick," Breegan interrupted. "I will sit and watch as you search for a stone."

"A stone?" Nigel looked at his smooth, rock-free beach. "What for?"

Padwick stepped up beside him. "Come, Nigel. I will tell you why as we look."

Breegan finally spoke to Nigel. "Give me your haversack." She extended her uninjured hand.

"Sure." Swinging it from his shoulder, Nigel handed his haversack to Breegan. "But I'm telling you, there are no stones on this beach. I specifically imagined a serene ocean setting. That means no birds, no wind, and no rocks."

Breegan wasn't listening. She was walking toward the knoll, Nigel's haversack under her arm. Her words drifted over her shoulder. "The setting is yours, but the world is not. All the requirements for a *baskaray* are here somewhere. You have only to look."

Nigel shook his head. *Does she have to make everything sound so easy and obvious?*

"So, Padwick," said Nigel, "why do we need a stone?"

"Breegan requires a solid object to transport the combination of energies," Padwick answered, inspecting the beach. "It must be a physical part of the Eras from which the *baskaray* is being created."

"So it can't be anything we've brought with us," said Nigel, thinking of his key ring and the other keys it held.

"No. It must be a natural piece of the land. Something small enough to carry yet sturdy enough to hold the concentration of energies formed by the *baskaray*."

"Okay." Nigel stooped to pick up a pale pink seashell. It had delicate veins and scalloped edges. As usual, Breegan was right. He hadn't conjured up an entire planet. His door had simply taken them to a pleasant world that had a nice beach at low tide.

"Gifts should come with a manual," Nigel muttered, putting the shell into a pocket.

"Has she done this before?" He glanced in Breegan's direction.

"Oh, no. But all Vengers are taught how to create a *baskaray*. First, Breegan will separate some of this world's Eras energies from the whole. Next, she will pull them into the stone. If I remember my history correctly, she will begin with the wind."

"I'm telling you," Nigel protested, "there's no wind."

A warm breeze ruffled Nigel's hair. Looking up, he stubbed his toe on a rock. "Damn!"

If a bird shows up, he thought, *Breegan will be three for three*. Aloud he said, "So she puts some Eras energies into a rock. Then what?"

Padwick walked along the edge of the surf. "Breegan will transform the stone into an orb and contain the energies with her Agenta Magic until they are needed."

"Needed for what?" Nigel found another shell.

"Immediate, explosive power."

Nigel stopped walking. "Are you saying a *baskaray* is a bomb?"

"I have told you, Nigel," Padwick said patiently, "it is combination of energies which, when released, cause an explosive reaction. It is used only if all of Atla is in peril. The last *baskaray* was used to alter the course of an asteroid."

"So it's a really big bomb."

Padwick nodded.

"But she's injured," Nigel objected. "Her Magics aren't working."

"They are. But manifesting them is painful and difficult right now." Padwick knelt and pulled a stone from the sand. "And dangerous," he added.

"Oh, great. And we're supposed to let her make a bomb?"

"Breegan is a Venger and the protector of Atla," Padwick stated. He stood up. "I believe she is preparing the *baskaray* in order to annihilate the Siskis. Breegan has said she is strong enough. It is our duty to assist her in every way we can."

"Do you think she's strong enough to do this?"

"I do. A good receptacle, however, is essential to the success of a *baskaray*. If the receptacle is weak, the bomb will explode before it is required. That is why we must find the right stone."

"Okay." Following Padwick, Nigel searched the sand for the perfect stone. He picked up another shell.

Ezamiah said Breegan is the Weapon, thought Nigel. *He couldn't have meant that literally, could he?*

Breegan said my entire being is the Key. What if Breegan's entire being is the Weapon?

Calm down, Nessel. Breegan's already fought and killed Fahgerdahl using her Magics. Now, she's just going to tidy up a loose end with a homemade explosive. Nigel paused to pick up two more pinks shells.

If you want to panic, Nessel, panic about not finding the right rock.

"Hey! How about this one?" Nigel scooped up a small rock. It was flat on one side, unevenly curved on the other. Dark brown lines marbled the beige surface. It looked like a muffin that hadn't risen properly.

Nigel weighed it in his palm, curling his fingers about the rock. It felt comfortable.

Taking the stone from Nigel's hand, Padwick considered it carefully. "It is a good stone," he decided. "We should find another so that Breegan can choose."

"Good idea."

They continued walking along the beach, occasionally kicking water at one another as the tide slid in. When they had found two more stones, Nigel and Padwick headed for the knoll.

Startled by how pale Breegan looked, Nigel tried to be unobtrusive as he sat down and emptied his pockets of his shell collection.

"We found three stones which may be appropriate," Padwick announced, placing the stones on the sand in front of Breegan. He, too, noticed her pallor.

Breegan glanced at the proffered pieces of rock, not touching them. "Padwick, make a fire. I am cold." Tension sharpened her words.

Padwick looked at Nigel, worry in his eyes. "I will. Immediately. And a meal."

"How about some *chessit*?" said Nigel.

"An excellent suggestion," Padwick agreed. He sorted through his pockets and began *fairowing*.

Nigel stretched out his long legs, sizing up Breegan's features as if he were about to paint her portrait. Tense jaw, furrowed brow, broad shoulders hunched forward as she rested her injured wrist on one knee.

"It's not that cold," Nigel commented, dragging a stick out of the sand. It was long and thin. *Just right for marshmallows*, he thought.

"You must be tired," Nigel continued. "I always get cold when I'm tired."

Breegan remained silent and motionless, wishing she could leap to her feet and fight Fahgerdahl again, strong and uninjured, the Venger of Atla. Instead she had to restrain her nature and remain calm, gathering her limited abilities for a far greater confrontation.

"I know I'm tired." Nigel moved alongside Breegan. "I'm never too tired to paint, though. Seascapes, storms on the horizon, doors. Whatever you like."

He looked at the sapphire blue sea, noticing how the waves curled and uncurled beneath the cerulean sky. *No matter how many doors I paint*, thought Nigel, *I'm always going to like seascapes best*.

"Hey, Breegan." Nigel looked at her. "Would you like me to erase the door?"

The question penetrated Breegan's thoughts. "The door?"

"Yeah." Relieved to have a response, Nigel took it like a fish on a line. "I could erase it, if you like. I'll make the next one a proper door.

I promise. With a keyhole or even a padlock, whatever you want. You can pick the color, too."

Breegan looked over her shoulder at the door, then back at Nigel. Her eyes were unfocused. "Do not erase it, Nigel. It is a proper door. It brought us here."

The compliment worried Nigel. He recalled when Breegan had been unconscious. He and Padwick had held her hands and it hadn't hurt. It may even have helped.

Taking the glass of *chessit* from Padwick, Nigel pushed it into Breegan's cold hand and wrapped his warm fingers about hers. With her guard down, he didn't get a shock.

"Drink this," Nigel urged. "It'll make you feel better."

The physical contact sent warming energy through Breegan's Aura, helping her to ignore the discouraging pain and focus on her goal.

Be strong, she told herself. *Be wary. Prepare. There is a war to win.* "And I will win it," Breegan murmured.

"What did you say, Breegan?" Padwick asked.

Releasing Breegan's hand, Nigel lifted the bottom of her glass, tipping it to her lips. She sipped then pushed the glass away.

"I said wake me at moonrise, Padwick. I will begin the *baskaray* then. With that stone." Breegan pointed at Nigel's piece of rock.

"Moonrise," Padwick repeated. He *fairowed* a pillow.

"I thought we were supposed to start at dawn," Nigel said to Padwick. "Not that I mind staying up late. As long as I get to sleep in tomorrow."

Taking the pillow Padwick offered her, Breegan lay down on the grass. "Moonrise," she repeated and closed her eyes.

"Why moonrise?" Nigel asked.

"It is when the energies of the Eras will be the most pliable," Padwick answered. He handed Nigel a bowl of soup. "Moonrise will make the transition from energy to matter easier."

"Oh." Nigel felt his heart beat faster. *Did anybody ever have an adventure that just went along pleasantly? Just a simple trip with pretty scenery?*

They ate their meal, confining their conversation to favorite foods and avoiding topics such as *baskarays*, Siskis, and Breegan's bad mood.

The sun surrendered to night. Soft black clouds parted like stage curtains, revealing a single full moon.

"Now, that's a moon," Nigel commented.

"It is indeed," said Padwick. He returned his attention to the stick he held over the fire, rotating it as Nigel had instructed and roasting his *rananin* evenly. A *rananin* was Padwick's substitute for the food Nigel had described: a sweet, sticky candy with a soft shell.

Nigel popped his *rananin* into his mouth. It tasted just like a marshmallow.

"We'd better wake her up," Nigel mumbled, mouth full.

Padwick looked at Breegan. "I hope she is feeling better." He leaned forward then sat back. "It is your world, Nigel. You wake her."

"It's not my world. It's a world. It just happens to have some of the things I like." Nigel pushed another *rananin* onto the end of his stick. "You wake her."

"It is your door and your Gift that brought us here." Padwick lifted his stick out of the fire, his *rananin* slightly charred. "You wake her."

"I am awake." Breegan raised herself on one elbow and looked at the pair, guiltily stuffing *rananins* into their mouths.

"Finish your food," she said, sitting up. She waved her hand in refusal when Padwick offered her a *rananin*.

"Listen to me," Breegan voice was stern. "You must both sit still and silent. Do not interrupt me or disturb me. The *baskaray* is my duty. I will be successful."

"No problem," said Nigel. "We'll just sit and watch."

"Yes." Breegan arched an eyebrow at him. "Silently," she added. Breegan looked up at the moon. "Only one?"

"Yup." Nigel tossed his stick into the fire. "But a big one," he pointed out.

Breegan stood up, stretching, eyes on the moon.

Nigel watched, fascinated as the stretching became dancing: rhythmic, flowing, sensual. For several minutes, Breegan seduced the moonlight, beckoning it toward her, leaning forward and back, side to side. She spun about like a ballerina then held a pose, arms extended, hands lifted.

A breeze raced across the tips of the long grasses. It hurried toward Breegan, sweeping up her legs, her torso, pushing her hair from her back and swirling it about her head. Breakers crashed against the knoll. The light from the moon intensified.

Looking up, Nigel thought the moon seemed twice as big, three times as big. Beneath it, the waves stilled until the ocean looked like glass, motionless, existing only to mirror the moon.

Nigel risked a peek at Breegan. She picked up his piece of rock and cupped it in both hands, holding it before her. The moon spotlighted Breegan and the stone shone impossibly bright until Nigel had to squint. The fire snapped, sizzled then disappeared.

"Padwick?" Nigel whispered. "Did you put out the fire?"

"No," Padwick whispered back from somewhere in the darkness. "I think the energy of the *baskaray* extinguished the fire. Look at the stone."

"Where?"

A small circle of light appeared to his left where Breegan had been standing. She was still there, holding the stone in her right hand. The light increased, casting a glow beneath Breegan's chin.

"I pulled the wind into the stone," Breegan said before Nigel or Padwick could ask. "The wind brought the ocean and the ocean brought the moonlight."

"All three at once?" Nigel had forgotten the power Breegan commanded.

"Yes."

"Are you well, Breegan?" asked Padwick, concerned.

"I am tired." Breegan drew the stone against her, holding it as if it were a baby bird. "The Eras Magic of this world is new and strong, untainted and untapped."

She sat down carefully, keeping the stone against her heart. "It is a peaceful place you have brought us to, Nigel. Free of Siskis, as I requested."

"Great. I'm glad you like it." Nigel waited for more information: a plan, an idea, even a suggestion. "Now what?" he prodded.

"Now we rest again," Breegan answered. "Until dawn."

"Of course. Can I make the fire this time?" asked Nigel.

"No, Nigel," said Padwick. "No fire. The Eras must rest as well." He began *fairowing* blankets and pillows, making Breegan's extra soft and fluffy.

Accepting his bedding, Nigel arranged it on the sandy grass. "That was really something," he remarked. "What happens at dawn? Or do I want to know?"

Breegan did not answer. She was asleep again, the stone cradled in the palm of her right hand. The light from it pulsed.

Like a heartbeat, thought Nigel. He heard a snore. Padwick, too, slept.

Nigel looked at his door. He wished Breegan had let him erase it. What if something sneaked in from the waterfall world?

Glancing at his sleeping companions, Nigel visualized a doorstop wedged beneath the door. Satisfied, he pulled off his glasses and lay down, deciding a manual for Gifts would be too complicated, like stereo instructions.

Chapter Fourteen

Before dawn, Breegan woke. Her heart beat in time to the pulsing of the Eras energies. She felt like the wind, the waves, the moon's light: insubstantial, dependent on outside sources for life.

Standing up, Breegan held the stone against her chest. The world clouded before her. She took a long, deep breath, forcing her heartbeat to slow, drawing on her *zinahday* with Atla to strengthen her Aura Magic.

"I am the Venger, Breegan," she whispered. The world around her solidified. Breegan looked up at the fading stars.

The first stage of the *baskaray* had not been successful. Breegan knew she had been right to choose energies of motion that were interdependent and accustomed to interacting with each other. She had been right to begin with the wind.

The physical incantation should have allowed her to slowly pull the specific energies away from the Eras one by one and then gently channel them into the stone. In that receptacle, they would combine naturally.

A verbal spell would have created an abrupt seizure of power. It would have taken an enormous concentration of Breegan's Magics to capture the small portion of Eras energies the *baskaray* required.

But Breegan had underestimated the fragility of her Aura Magic and the potency of this world's Eras energies. They had started combining before she could complete the transfer to the stone, overwhelming and exhausting her.

Now the energies were interfaced between the stone and her heart, shifting in their combinations, out of balance and incomplete. Breegan knew she had to transfer them before the Eras Magic strengthened. Before dawn.

I need something of this world, thought Breegan. *A corporeal piece of Eras that will attract the energies. Something yielding, but strong. Something adaptable.*

She looked around her. *A flower, perhaps? A plant?*

Breegan stepped forward. A delicate crunching beneath her boot made her stop. Several shells were stacked near Nigel's haversack. Stooping, Breegan picked up one. She turned it over, noticing the thin residue of tissue stuck to one side.

"Wake up, Nigel," Breegan said.

Nigel mumbled and rolled over.

"Wake up!"

Padwick sat up. "What is it, Breegan?"

"Nigel!" Breegan stamped her foot, pelting his back with sand.

"Hey!" Nigel threw back his blanket and glared around him. "What the hell?" Grabbing his glasses, he focused on Breegan. She was still too pale and her beautiful eyes looked feverish.

"Nigel." Breegan pointed at his shells. "Are any of these shells occupied?"

"Occupied?" Nigel looked at his shells. "You mean, with oysters?"

"If that is what they are called, yes." Breegan held the stone closer to her heart, feeling unsteady. "Look for me."

"Okay. I think I pocketed a couple that were closed, but even if they're still alive, they won't be fresh."

"I am not going to eat them."

"We could look for more," Padwick offered.

"I need one now." Breegan glanced at the sky. "Before the dawn."

Padwick, helping Nigel search the shells, looked up at Breegan. "What is wrong, Breegan? Is it the *baskaray?*"

"Yes," Breegan admitted. "The energies overpowered me. They combined before I could finish the first stage."

"And?" Nigel asked, suspicious and afraid.

"And they are now split between my heart and the stone."

"You mean you're part of the bomb?" Nigel unintentionally cracked the spine of a shell, horrified that Ezamiah's words might come true.

"If I do not transfer them out of my body before dawn, yes."

Padwick and Nigel exchanged worried looks.

"Why didn't you say something last night?" Nigel demanded.

"I had hoped the energies would continue passing through me and coalesce inside the stone as I intended." Breegan answered Nigel's fear and anger with a calm she did not feel. "It is my first *baskaray*."

"Oh. Well. It'll be okay. It's a good start. We'll just find an oyster and …" Nigel paused. "Why do you need a piece of seafood?"

"I need a corporeal piece of this world's Eras. I can project the energies into its body temporarily. Then, when I am stronger, I will complete the first stage of the *baskaray*."

"That is all of them," said Padwick. "We must find more."

"Wait!" Nigel fumbled in a pocket of his jeans and pulled out a sand-covered seashell. Inspecting it, he held it out to Breegan. "This one's occupied."

Breegan took the shell from Nigel. She nodded and stepped away from where he and Padwick sat. "Stay there," she commanded.

"What's she going to do?" Nigel whispered to Padwick.

"I do not know."

"Does she?"

A strand of sunlight silenced them.

Breegan held the shell in the palm of her left hand and lanced it with a dart of Agenta Magic. The oyster inside pulsed and opened its shell.

Focusing on the Eras energies within her heart, Breegan channeled them into the oyster. The shell glowed white for an instant then snapped shut.

Padwick and Nigel hurried to Breegan.

"Are you all right?" asked Nigel.

"Breegan!" Padwick gasped. "Are you well? Are you safe?" He glanced at the horizon. Pale blue and pink traded places along the horizon's edge.

"For now. Yes." Breegan drew a deep breath. "The energies are split between the organism—what did you call it?" she asked Nigel.

"Oyster."

"Between the oyster and the stone. As I am, however, I cannot complete the *baskaray*. I must heal my injuries first."

"Injuries?" Nigel looked her over. "What's injured besides your wrist?"

"My heart," whispered Breegan. She turned away, moving slowly back to their campsite, her arms crossed over her chest, the stone in one hand, the shell in the other.

Padwick hurried ahead of her and *fairowed* fire and breakfast. Nigel watched the sky and waited for instructions.

The pink of dawn brightened, lightened, dispersed. Nigel had painted dozens of sunrises, but this one was best because Breegan was still alive. He finished eating.

"So." Nigel tried on a smile. "Where to?"

"Home," Breegan whispered. "We must return to Atla. To Karn."

"Karn?" Nigel objected. "Why Karn? Wouldn't it be safer to return to the Hall of Doors? I've been practicing. I think I could pull it off."

"No. We cannot risk our presence being detected. The Siskis may be focused on Atla, waiting, like the *carolaks*. We must return secretly and leave quickly."

With the shell and the stone on her lap, Breegan pulled a stick from the sand and drew a map. "Look," she directed Nigel.

"Here is Karn. Here is the Well"—Breegan marked a spot with two circles—"and here, extending south of Karn, is a line of small, uninhabited islands." She drew several ovals in a long line south of the Well.

"These islands are little more than coarse sand and black rock," Breegan continued. "Your door must blend with the landscape. The outline should be black and resemble a boulder and it must have a keyhole."

"A boulder with a keyhole?"

"To make it more secure, yes. Once there, I will swim into the ocean and create a *donaderas*. When I am healed, we will depart Atla, returning when I have completed the second stage of the *baskaray*."

"Will the *donaderas* be detected?" asked Padwick.

"If it is sensed at all, it will be as a natural part of the ocean's currents."

"What about my door? Uh, boulder?"

"If it looks like a boulder, it will be safe. I will camouflage you and Padwick so that your presence is undetectable."

"Camouflage?" Nigel looked to Padwick.

"It is a type of *zinahday*. Breegan will temporarily cloak our Auras with hers," said Padwick.

Standing, Nigel hoisted his haversack onto his shoulder. He wished he could offer Breegan a hand; she had dark circles under her eyes.

"Okay." Nigel took a deep breath. "I guess I'm ready."

"Padwick?" said Breegan.

"Almost."

Nigel still got a kick out of watching Padwick pack away his Prime ingredients. It was like watching a movie in reverse; everything that had bloomed from the mists of combined Magics contracted into pocket size, shape, and form.

"There." Padwick brushed his hands together. "I am ready, Breegan."

"Wait." Breegan frowned. "I need to protect these." She held up the shell and the stone. "Did you leave an inside pocket vacant?"

"Yes, Breegan." Unbuttoning the neckline of his jumpsuit, Padwick folded back one wide lapel. He took the shell and stone from Breegan, carefully placing them into a deep inside pocket.

"Excellent," said Breegan as Padwick did up his jumpsuit. "Now we are ready."

The trio left the beach and returned to Nigel's purple door. Breegan noticed the doorstop at once. She made no comment.

"Erase your door first, Nigel," Breegan instructed. "Then paint the boulder."

Like I do this every day, Nigel thought. Erasing the door, Nigel held up the bottle of turpentine. "I'm going to need more of this if we keep hopping from world to world."

"If we need more, I will *fairow* it," said Breegan, standing well back from the offensive smell.

"Okay." Nigel sat down and concentrated on painting a small door that resembled a boulder. A boulder with a keyhole.

He pictured the last island at the end of the archipelagos as their destination. He had some experience with rocky shorelines in his seascapes, but the result still looked clumsy to his eye and the keyhole really spoiled the effect.

"Is it complete?" asked Breegan.

"More or less."

"Is it level with the land?" asked Padwick.

"I hope so," said Nigel.

Breegan placed her right hand on the keyhole. "*Spesivah*," she said. The outline of the keyhole sparked.

As it did, Nigel felt a ripple of energy run down his spine. "Did you feel that?" he asked Padwick.

"Yes. It is the camouflage of the *zinahday* working. *Spesivah* means 'for my eyes alone'. You and I are now visible only to Breegan and each other."

"What about Breegan?"

"She must remain visible in order to sustain the camouflage."

Breegan looked at Nigel. "Open your door."

Pointing his right index finger, Nigel inserted it into the keyhole. Nothing happened.

"Try turning your wrist," said Padwick.

Nigel turned his wrist. Again, nothing.

"What were you thinking when you painted the keyhole?" asked Breegan.

Nigel shrugged. "I don't know. I guess I was thinking about not being noticed."

"What else was in your mind?" she prodded.

"I was wishing I didn't have to use a keyhole. I thought why can't I paint a door that opens with a magic word? Like, hocus-pocus?"

The door opened.

Nigel looked at Breegan. "Did I do that?"

"Yes," she answered.

"Sorry."

"Do not apologize. It is an unusual application of your Gift and yet it may prove helpful if we are in need of your hasty exit."

Padwick inhaled deeply. "It smells of Atla," he sighed, feeling happy.

"I will go first," Breegan announced. Stepping up to the door, she crouched and peered around its uneven edge. "We are on a narrow strip of beach," she whispered. "Stay close to me."

Breegan crept across the door's threshold, closely followed by Padwick then Nigel.

Nigel glanced around. Large rocks rose overhead, like black talons clutching at the brilliants colors of Atla's sky. His door squatted among an outcrop of smaller rocks and boulders. Waves slapped at its edge.

"Shut the door, Nigel," Breegan ordered. She led Padwick into the shadows of the large rocks. "And lock it."

Nigel frowned at his door, resenting the lovely seashore he could see just inside the harsh black frame. "Abracadabra," he quipped.

The door shut.

"Geez!" Nigel started. "This is one spooky talent."

"Wait here," said Breegan. "When you see me returning, paint another door against this wall of rocks."

"Why not start now?" asked Nigel.

"Because of our nearness to the Siskis."

"Well, what's our next destination?"

"An unexpected place of refuge, isolated, with water." Breegan pulled off her boots, thinking. "Someplace tropical."

"Tropical?"

"Your Gift heightens your creativity, Nigel. You were successful with the seashore world. I am certain you can be successful again." Breegan saw the doubt in Nigel's eyes. "Remember, anything you can imagine exists. See it in your mind."

Nigel put his trust in the emerald gaze. "Tropical. Okay. I'll give it a shot."

Sitting with their backs against the rocks, Padwick and Nigel watched as Breegan strode into the surf. When the water reached her shoulders, she dove beneath, surfacing several feet out to sea. Gentle waves glowed gold and formed a circle around Breegan as she began to tread water.

It looks like a slow-motion whirlpool, thought Nigel. "Will she be all right?" he whispered to Padwick.

"I believe so. I have never seen a *donaderas*. It is beautiful, is it not?"

"Yeah. In an incredibly scary kind of way. Sure."

The waves rose and fell around Breegan, gold shifting to copper then back to gold. Breegan floated within the swirling energy of the *donaderas*. It buoyed her from underneath and healed her from within, making her tilt her head back and rest for the first time since she had left Atla. Her *zinahday* with Atla washed over her like the ocean. Her wrist stopped aching; she could flex it again and make a fist.

Breegan breathed deeply. The pain in her heart dissipated. She basked in the peacefulness of the *donaderas*, letting it lull her senses, wanting to stay in its embrace. Safe, free of pain, free of responsibility.

I am home, Breegan smiled. She thought of Judson, missing him.

Breegan dove underwater, clearing her mind and ending the *donaderas*. *I am the Venger, Breegan*, she told herself. *I cannot yet rest. I have a war to win.*

Surfacing, Breegan noticed the rhythm of the waves had changed. The water was colder, rougher. A hiss of rain spattered her face. The *donaderas* had pulled her farther from shore than she had anticipated.

Breegan focused her thoughts on Padwick and waved her right arm. Did he see her? What about Nigel?

Splashing to discourage *fekinats*, Breegan swam toward shore, hoping Nigel was painting their exit.

On the narrow beach, Nigel and Padwick stood up in unison. "There's a storm brewing," Nigel warned, seeing the waves churn. "Is that from the *donaderas*?"

"I do not know. The increase of Eras required could have started a storm."

Worried, Nigel squinted as rain swept across the oceanfront, cold and unwelcoming. "Do you see her?" he asked.

"I think so."

"I think I saw her splashing around. Is she in danger?"

"Splashing repels *fekinats*," Padwick explained. "You should paint your door now, Nigel. I will keep watch."

Padwick peered through the rain, ignoring the surge of waves against their tiny beach. He surveyed the ocean. Where was Breegan?

Trying to recall Breegan's directions, Nigel painted a high, narrow door, intent on keeping their presence and departure secret.

"Hey, Padwick." Nigel painted a skeleton keyhole, long and thin like the door.

"Yes?"

"What are *fekinats*?"

"Large, carnivorous sea creatures. They live in the depths and swim with fierce speed to the surface when they detect prey."

"Like a *seniya* resting?"

"Yes, my friend."

"But doesn't splashing attract them?"

"No. *Fekinats* dislike noise and motion."

Nigel stepped back from his door. "No kidding." Packing up his haversack, he changed the subject. "Any sign of Breegan?"

Padwick was silent, watching. "I see her now," he whispered. "She is almost here."

"Great stuff." Nigel shouldered his haversack. "We're ready for action."

Breegan's foot touched the island's sandbar. A heavy wave shoved her forward. Stumbling, she struggled free from the ocean's weight. "Are you ready?"

"We are," Padwick smiled, feeling Breegan's renewed energy and health. He handed Breegan her boots.

"Nigel?" Sensing his anxiety, Breegan half turned to follow Nigel's shocked stare. "What is it?"

A *seniya* dived low to the ocean where Breegan's *donaderas* had been. A dark, nasty shape leapt to catch it.

"Let's get out of here," said Nigel. He pushed his finger into the keyhole. The door shuddered. Its outline glowed.

"It won't open," he panicked.

"Try a word, a phrase," Breegan ordered. Tugging on her boots, she scanned the sky for other *seniyas*. "Hurry."

"Uh, what did I say before?"

"Hoe-kaw-poka," Padwick tried to help.

"Hocus-pocus," Nigel sputtered, pushing against the door with his left shoulder as he spoke. The door creaked then gave way. Nigel hesitated at the blur of greenery before him.

"Go through!" Breegan ordered. Nigel stepped through the doorway. Padwick and Breegan hurried after.

"Close it and lock it!" Breegan had to shout over wind and rain.

"I can't think of any more mumbo-jumbo," Nigel yelled back.

The door lurched shut and locked.

Chapter Fifteen

The wind and rain ceased.

Dropping his haversack to the ground, Nigel rubbed his shoulder. A clammy, claustrophobic feeling slid over him. He was surrounded by an amalgamation of forest and jungle. It was dense with foliage that looked like giant ferns. Bright orange flowers dotted vines that looped and intertwined overhead, making the sunlight green.

Padwick and Breegan stood shoulder to shoulder with him in the humid silence.

"Where the hell are we?" Nigel held up a hand. "No. Don't say it. I know. What was I thinking when I painted the door?" Nigel looked around. "Not this."

Relieved that they had escaped Karn, Breegan made no comment. "Padwick, what can you sense?"

Padwick closed his eyes, shutting out the peculiar scenery. "The Eras is dim, like a memory. Old, I think. I sense no Siskis."

Opening his eyes, Padwick looked at Breegan. "It feels unreal, like a mixture of ideas. I sense we are very far from Atla."

Wringing out her tunic, Breegan turned to Nigel. "Well?"

Nigel shrugged. "I tried to focus on a tropical destination, but all I could think of were desert islands. The kind I used to see in old cartoons.

I didn't like that. So I tried to visualize a rainforest or a jungle." He frowned.

"That got me thinking of freshwater, rivers and lakes. It all got mixed up in my mind. I must have brought us to a place with the best of all three things."

"Which would be?" asked Breegan, untying her sash from her mended wrist and wrapping it about her waist.

"An isolated, tropical refuge." Nigel tilted his head back. He could just see bits and pieces of blue sky between the greens of foliage.

"An oasis," Nigel announced.

Breegan considered Nigel. He had inadvertently merged concepts and manifested a destination. It was a sign of his Magic increasing in power. Making a decision, she moved closer to Nigel. "Stand still, Nigel. I need to sense your Gift."

Nigel glanced at Padwick, but stood still. He felt a soothing warmth as Breegan held her hands on either side of his forehead. She touched him with her fingertips.

"Ow!"

Breegan dropped her hands. "Your Gift is maturing rapidly, Nigel," she said. "You need to control it better."

Nigel resented the criticism. "I think I'm doing pretty damn well under the circumstances."

"I agree." Breegan's soft tone undermined Nigel's defensiveness. "But a strong Gift can be difficult to control. Even dangerous. You must let me know immediately if at any time you feel ill effects. Magics are usually slow to develop, allowing the bearer time to adjust and adapt to the Gift's power. Gifts such as yours and mine require years of training in order to wield them successfully. The correct application of our Gifts also requires practice."

"What correct application? I've been painting doors right and left."

"Learning to sense how much Magic is needed and in what combination."

Breegan recalled the flood that had resulted on her first attempt at channeling water. She had created a large lake.

Too large, Breegan admitted to herself. She had been anxious to jump ahead of her schooling and evoke a *donaderas*. She had not considered the energy of currents and tides in such a large body of water, or the intense surge of power that overwhelmed her. The resulting whirlpool nearly drowned her tutor and flooded a small area of the province of Sunderland.

"Perhaps it is because you are human that your Gift is unpredictable in its growth," Breegan said. "I do not know. If we are successful …"

"When we are successful," Padwick interjected.

"Ezamiah may know of someone who can assist you in refining your abilities," Breegan continued.

"Ezamiah?" Nigel took off his glasses to steady himself, wiping the water-streaked lenses against his shirt. "Are you saying I can stay?" He put his glasses back on.

"Stay?" Puzzled by Nigel's question, Breegan looked at Padwick.

"Why would you wish to remain here, Nigel?" Padwick asked.

"Not here. Atla!"

Padwick's round face lit with happiness. "By the Light! An excellent idea. You can spend more time with me in Atla, my friend."

Breegan folded her arms. "You may stay or go where you please. For now"—she glanced at the tangled mess of trees and shrubs surrounding them—"to complete the second stage of the *baskaray*, I need water."

Nigel grinned. "Wonderful! Okay." He paused. "Wait a minute. You didn't say what kind of ill effects I might get."

"Headaches that are unusually severe, prolonged fatigue." Breegan remembered when her Gift of Agenta was new to her. "Sudden anger or dismay without provocation. Nausea."

"What am I, pregnant? Next I'll be expecting food cravings."

"That, as well." Breegan nodded to Nigel's haversack. "I will *fairow* more chocolate when this stage of the *baskaray* is successful."

She took a short step away from Nigel. "What kind of water did you visualize?"

"Small," Nigel said, not paying attention. *How much Magic do I have? Will I always have it? Does it only work on doors or will I become a better artist?*

Padwick pulled aside several long leafy branches. "It is sunnier in this direction and the trees are farther apart. Perhaps your small water is this way? Nigel?"

Padwick's voice penetrated Nigel's musings. "What?" Nigel looked at the opening Padwick had created. "Oh, sure. Let's go."

The trio pushed their way through the undergrowth, winding

around tree trunks and stepping over vines thick with flowers. Nigel led, followed by Breegan then Padwick.

Previously, Breegan had stayed last in order to keep watch; now she wanted the other two where she could easily pull them to safety, one in front and one behind.

"Any idea why my door stuck?" Nigel threw the question over his shoulder.

"Because of the unique qualities of our destination," Padwick answered, excited. "The farther you journey, the greater the blend of Magics required. Remember when you first arrived in Atla? There was a storm on your world. The Magic of your Gift blended with the Eras Magic. In a sense, you created an invisible door."

"That's right," said Nigel. "An invisible door." He spun about, almost bumping into Breegan. "The door!" Nigel strained to see behind her. "How will we find it again in this maze? I didn't erase it."

"Calm yourself. I heard it lock. You will find it when we need it. First, find the water."

"Right, right. The water." Nigel turned around. He stepped over a vine and slapped away a frond, continuing the expedition. "I know I pictured a pond. Nothing fancy, not too big and no ducks. Just calm water, sans waterfalls or raging rivers."

Nigel stopped. He stared. Breegan and Padwick struggled through the undergrowth and came up beside him. Pearl white sand stretched into dunes that seemed to hold the sky aloft. The sun's heat, unimpeded by leaves and trees, slapped against their faces.

It reminded Breegan of Jeraj and, for a moment, she thought of Judson. Breegan frowned and forced herself to focus on her goal. "Where is your pond, Nigel?" she asked.

Nigel looked right then left, following the rim of trees. The contrast between the forest and the ocean of sand was as sharp as an artist's pencil.

"Well." Nigel rubbed his chin. "I know when you said someplace isolated I thought someplace small. So … Let's try the other side. After all, it's an oasis. There's got to be a pond around here somewhere."

Somewhere! Breegan swallowed her impatience and motioned Nigel ahead of her. "Try again." She stepped behind him and Padwick followed.

Nigel led them back along their trail of crushed leaves and broken flowers. As they passed his door, he stopped. "Do you want me to erase it now?" he offered.

"No. You must not paint a new door here. The second stage of the *baskaray* is volatile and your Magic could interfere with it. We will use this door, then the door we left on Karn. We will be moving quickly, with little time to paint or erase."

"That's why you wanted keyholes," said Nigel.

"Precisely."

"Which way should we try this time, Nigel?" Padwick asked, feeling hot and thirsty. The forests of Penkas were spacious and the air cool. The closeness and humidity of their current environment made Padwick uncomfortable.

"Let's try that way." Nigel pointed directly across from the door. The forest was darker in that direction, almost foreboding, but Nigel was determined to find his pond. He poked and pushed his way through a group of fronds. Breegan and Padwick followed.

The battle against the leaves and branches eased and the forest brightened.

"Hey, look!" Nigel pointed. "Up ahead! See? It's sunlight reflecting off water." Feeling like a triumphant explorer, he tried to hurry forward, no longer watching where he stepped. Tripping over a vine, he fell into his pond. It was surprisingly cold and deep.

Nigel surfaced with a gasp. "What the hell? Don't they have beaches here? We know they've got the sand."

As he floundered in the water, invisible arms reached around his waist, lifted him up, and set him on the grass.

Nigel sat down. "What was that?"

Memories of Fahgerdahl made him shiver. Fahgerdahl's touch, however, had been cold and painful. This one had been warm, gentle, familiar: Breegan.

"That was Breegan's Aura Magic, Nigel," said Padwick, sitting next to him. "She is well again, remember? Sit still and I will dry your clothes."

Breegan knelt in the long grass at the edge of the pond. She skimmed her fingertips across the surface. It was small and oval, encircled by tall grass and open to the sky.

"This will do," Breegan decided. "Padwick? Please give me the shell and the stone."

She held out her hands, side by side, palms up. "Place one in each," she instructed.

Carefully, Padwick gave the items to Breegan. "Should we wait at the door?"

"No. You will be safer near to me."

"What's going to happen?" asked Nigel, watching as Breegan dipped first the shell, then the stone into the pond, rinsing them.

"I merge the shell into the stone," Breegan said. "The energies within will unite and divide, gradually becoming toxic. I then wrap the stone with a strand of my Agenta Magic. It will keep the orb from exploding until the proper time."

Her voice was as calm as the surface of the water, but the shell and the stone vibrated as she spoke.

"What is this?" Breegan held the oyster out to Nigel. The shell had opened.

Nigel peered at the oyster. "It's a pearl."

"A pearl?"

"What is a pearl?" asked Padwick.

"An over-priced piece of jewelry formed by an irritated oyster," Nigel commented. He poked at it. "Nice one, too."

Breegan spoke to Padwick. "Tip the shell. Make certain the pearl drops into my hand."

"I think you'll have to pry it loose," said Nigel.

Padwick tipped the shell; the pearl dropped into Breegan's waiting hand. She wrapped her fingers around it. "Excellent," Breegan said. "The Eras energy I transferred into the oyster is concentrated in this pearl."

Surprised, Nigel reminded himself that it wasn't an Earth oyster. Who knew how different it was?

"This was a fortunate choice of yours, Nigel," said Breegan. "The pearl will meld more easily with the stone and I will not have to sacrifice a living creature. We will return the oyster to the seashore world when we are finished here."

Nigel thought she sounded relieved. He smiled. "Good. Great. Fine by me. Anything else I can do?"

"Sit next to Padwick and remain still." Face stern, Breegan looked at Nigel. "And silent," she added.

"Got it." Nigel sat down next to Padwick.

"Is this not exciting?" Padwick whispered.

"You know, this time it is."

At Breegan's quick glare, the two sat still and silent.

Breegan turned her attention to her Prime ingredients. Taking a deep breath, she began to sing, her low voice melodious, coaxing. Lifting one hand above her head, Breegan lowered her other hand into the pond, she repeated the alternating motion again and again, still singing.

The pearl and the stone began to glow white, emanating a heat Nigel could feel a foot away. Each time Breegan dipped one in the water, the heat lessened, increasing as she raised them up.

A mist formed within Breegan's cupped hands. She stopped singing.

"*Denivah*," Breegan whispered. *Separate.*

Like a magician's act, the pearl and the stone disappeared in a puff of smoke. She lowered both hands together into the water. The surface of the pond rippled.

"*Ahrolai!*" *Join together.*

Breegan lifted her hands. A single orb the size of a baseball rested in her hands. Pearl-white, it glistened in the sunshine. Drawing it to her chest, Breegan put the index and middle finger of her right hand together. A small point of purple light appeared at her fingertips.

She extended her Agenta Magic, wrapping it in a thin band of purple around the middle of the orb. It pulsed for a moment then glowed white.

"*Su*," said Breegan. "*Enivah.*" *Stay. Wait.*

She rose awkwardly, off balance from the orb's weight. "Nigel?"

Still spellbound from what he had seen and heard, Nigel stood up.

"I require your haversack."

"Oh, sure. Sure." Nigel flipped back the leather flap, holding the bag open like a trick-or-treater.

Breegan placed the orb inside and took the haversack from Nigel's hands. "Now we must hurry."

"Back to Nigel's door?" asked Padwick, rising.

"Yes. And then to Nigel's seashore world. We will rest there while I think about what to do next and how."

"Think?" Nigel's anxiety jumped at him. "What's there to think about? We ditch the oyster and blow up the Well. Right?"

Ignoring his outburst, Breegan gently pulled the strap of Nigel's haversack over her head and across her chest so the contents rested against her abdomen.

She looked past Nigel to Padwick. "Is the oyster safe?"

"Yes, Breegan."

"Then follow me." Breegan headed back along the path they had made.

"What if there's still a storm when we reach Karn?" Nigel worried.

Breegan stopped suddenly. The three bumped into one another like railroad cars.

"Ouch!" Nigel winced as their Auras collided.

"My apologies, Breegan," said Padwick. Turning, he apologized to Nigel as well.

"It's okay." Nigel held up a hand. "I'm okay."

He noticed Breegan's look of apprehension. "Now, what?"

"A storm. You might need a storm of Eras Magic to assist you in opening the door. I had not anticipated that."

"So?" Nigel said.

"I cannot risk disturbing the *baskaray*."

"Right. Well, you know, maybe you won't need a storm. I think I can handle it."

Breegan straightened her shoulders as she realized the solution. "Nigel, you can use the storm in Atla. You can connect with it when you put your finger in the keyhole, it should provide any necessary boost of Magic."

Nodding to herself, Breegan strode forward again.

"I can connect with a storm?" Nigel caught up with Breegan. "How?"

"Open your Aura to the Eras."

"Oh, that's a big help."

"You connected with a storm when you first came to Atla, Nigel," said Padwick.

"Yeah, yeah." Nigel sighed. "I didn't do that on purpose, you know."

They reached the door and Breegan moved aside.

Nigel stepped up. "Any other suggestions? I haven't reused a door yet, let alone deliberately connected with a storm."

"Concentrate on the storm beyond the door," Breegan instructed.

"Visualize its strength and its colors. Beckon it to you. Then put your finger inside the keyhole and pull."

"Okay."

Nigel pushed his finger into the skeleton keyhole, crooking it. "Hocus-pocus."

The outline of the door flickered.

"Very good, Nigel," Padwick encouraged. "You are evoking the Magic of your Gift."

"Concentrate," said Breegan.

Nigel leaned close to the keyhole, closing his eyes. He remembered the sudden storm, the muting of Atla's multicolored skies, the cold wind blowing across the ocean, the rain. "Hocus-pocus," he whispered.

The door snapped open, knocking Nigel down. An ocean wave swept into the tropical forest.

Breegan snatched Padwick's arm before he fell. "Nigel!" she shouted.

Soaked and shivering, Nigel struggled to stand. Another wave hit him, but he grabbed for the doorframe. "I'm here. Now what do we do?"

"Go through and get to the other door. We will follow."

"What about this door?"

"You can close and lock it when we are safely through the other."

"Oh, sure!"

"Go!" Breegan commanded.

Pulling himself across the doorstep, Nigel stretched out a foot, relieved to feel the shore beneath even though he couldn't see it. He shoved his way through the knee-high waves, glad he didn't have to swim.

The outline of his boulder was barely visible. Nigel sloshed toward it. Grabbing the narrow frame, he felt for the keyhole. It was underwater. "Great."

Still hanging onto Padwick, Breegan joined Nigel. She saw the problem at once. "Chant your words in your mind like a litany," she said. "Hold your breath, duck under the water, and pull. This door should open easily."

Nigel didn't take the time to argue. Pushing at his glasses, he followed Breegan's instructions. The ocean pressed against the door, but Nigel's Magic prevailed. The door opened.

A torrent of water carried Nigel, Padwick, and Breegan through the doorway. Atla's ocean surged onto the meadow of sea grass, taking the trio with it.

"Abracadabra!" Nigel yelled.

The door shut. Instantly, the water calmed and began to dissipate.

Nigel tried standing. "We made it."

He looked up at the blue sky. "We're safe!" Wishing he could hug somebody, he settled on a happy whoop and kicked at the water that was already forming puddles.

The splash hit Breegan as she walked toward him. Nigel braced for a diatribe.

Breegan remained calm. "Close the other door, Nigel," she said. "And lock it."

"How?" Nigel looked at his boulder. "I can't see it now."

"See it in your mind." Her voice became quiet and gentle. "As you have done previously. See the door. Close it. Lock it. The Magic is yours to hold and command. Use it well. Use it now."

Nigel looked into Breegan's emerald eyes. "Do you really believe I can do that?"

"Do you?"

Nigel walked over to his door. He folded his arms and closed his eyes, visualizing the green waves of Atla's ocean. He saw his narrow gray and black door against the rock wall. Concentrating, Nigel chanted his litany in his mind, pulled the door shut, and locked it.

He plunked to the soggy ground. "That's it. I've had it. Enough already."

Wet but smiling, Padwick joined them. He beamed at Nigel. "Congratulations, my friend. That was Magic indeed. Was it not, Breegan?"

"It was," she said absently, looking at the seashore. "We will camp where we did before, Padwick. A small fire will do, and something to eat, if you please."

"Gee." Nigel flicked some mud off his jeans. "Try not to gush."

He pushed himself to his feet. "And speaking of eating"—he pointed at his haversack resting on Breegan's hip—"you owe me some chocolate."

Chapter Sixteen

Breegan climbed the slope of a dune. Reaching the top, she stared out to sea. She had eaten, but not rested. The glow from the campfire below did not inspire her to seek the company of the two who chortled and drank and roasted marshmallows.

I cannot think how to accomplish what must be done next, thought Breegan. *I need a voice outside myself to help me. I cannot solve this problem alone.*

She thought of Nigel and the amazing depth of his Gift. Could he help her?

"I have been impatient with him," Breegan told the night, "and he has not become bitter toward me." She sat down.

He keeps trying, however much he fears the task. It is his nature. She smiled. *Like his grumbling and objections. In the deep zinahday we shared, I felt his desire to be a part of something greater than himself. He has been so long alone with his paintings and his dreams.*

Breegan looked up at the single moon. *Nigel fears disappointing us, Padwick and me. What is the phrase Nigel would use? Letting down. Yes. Nigel does not want to let us down. Even now, I sense his anxiety. To ask for his help will only add to it.*

Running a finger across the sand, Breegan sighed and stood up, wishing she could cleanse herself of pain as easily as the oyster.

When she returned the small creature to what Nigel called an oyster bed, Breegan had felt a sense of accomplishment, but it had not been her victory; it had been Nigel's.

He is from another world. He has seen things I had not even imagined until the deep zinahday. He is the Key.

I have to ask for his help, Breegan decided. She walked down the side of the dune, careful not to make the sand slide.

"There you are!" Nigel waved his flask. "Did you know Southern Comfort mixes with tea?"

"I did not." Breegan glanced at Padwick's cup as she joined them. "Is there any left to share?"

"You're kidding." Nigel peered at Breegan across the fire. "She's not kidding," he said to Padwick.

"Indeed." Padwick *fairowed* another cup of tea and Nigel added the liquor.

Breegan drank the tea without stopping. "I cannot think," she explained, holding out her cup for more.

"This won't help you think," Nigel cautioned. "It mostly just helps a person to forget and even that's usually temporary."

"Then let us think together," said Breegan.

"Really? About what?" Flummoxed by Breegan's willingness to talk, Nigel had nothing to say.

"I must decide how to deploy the *baskaray* effectively, ensuring the Siskis in Atla is utterly destroyed."

"Don't we just sneak up behind the Well and drop it in?" asked Nigel.

"No. The Siskis is intelligent. Already it has demonstrated power and malice when it tried to kidnap you. We must assume it will be on guard against our return. It will defend itself. It may even be seeking other ways to gain access to Eras Magic."

"Access to Eras Magic," Nigel repeated, mulling over what he had learned about the Siskis so far.

Breegan straightened her shoulders. "I feel certain the Siskis will subsume anything it senses to be weak or vulnerable and use that to protect itself. Our plan must be flawless. We will not have a second opportunity."

"Nigel could paint a door that would open directly beside the Well," said Padwick.

Breegan shook her head. "The proximity to the Siskis could interfere with the door's materialization. We could end up in the Well. What do you suggest, Nigel?"

Feeling like a child called on by a teacher, Nigel resisted the urge to shrug off the question and the responsibility. He remembered how sly the Siskis had been, using misdirection and subterfuge to gain power. Using whatever and whoever was available. Infiltrate and overtake, he realized. Very nasty indeed. And effective.

"And I thought Fahgerdahl was the megalomaniac," Nigel said.

"Pardon?" Padwick leaned forward. "What did you say, Nigel?"

"Megalomaniac. A person who is hungry for power."

"The Siskis is not a person," Breegan said.

"No." Nigel poked at the fire with a stick. "But it thinks like one. We know it's a life form. We know that, under the right conditions, it contaminates and spreads like a disease. What if the *seniyas* and *fekinats* are carriers? What if Fahgerdahl was just a victim ... an experiment? An opportunity for the Siskis to practice?"

Uneasy, Padwick looked over his shoulder. "What would the Siskis practice?"

"Manipulation and disguise," Nigel answered. He looked at Breegan. "How long has the Siskis been around?"

Breegan frowned. "The Seers believed the Siskis Magic existed in Karn long before the time of Fahgerdahl and Fahdra. Sensing the dangerous nature of the Magic, the Seers warned Atlans to avoid Karn."

"How did they sense that the Siskis was dangerous?" asked Nigel. "Ezamiah said Atlans used to go on sabbaticals to Karn. Have any of the Seers been there?"

"I do not know. Seers rarely journey beyond their home province because they are telepathic. Their thoughts are easily sensed by each other and their Auras are often uncomfortable to be near. They live in seclusion. When the Seers wish to communicate privately, they use a Well of Thoughts."

Nigel remembered. He and Padwick had passed one on their way to the Inn of Sunderland. To Nigel, it looked like a giant bowl of soup. Padwick had explained that a Well of Thoughts allowed a person to speak to someone in another province.

These special Wells contained a mix of liquefied Magics that distilled the Aura of the person sending the message, preserving their energy and privacy. There were several Wells in every province of Atla and anyone could use them.

"Telepathy and seclusion," Nigel said, thinking out loud. "So, nobody keeps in touch with the Seers and nobody sees much of them."

Breegan spoke carefully. "When the Seers have an important vision to share, they attend the Council's meetings. Their guidance and advice have aided Atla countless times. The Seers have always been worthy of our trust. Their visions have always been accurate."

"Until now," said Nigel.

"Yes. Until now," Breegan sipped her tea. "The Seer who sent me to destroy Fahgerdahl did not speak of another Well of Siskis. It was Ezamiah who warned me, and he was right. I believe if I destroy the Well in Karn, anything tainted by the Siskis will be eliminated. Just as destroying Fahgerdahl eliminated the Well on the other world."

"I agree," said Nigel. "But the Siskis on Atla isn't draining Eras. It can't. Your *zinahday* with Atla prevents that direct approach. Instead, the Siskis has been infecting birds and, we suspect, fish. It's been altering their genetic makeup on command. I think the Siskis has something planned in its gooey little mind."

"Which would be?" asked Breegan.

"An invasion? A hostile takeover of Atla? Suppose the Siskis has already contaminated some of the people of Atla, people who would be the least likely to come under suspicion. That would make it very powerful. You wouldn't know your enemy until it was too late."

"No Atlan could be so vulnerable," Padwick objected.

"Fahgerdahl was," said Breegan, intent on Nigel's hypothesizing.

"Right," nodded Nigel. "And maybe he wasn't the first opportunity for the Siskis to infiltrate a person."

"Oh?" Breegan kept her thoughts silent. She set her cup down in the sand. Without asking, Nigel poured more liquor into it.

"Padwick told me the Seers were blind to everything but their visions." Nigel said. "At the time, I said that sounded scary. Think about it now. Fear is isolating. It makes a person vulnerable in all sorts of ways. It could even create a hollow place inside them."

"Breegan would have felt it," protested Padwick.

"How? When? No offense, Breegan," Nigel apologized, "but you didn't know about the *seniyas* until they were transformed into *carolaks*. Just as Ezamiah didn't know about Fahgerdahl until the Siskis revealed itself in the duel with Fahdra."

Nigel paused, worried he had said too much.

Listening to Nigel, Breegan knew she had chosen well. She lifted the cup, but without the tea to dilute it the smell of the liquor was too strong. A tiny movement of her forefinger returned the liquor to the flask without Nigel even noticing the slight flicker of Magic.

"Continue," Breegan said.

Encouraged, Nigel leaned forward. "Like a disease, the Siskis may have infected one or more of the Seers directly. Its presence would go unnoticed because of their seclusion. While we chased after Fahgerdahl, the Siskis was really plotting to use the Seers to access Atla's Eras."

"It is an interesting theory," Breegan said. "It has always been the Seers who determine Atla's future. They have an unacknowledged power. Control over them and their telepathic abilities would be a great advantage in a war or an invasion."

"I bet that's how they got infected in the first place," Nigel said.

"Explain," said Breegan.

"Telepathy. The Seers probably used their telepathy to keep watch on the Siskis. At some point, it became aware of them and infiltrated their bodies through their minds."

"It was one of the Seers who sent you after Fahgerdahl," said Padwick, worried. "Not Ezamiah."

"Yes. The Seer, Dalyse."

"Sounds like the Seers wanted you away from Atla," Nigel pointed out.

"A wild goose chase," exclaimed Padwick.

"Yeah." Nigel nodded at his friend. "Get the most powerful person out of the way."

"What about your power, Nigel?" Padwick poured more tea, unaccustomed to the anxiety and tension generated by Breegan.

Nigel shrugged. "I wouldn't call it power. It's more of a knack, so far. Hardly something for the Seers to worry about. They probably figured I wouldn't be of much help. There was a very good chance that Breegan might never make it back to Atla. And even if she did, by then the Siskis would have spread further, ingesting Eras Magic through the Seers. It could even be manipulating their visions, so they're completely unaware of their actions. Eventually, it could contaminate everyone. Like a plague."

"Poisoning the Eras," said Breegan. "My *zinahday* with Atla would become toxic to me and all of Atla would succumb to the Siskis."

Nigel saw Breegan's eyes turn a dark jade green with anger. "I think the Seers set you up," he said quietly. "Pursuing Fahgerdahl was just a ruse."

"Classic decoy," Breegan snapped. For a moment, a purple light danced like fire in her hair. The campfire roared brighter.

Nigel braced himself against a rush of energy as Breegan's Agenta Magic swept uncontrolled around their tiny camp. Then it was gone. The fire, too.

The beach was silent except for the whine of the wind and the whisper of the waves.

"I am calm now, Padwick," Breegan spoke from the darkness. "You may light your fire again."

"*Kesla!*" The campfire popped back into existence. "Breegan?" said Padwick.

"Yes?"

"We have something the Seers did not foresee."

"What is that?" asked Breegan.

"Nigel's talent for strategy."

"My what?"

"You are perceptive as always, Padwick," Breegan said. "And you are right."

She pierced Nigel with her stare. "What would you do, Nigel, if you wanted to create a 'classic decoy' in this situation?"

"Me?" Nigel fidgeted. He didn't want Breegan to get upset again, but he did have an idea. "A first strike," he said. "Something unexpected. Maybe an aerial attack. Fly the bomb over the Well and drop it in. Kaboom!"

"How would we achieve such a plan?" Padwick asked. "Even with all her Magics, Breegan cannot fly."

"What about taking over a *seniya*?" Nigel suggested. "It works for the Siskis."

"My Magics in the *seniyas* would be detected," said Breegan.

They sat silent.

"What if it were something that only resembled a *seniya*?" said Padwick.

"Something in disguise?" offered Nigel.

"What could that be?" Breegan asked.

"You were going to breathe life into a painting of a boat," Padwick said. "Why not a painting of a *seniya*? It would be created from a Prime ingredient of Atla and therefore could only be detected as a part of the Eras."

"Hey, that might work," Nigel agreed. "I can paint a bird."

He looked at Breegan. "Of course it won't be much of a bird, but it doesn't have to be. It just has to fool the Siskis long enough for you to maneuver it into position and drop the bomb."

"How would I maneuver it? I would have to use my Magics to control it."

"You've already wrapped a string of your Agenta Magic around the orb." Nigel organized his thoughts. "I could paint a picture of a kite that looks like a *seniya*. We attach the bomb to the kite; you guide the kite to the Well. You'd only have to use your Magics long enough to drop the bomb. I mean, the *baskaray*."

"What is a kite?" Padwick inquired.

"A large, colored piece of paper that floats on the wind," Breegan answered.

Surprised, Nigel looked quizzically at Breegan. "How did you know that?"

"In your mind there is a vivid memory of an ocean shore with kites sailing like ships in a cloudless sky."

"The deep *zinahday*," Nigel muttered. "What other memories did you tap into?"

Reaching for Nigel's haversack, Breegan set it on the sand in front of her and removed the orb. "I did not 'tap into' your memories, Nigel," she said, placing the orb beside her and scooping sand around it.

"I only touched your true self. Your true self sees the world as an ocean waiting to be painted. Colors and motion attract you, whether they are on land, water, or in the air. The recreation of them is part of your Gift."

"I see." Nigel watched Breegan half bury the orb. "Is it safe to do that?"

"Yes. The second stage is complete. The orb has stabilized."

"Okay." Nigel thought of something Breegan had mentioned on the oasis world. "What about all this magic we're planning on doing? You know, poof! It's a swan! Presto! It's a door! Won't the *baskaray* cause interference?"

"Not on this world. The energies are from here. They are grounded."

"That's why the orb is stable," Nigel concluded.

"Yes." Breegan looked across the fire. "Padwick? Please *fairow* pillows and blankets."

"Wait a minute, wait." Nigel held up his hand. "We're forgetting something important."

"And what is that?" asked Breegan.

"We need wind to fly a kite. It was a windy day at the beach that you're recalling. What if it isn't windy when we get to Karn? No wind, no kite flying."

Breegan almost smiled. "You forget, Nigel, as did I."

"What did I forget?"

"My *zinahday* with Atla. The Eras of Atla is mine to access. My *zinahday* is unbreakable. I control the elements."

Satisfied with their plan, Breegan gave Nigel his haversack. "I will evoke the wind to fly our kite and guide it to the Well. The final stage of the *baskaray* will be completed when we deploy the orb."

"Great stuff! So." Nigel drained his cup of tea. "When do we start?"

"At dawn."

"Dawn again?" Nigel complained. "When do we get to sleep in?"

"When we have won," said Breegan.

Chapter Seventeen

Nigel scowled at his painting. His bird looked like a mutant duck.

"Another piece of paper, Nigel?" Padwick asked.

"Yes, please." Nigel sighed. "Damn swans." Taking the new piece of paper, Nigel began again. Pointed beak, small head, long neck like a giraffe. *No, no! Like a swan!*

Fat body? No, elongated. Big wings. Goofy feet.

"Dammit! I forgot the legs."

Padwick handed him another piece of paper.

Breegan paced back and forth in front of Nigel's boulder, holding the orb against her body. The pink sky overhead disquieted her. She missed Atla. How long had she been away? In her absence, how much harm had the Siskis accomplished?

She peered at Nigel's painting, but made no comment, more concerned with their return to Karn. They would have to materialize at the foot of the southernmost mountain circle, Breegan decided. A short climb up its western slope would take them to a vantage point where she would be able to see the Well and launch the kite with accuracy. Their only problem would be real *seniyas*. And *carolaks*.

"Hey, not bad this time." Nigel held up his painting for approval.

"It will suffice," said Breegan. "Now you must paint a door."

"Oh, there's a surprise." Nigel gave himself a mental kick for expecting praise. As they had formed a plan of attack, he had felt a kinship with Breegan. Now the hierarchy was back again; Breegan was in command and he and Padwick were the troops.

Handing Breegan his painting, Nigel jerked his head in the direction of the boulder. "Do you want me to erase this door?"

Breegan shook her head. "Not yet. We may need it as an emergency exit. I do not know how much destruction will be caused by the third stage of the *baskaray*."

Nigel decided he liked it better when Breegan didn't volunteer information. He changed the subject. "What kind of door would you like? Any particular color or style? Any favorite shape or size?"

"Something large."

"How large?"

Breegan spread her arms wide. "Large enough to fit a paper *seniya* through it."

"You're going to make it here?" asked Nigel.

"The Siskis may notice a door so large," Padwick pointed out.

"We will arrive far enough away from the Well that the Siskis will not be aware of our presence," said Breegan.

Before Nigel could protest, Breegan knelt down and touched his forehead with her right index finger.

Nigel couldn't move. Frozen, he saw a dark mountain ridge. The walls and cliffs looked familiar, as if he had scaled them once. A gouge in the mountain's side provided an outcrop of rock that looked like a ledge. *A lookout*, thought Nigel.

"What the hell was that?" Nigel demanded as Breegan released him from the *zinahday*.

"It was necessary to ensure the precise location of the door. The simplest way to do so was to share my memory of an earlier exploration through a brief *zinahday*."

"You could have warned me," complained Nigel. A wave of nausea silenced him.

"When you expect something, you tense your mind," Breegan responded.

Nigel rubbed his forehead, feeling disoriented. He struggled to make sense of the images Breegan had transferred to him: a ship, a jagged coastline, a mountainside, a *seniya's* nest. Nigel saw a hidden inlet that led to a narrow gorge between the southernmost mountain range.

He felt himself climbing a rough slope until he came to a small cave with a ledge. It gave him an excellent vantage point of something familiar. What was it? The Well!

"You've been to Karn before," he accused Breegan.

She nodded. "Of course I have, Nigel. Karn is part of Atla. Its mountains are the homes of the *seniyas*. They are part of Atla. All is mine to know and protect."

"Why did you look at the Well?" Nigel asked even as the knowledge left by Breegan's intense *zinahday* answered his question.

"You know why."

Nigel nodded. "Yes." He felt guilty for suspecting collusion between Breegan and the Seers. "You check the Well regularly to see if the Siskis has changed, if it's expanded beyond the Well. If it's a threat to Atla."

"And now it is." Breegan's voice was solemn.

"Yes." Nigel felt a chill. "I'm sorry."

He didn't know why he said it, except that he felt a great sorrow and fear. He realized he was experiencing what Breegan had felt the first time her duty had taken her to Karn. "Is protecting Atla always so difficult?" he asked, discouraged.

"No." Breegan's soft tone made Nigel look deep into her beautiful eyes. This time he understood her aloneness.

"Now listen closely to me, Nigel." Breegan began to pace. "As you paint this door, allow my memories to guide you. Make the door large, but fragile. It must be easily destroyed when we complete the *baskaray*."

"We?" Nigel hesitated. "You mean, you and me?"

"Yes. The Magic in your painting will intertwine with mine when I bring it to life. Our Magics will blend together in the final stage of the Baskaray."

Listening, Padwick smiled. "By the Light! This is exciting, is it not, Nigel?"

Nigel pulled a new paintbrush from his haversack. "Exciting, unnerving."

He reached for his palette.

"Scary?" Padwick suggested.

"You bet." Nigel thought a moment. "But not as much as before."

He smiled back at Padwick. "Maybe I'm getting the hang of being a 'born adventurer' and all. A door here, a swan there. What's to worry about?"

Carolaks, thought Padwick. He stayed silent and watched Nigel mix paints. Padwick felt again the dismay he had experienced when he and Nigel held Breegan's hands after the first battle with Fahgerdahl. Until that moment, it had never occurred to Padwick that Breegan might not survive, that he and Nigel and Breegan might not win.

Why do I worry now? thought Padwick. *It must be because we face the Dark Magic itself.* He took a deep breath. *At least we face it together.*

Breegan stopped her pacing. "Padwick! Let him paint. Come and help me, please."

"Yes, Breegan."

"I do not know how long we will be safe when we return to Karn, Padwick," Breegan said. "Stay close to Nigel and me. Be prepared to run or fight."

"Perhaps some fireballs," Padwick suggested. "I have a good aim if I have the time to concentrate."

"Excellent. But I cannot promise you time."

"Fight?" Nigel looked up from the beginning of his door. "When did we discuss fighting?"

Breegan pointed at Nigel's paintbrush. "Stay focused," she ordered.

Grumbling out of habit, Nigel concentrated on the images Breegan had placed in his mind. He turned his complete attention to his door.

Breegan motioned to Padwick to follow her, walking several feet away from Nigel. She gave the painting of a *seniya* to Padwick. "Hold this up as high as you can reach," she instructed.

Padwick looked about, found a rock, and stood on it. He stretched one arm above his head, holding Nigel's painting up to the dawn.

Breegan set the orb gently down in the sea grass directly beneath the painting, as if it were an egg. She faced the picture and swept her right hand in front of it.

"*Malinay,*" she whispered, repeating the motion with her left hand. "*Malinay.*"

The picture in the painting pulsed then glowed.

"*Malinay.*" *Metamorphosis.*

Leaning close to the paper's edge, Breegan breathed upon it. "*Pethlinay.*" *Exist.*

The paper crumpled into a ball and disappeared into a purple mist. A loud popping noise preceded the appearance of a brilliant white *seniya* with emerald green eyes. Its lines were stiff, like origami, and a breeze almost knocked it down.

Breegan walked slowly around the paper bird. As she moved, the proportions and details of the kite altered and solidified. With a sweep of her right hand, the kite rose and floated overhead. Breegan placed the orb within the framework, leaving the purple string of her Agenta Magic to dangle underneath.

"What do you think of it, Padwick?" Breegan asked.

"It is both disturbing and beautiful, Breegan," he answered. "Do you think it will deceive the Siskis?"

"Let us see," she answered. Taking the end of the kite tail, she led it and Padwick back to where Nigel painted.

A large shadow interrupted Nigel's light. "Hey!" He looked up, expecting a cloud. "What the hell?" Nigel scrambled away from the fake *seniya*.

Breegan suppressed a smile. "Do you not like your kite, Nigel?"

"Oh, sure." Nigel steadied himself. Breegan's sense of humor was as skewed as it was unexpected. "It's just great."

"And your door? Is it finished?" Breegan asked.

"More or less. You wanted it fragile, so I guess, yes."

Padwick studied the irregular edges of the black double door. "It looks scary," he said, turning his eyes to Nigel. "Is that because of our destination?"

"Exactly."

"Is it wide enough?" Breegan considered the wingspan of their false *seniya*.

"It will be when it's open," said Nigel. "I didn't think we'd need a keyhole since we're only going to blow it up or disintegrate it or whatever."

Breegan nodded. "Very well. Pack your haversack."

Breegan pulled on the kite's string, lowering it to her shoulder. "Are you ready, Padwick?"

"Yes, Breegan."

Snapping her fingers, Breegan miniaturized Nigel's haversack and placed it in his shirt pocket. "We will go together," she said. "Open your door, Nigel."

Nigel straightened an imaginary tie. "Hocus-pocus," he ordered, voice firm.

The doors opened inward. A gray rain spattered their faces. Wind blew a faint smell of something each of them had experienced: Siskis.

***

Far from the Mountains of Karn, the Seer Dalyse knelt before a Well of Thoughts in Hardisty and turned her blind eyes to the south. "She has returned," Dalyse announced.

Four other Seers murmured. Each stood at a Well in their home province. They, too, were under the influence of the Siskis and ignorant of the contamination. Each had experienced the same epiphany after a journey to Karn: the Venger, Breegan was evil. It was their duty to secure her destruction.

The deliberate insurrection against a Venger had been necessary only once before. It was a violation of all that Atlans held sacred. The success of a plan to overthrow Breegan's power depended on its secrecy.

Afraid other Seers might overhear their thoughts, the Five did not use their telepathy to discuss their subversion. They used the Wells of Thoughts.

The Five agreed it was a righteous defense. It was their duty to save all Atla from Breegan. Each felt a deep patience they had never experienced before their sabbaticals. They meditated on how to succeed at their task, waiting for the opportunity to be revealed to them, never thwarting the Venger openly.

Occasionally one of the Five would present a vision to the Council suggesting that Breegan's abilities be tested. All plots failed, but the Five persisted, determined to bring Atla under their personal protection.

It was Dalyse who experienced inspiration. The Siskis directed her thoughts to Atla's past. As it had touched her telepathic observation years before, the Dark Magic whispered to Dalyse in her dreams. A Venger. An equal to Breegan. A true threat. A decoy.

Over and over the Siskis entwined images in the Seer's mind until, when she woke, Dalyse believed the idea was her own. They would resurrect the fear of Fahgerdahl. Dalyse would direct Breegan to find Fahgerdahl and destroy him. The Five agreed that Breegan would either perish or be unable to return.

"Is she at the Hall of Doors?" one of the Five asked.

"Is she with the others?" another questioned.

"Perhaps she is in Karn and vulnerable to the Siskis," another said.

"I cannot yet tell," Dalyse answered.

She stirred the waters of the Well with the tip of a bloodstained finger. The blood belonged to Halinan, a young man of Hardisty who had the misfortune to be near the Well of Thoughts when Dalyse needed it.

Dalyse had allowed Halinan to assist her to a bench near the Well, let him bend near to help her with her shawl, then slit his throat, telling herself the killing was necessary. The Siskis inside Dalyse soothed her, remedied the momentary discomfort she felt at the murder of an Atlan, then sent *carolaks* to dispose of the corpse.

"Be patient a little longer," said Dalyse, her voice hollow. "No doubt, if we are patient, we will experience new knowledge of how to defeat the Venger, Breegan and rule Atla ourselves. Forever."

"Forever," the others agreed.

"Stay in your Provinces," Dalyse ordered. "Use your visions to misguide and misinform.

"I myself will travel to Eshref. I will tell Ezamiah that I had another vision. I will say that she has already failed. It will gain us a little time. We will not speak again until the Venger, Breegan is dead."

***

"You know," said Nigel as he struggled up the slope of the mountainside, "I could have made the door open right into the cave."

"It is not big enough," Breegan said over her shoulder.

Trailing, Padwick looked up at their kite. It floated just above Breegan, bobbing up and down on the breeze she was creating.

"If we take much longer," Padwick said, "we will be noticed."

"We are almost there," said Breegan. She had sensed Padwick's anxiety earlier and distracted him. Now she projected reassurance to him. "And what is more natural to these mountains than a *seniya* drifting on a breeze?"

"A *carolak*," Padwick said beneath his breath.

"I heard that," Nigel said.

"Be silent," said Breegan.

The trio continued their ascent. The rain had stopped, but the sky's colors were still mixed with gray and the air was cold.

"I remember Karn being warmer than this," said Nigel.

"It gets cold at night," Padwick reminded him.

The Siskis is drawing into itself, thought Breegan. *Is it because of the storm passing or does it sense my presence?*

She reached the ledge and stepped quickly into the confines of the cave, drawing the kite down so it appeared as if the *seniya* was nesting.

The paper *seniya* was soaked, held together only by the Magic already present in Breegan's string. Its brave lines sagged, making the orb visible.

Breegan felt an unaccustomed panic. "Nigel! Padwick!"

Fearing carolaks, Padwick clenched his fist in case a fireball was needed. He pushed himself to catch up to Nigel. "Hurry!" he urged.

Breathless and muddy, the two men arrived at the cave and rushed in. The sight of the waterlogged kite stopped them.

"Oh, Breegan," Padwick said, dismayed. "What are we to do?"

"I do not know," she whispered, tired beyond tired. "I do not know."

Nigel looked from Breegan to Padwick and back to Breegan again. "You're kidding me, right? Come on. We can't give up now."

He walked up to the kite and poked it. "It's not so bad. We'll just dry it off."

"We cannot risk the Magic," Padwick explained.

"Sure we can." Nigel sat down next to the kite. "Here's what we do. We wait until sunset, when the Eras is weak, right? We bring back the storm …"

Nigel looked at Breegan. "You can do that."

She nodded.

"Good. Then we dry out the kite using the storm's disruption of the Eras to cover our Magic. Simple."

Breegan sank down against a wall of the cave, stunned. "Brilliant," she whispered.

"Brilliant," Padwick echoed.

"It is?" Nigel straightened his shoulders. "I mean, it is."

"Move further back into the cave, both of you," said Breegan, taking charge once again. She stood up. "I will watch for the right moment to begin another storm.

"Padwick, when the storm is overhead, you will be in charge of drying our kite."

"How will we keep the kite dry, Breegan?" asked Padwick, recovered from his shock. "It will not fit in this cave, as you said."

"Nigel has something in his haversack." Moving quietly toward him, Breegan reached into Nigel's shirt pocket and removed the tiny bag.

As her fingers brushed against his chest, Nigel shivered. "What?" he asked.

"I do not know what it is called, but you used it often as a child. You still like to carry some as a keepsake. It made watercolors shiny and stiff so that your pictures almost repelled water. I can enhance that property, strengthen our kite, and make it waterproof."

"These *zinahdays* are an invasion of privacy," Nigel grumped. He folded his arms across his chest. "It's called shellac and I don't know how I could apply it to that." He pointed to the kite.

"I know how." Breegan went to the front of the cave. "After I bring the storm, I will create a bubble of shellac about our kite as it dries. The sun is setting even now. We will launch the kite at moonrise."

"*Seniyas* and *carolaks* could notice the Magics," Padwick said.

"I do not sense any in this area," said Breegan. "Do you?"

"Not yet."

"Then we will proceed. After my storm, Nigel and I will create the last stage of the *baskaray*."

Chapter Eighteen

Breegan's storm blew in like a hurricane.

Inside the cave, Padwick *fairowed* a small fire to help him see better as he dried the kite. Breegan snapped Nigel's haversack to full size.

Finding his shellac, Nigel offered the bottle to her. "Nice storm."

"Thank you." She looked into his eyes and Nigel felt a warm familiarity.

Maybe zinahdays *aren't so bad after all,* he thought. He watched the two Atlans work with their Magic, feeling a little left out. His Gift of Colors was surprising in its scope, but the current task required speed and experience.

Nigel realized that he had some serious practicing to do if he wanted to master his Gift as Breegan had. He studied her as she created a bubble of shellac around their kite, admiring Breegan's control of her Magics.

I wonder how long she had to practice, thought Nigel.

Padwick stepped back from the kite and looked out at the wind and rain.

"Breegan," he whispered.

"I know, Padwick. If they approach closer, use fireballs from your fire."

"Do I want to know who they are?" asked Nigel, getting up and quietly joining Padwick at the mouth of the cave.

"You do," said Padwick. "They are *carolaks*. If they were once *seniyas*, I cannot tell. They have sensed the Magic even though we have evoked very little. They are coming along the trail."

"There was a trail?" Nigel whispered back his indignation, trying to keep his anxiety in control. "What should I do? Paint a door? How about a big stick?"

"That might do well enough, my friend. They are closer now. A hunting pair of true *carolaks*. They will not press an attack until they are certain we are vulnerable."

"So basically, we have an audience."

Padwick nodded, glad of Nigel's perspective. "Yes."

With a final whispered word, Breegan moved away from the kite. "It is finished, Padwick, but keep your fire burning. You can use it to ignite fireballs instead of generating more Magic. Stand guard now."

"Understood."

"How long until moonrise?" Nigel asked Breegan.

"My storm is ebbing now."

Not exactly a precise answer, thought Nigel. He stood still, listening to the wind. It was quieting. Looking over Padwick's head, Nigel could see the clouds thinning. Did he see a glint of color or was he imagining it?

Nigel felt his insecurity undermining his anticipation. "Uh, Breegan?"

"Yes, Nigel."

"You said we would be doing this"—Nigel waved one hand helplessly—"this blowing up thing together."

"Yes, Nigel."

"What exactly do you want me to do?" Nigel pressed for details, hoping it was something he actually could do.

Breegan took Nigel's hand. Immobilized, he listened to her voice in his mind.

Stay close to me. We will stand on the threshold of the ledge and I will guide the kite. When I have anchored it directly over the Well of Siskis, I will release the orb.

At that instant, you will say a Magic Word aloud. That will detonate the orb and the baskaray *will be complete.*

Breegan released Nigel's hand and looked at him. "You have questions," she said.

Nigel jerked as if he had been hypnotized. "Yeah. Do we have to stand on the threshold of the ledge? I mean, couldn't we just peer out from here? You know, be stealthy instead of drawing attention to ourselves?"

Breegan took Nigel's hand again, this time speaking directly to him. "You will be safe, Nigel. I will hold your hand as now. It must be so because you participated in the creation of this *baskaray*."

"Me? What did I do?"

"It was the Magic of your Gift of Colors that took us to the seashore world. It was your oyster I used. It was your picture I brought to life. You must say the Word of Magic, Nigel, or the orb will not explode and you will not have the happy ending for which you long. Do you understand?"

"I think so. You've been getting me used to your touch from the beginning, haven't you? You've suspected all along that Dalyse and some of the other Seers had been exposed to the Siskis."

"Yes."

"You knew you'd have to destroy the Siskis sooner or later. Hunting Fahgerdahl was sort of a fact-finding mission. Learn your enemy's weaknesses. You just didn't count on your enemy being alive."

"No, I did not. Nor did I suspect it would be so powerful. Too powerful for me to face alone," Breegan confided.

"So I lend you a hand, literally, and you and I kill the Siskis together. That'll get rid of the infected Seers, too. Right?"

"Yes, Nigel. When we destroy the Siskis, the Seers will be destroyed."

"Just like the Well on the pink world when Fahgerdahl died."

"Yes."

Breegan dropped Nigel's hand and turned to face the clearing sky. "We will do this together," she said, back stiff, voice soft.

"Does Padwick know about any of this?" Nigel asked.

"No. I protect him from the terror and sorrow of the truth. As you did when we found the dead swallow. I protect all Atla. It is not for Atlans to know of peril. They cannot live their lives in fear. It is for me to know. And now you."

"The storm," Nigel said half to himself. "You created the storm that brought me to Atla." He tried to turn Breegan to face him.

"Ow!" It felt like a field of electricity cloaked Breegan.

Padwick looked over at the two, incredulous that his friend would be so rude as to touch Breegan.

"Continue your guard, Padwick," Breegan ordered. "All is as it should be."

Nigel leaned close to Breegan without touching. "Physical contact may be a one-way street," he whispered, "but *zinahdays* aren't. You told Ezamiah that thoughts and Magics can travel where the body cannot. You sent an incantation through some sort of portal and disturbed the Eras Magic of Earth."

Breegan did not respond.

"Didn't you?" Nigel demanded. "Answer me, Breegan."

She whirled to face him and Nigel saw fear in her eyes. Fear of what was to come. Fear of failure. Her world entire was under attack and their plan was Breegan's only hope.

"You know the answer," she whispered.

"Tell me anyway," Nigel persisted. "Is the Gift of Colors really mine, or am I impotent without you and your Agenta Magic, like Fahgerdahl and the Siskis? Will my Gift disappear once you've achieved your goal?"

"Your Gift is true, Nigel. Its Magic is yours to command and to share forever. I only created the opportunity for you to use it. I needed help. Your help."

"Are you telling me the truth?"

"You know I am."

Nigel reached out in his mind, through the intimate *zinahday* Breegan had created between them. She was telling the truth.

Reassured, Nigel nodded. "Okay. Good. Great. I'm sorry I was rude. I had to know."

"Of course you did. I have taken you too much for granted." Breegan looked up, searching for her moons. "I did not realize at the time, but I needed more than your Gift, Nigel. I needed you."

"Me?"

"Yes. Your sensibility, your intuition, and your perseverance."

"I thought I was just a pain in the ass."

"You are not 'just' anything."

"Thanks." Nigel thought for a moment. "One more thing."

Breegan did not turn around. "Yes?"

"What Magic Word should I use?"

Breegan smiled, glad that Nigel could not see it, knowing he could sense it. "Your middle name."

***

Ezamiah pretended to listen as Dalyse described her vision of Breegan's death. The lie was as palpable as the Siskis that glittered occasionally in the Seer's eyes.

How long had the Seers been stained by the Dark Magic, he wondered. No doubt that was what made their Auras unpleasant to be near.

I must send word to the members of the Council I have chosen, Ezamiah thought. *Already they are on guard against the five Seers whom Breegan suspected of treason. Worse than treason, the decimation of all Atla by the Siskis Magic.*

"Be wary, Ezamiah," Breegan had said when she came to warn him a year before. "The Siskis is like a disease. These five Seers may not know they are ill. Perhaps there is a way to save them."

"It is not a disease that can be cured, Breegan," he had answered. "This evil must be completely annihilated."

Breegan straightened her shoulders. "Then I will do so. I do not yet know my enemy well," she confided. "The Siskis Magic may be elsewhere in Atla. I cannot tell. You must choose whom to trust, Ezamiah. The Council cannot be convened again until the danger I face has passed. I know you will choose wisely."

"And what of Fahgerdahl?" Ezamiah had asked.

"Fahgerdahl is a possible threat. I will confront him. When I have defeated my true enemy, you will know."

"I will feel it in the air of Eshref," he had answered.

Breegan nodded. "I will create a portal," she said, "and use an incantation to rouse the Eras on the Key's world. Thoughts and Magics can travel where the body cannot."

Bringing himself back to the present, Ezamiah rose, walking slowly, as if in grief. "What you tell me, Dalyse, is a great sorrow. Still, I interpret your vision as what may come and not as what has already occurred."

He turned to face the Seer. "Wait with me a while," he encouraged. "There may yet be better things to see."

***

Breegan extended her hand to Nigel.

He took it. They stood together on the threshold of the ledge.

Padwick remained near the entrance of the cave. The two *carolaks* had disappeared when the artificial *seniya* took flight. He stood guard against their possible return.

"It looks beautiful," Nigel remarked, watching his ducklike swan sail on a strong breeze created by Breegan.

"It is. You painted it well."

Nigel shifted on his feet. He still wasn't accustomed to praise, especially from Breegan. "Is it there yet?" Nigel asked.

"Not yet."

Padwick called softly to them. "Is it there yet?"

"No!" they answered.

Nigel squinted into the distance as the kite became like a line of paint in a picture.

Breegan could see it clearly. Her hand tightened about Nigel's. "The kite is nearing the Well. I intend to make it circle as I check the positioning."

Nigel tensed.

At the cave's entrance, Padwick tensed as well. "Breegan? The *carolaks* are returning."

"Come and stand behind us, Padwick." Breegan's voice was calm, but her tight grip on Nigel's hand increased. "We stand back to back. The kite is at the Well."

"Is the kite in position?" Padwick's worried question came from directly behind Nigel, startling him.

"Padwick! Dammit. You startled me." Nigel turned his head to glance down at his friend. "Hit them with a fireball, would you please? I'm kinda busy here. I've got a bad guy to blow up."

"Certainly, Nigel."

"Thank you." Nigel faced forward again.

Behind him he heard a whoosh and a yelp from a *carolak*.

"I think I have discouraged them," said Padwick.

"Great stuff," Nigel whispered. He kept his eyes on Breegan, and for a moment it seemed as if he was with the kite, looking down at the Well, spiraling closer. Dizzy, Nigel felt a familiar panic until Breegan pulled him next to her.

"The kite is in position, Nigel. I will release the orb … Now!"

"Buckaroo!" Nigel shouted at the top of his lungs.

The bomb exploded.

A shock wave hit them even as Breegan pulled both Nigel and Padwick back against the mountain's wall.

Nigel. Breegan's voice was in his head. *Listen to me,* she whispered in his mind. *The cave is your door. Your door. The one we left behind.*

The boulder?

"Yes!" she yelled aloud as another shock wave pelted them with rocks.

A piece of the ledge split off and dropped to the valley floor one hundred feet below.

Breegan pulled herself under control. Again, she spoke to Nigel through their *zinahday.*

Nigel, listen to me.

What?

This cave is your door. The door you created. See it with me and the three of us will escape and run into the sunlight of your seashore world.

Your Gift is true. Breegan's voice in his mind was clear and strong. *Believe me, Nigel. Believe in yourself. There is no time for doubt. The cave is the door you painted.*

The cave is my door, thought Nigel as the ground beneath his feet shuddered. He remembered his boulder. It would blend perfectly with this landscape, but it was miles away. At the end of the archipelagos.

No! Breegan forced him to listen. *It is here. It is why we left it behind. It is your door, Nigel. You have the Gift of Colors.*

"I am taking us through the door," Breegan screamed against the rain of rocks and rush of angry wind. "Say the words, Nigel."

"What door?" Padwick asked even as Breegan dragged him behind her like a child. She still held Nigel's hand as well. The three of them ducked into the cave.

"Hocus-pocus!"

They stumbled and fell into sea grass and sand. A soft breeze rushed across their bodies. High overhead, a gull cried.

"I knew there were birds here," Nigel complained, cheek against the sand. He lay still. "Are we there? Here? Safe?"

Padwick jumped to his feet. "You did it, Nigel!" He almost danced.

Nigel sat up, brushing sand from his shirt. He looked around. "Not bad for a guy with a weird name."

"Your middle name is Atlan," Breegan told Nigel, shaking sand from her hair. "I have never heard it before, but it proved more worthy than your memories ever credited."

Nigel stood up and removed his glasses carefully. One of the lenses had finally cracked. "Yup. My father used to call me his little buckaroo. He said it was a family tradition. I didn't know he was serious until I saw my birth certificate."

"It means your ancestors came from the Province of Biachin," said Padwick.

"I'm speechless," said Nigel.

"I doubt you are," Breegan commented. She turned away. The double doors had disappeared. The smaller boulder door remained steadfast.

"Look through the keyhole, Nigel," Breegan said. "Tell me what you see."

Apprehensive now, Nigel walked over to his boulder and crouched down. He peered through the keyhole. "I seem to be looking down instead of across. Maybe the explosion caused a tectonic shift? Anyway, there's something in the distance. It looks like a big black boat sinking."

Nigel sat down. He looked at Breegan. "I think we sunk Karn."

"But where will the true *seniyas* make their nests?" Padwick's anxious question interrupted the shared triumph between Breegan and Nigel.

"On the archipelagos," Nigel answered. "It looks like most of them survived the explosion. They're just slightly higher and different shapes. Take a look for yourself."

Padwick looked through the keyhole then at Breegan and Nigel. "You were successful."

"Of course we were successful." Nigel pushed himself to his feet. "We all were."

He turned to Breegan. "Weren't we?"

"I believe so. I will know for certain when we return to Atla." Breegan gazed at the peaceful world around them. "You will have to paint a picture," she began.

"Of a boat," Nigel finished her sentence. "And let me guess. Another door, too."

"Do we have time to roast some marshmallows?" asked Padwick.

Chapter Nineteen

Ezamiah watched as Dalyse, face frozen in horror, shriveled and died, leaving only a small puddle of blue slime on the ground where she had been sitting.

"You may come down now, Judson," Ezamiah said.

Tree branches rustled as Breegan's *casielle* jumped to the ground.

Ezamiah nodded to him. "You heard?"

"Yes. And watched. But why tell me to hide when Dalyse came to you?" Judson asked. "She cannot see me."

"Not with her eyes, but Dalyse could have sensed your Aura. It is stronger since you made the Pledge and Dalyse would have felt your *zinahday* with Breegan. As Breegan's *casielle*, you are a liability. The threat of harm to you, Judson, could cause Breegan to react instead of act. You make her vulnerable. It is why I sent for you."

"To order me to break our Pledge." Judson's voice was strained, but his eyes did not waver from Ezamiah's gaze. "Then I will challenge you."

"You will not." Ezamiah turned away. "There is no need for your passion now. The danger has passed."

He paused, voice weighted. "This time. This danger. Never forget, however, you are Breegan's weakness."

Judson moved in front of Ezamiah. "You are wrong, Ezamiah. I am her strength."

Ezamiah studied the young man. He showed neither desperation nor fear, only calm and love. Loyalty and devotion. He was worthy of a Venger.

Stepping around Judson, Ezamiah walked away. Thinking, he spoke aloud. "I am going to meet Breegan on Eshref's peninsula. She will be coming across the ocean. It will take her several days."

"I know," Judson said. "I have twice sensed her presence in Atla since she left. I thought I was dreaming."

Again, Ezamiah paused. "That is a strength," he conceded. He started walking. "You will not be dreaming this time," Ezamiah called over his shoulder. "You may wait with me if you wish."

Judson smiled. He hurried to catch up.

***

"Why can't I paint a door that will take us back to where we started?" Nigel argued.

"Because the destruction of Karn disrupted the Eras," Breegan said, impatient at the need for explanations again. Her *zinahday* with Nigel had not survived the shock waves of the *baskaray*. "Because I must search the area where Karn existed to ensure we have truly been successful. Because the journey across Atla's ocean will allow me to sense if any Siskis remains anywhere. And because ..." Breegan tightened her sash.

"Because you say so," Nigel finished.

"Yes." Satisfied, Breegan ducked through the boulder's doorway. Padwick followed.

Nigel stayed behind for a minute. He took a last, loving look at his seashore world.

"Nigel!" Padwick's joyous call brought Nigel out of his reverie.

Shouldering his haversack, Nigel stepped through the door and onto a long stretch of beach. "What the hell?"

Nigel looked around him. Padwick was admiring the pastel sky of Atla's dawn. Breegan was standing knee-deep in the dark green ocean.

"What happened to the rocks?" Nigel asked.

Padwick pointed. "They are up there, Nigel."

Turning, Nigel looked up at high cliffs and escarpments. "Why didn't my door open up there? Not that I mind the beach, but I don't understand."

"Breegan says the Eras is shifting in this vicinity and rearranging the landscape. It has filled in the area where Karn once existed," explained Padwick, joining Nigel.

"And changed the location of my door," Nigel said.

"Yes. This small island will now make an excellent home for the *seniyas*."

"Glad to hear it," said Nigel.

In the shallows, Breegan stood still, letting the waves rush against her. "My heart beats for you." She spoke to Atla, but thought of Judson. Breegan spread her arms wide then hugged them about herself, embracing the Eras with the dawn.

"Pethlanah," she whispered. *Live.*

The wind increased, the waves rose higher, the colors of the sky deepened as violet and amethyst intertwined with them. Satisfied, Breegan placed the painting of a boat upon the ocean's surface and clapped her hands above it.

A purple mist engulfed the paper for a moment. Breegan blew upon it and Nigel's boat came to life. Small but sturdy, it bucked the waves, its lone white sail reflecting the colors of the sky like a prism.

"Hey, my boat looks great," Nigel enthused.

The night before he had worried it might not stand up to the rigors of magical transformation, not to mention an ocean voyage. On paper, it had looked more like a large rowboat with half a triangle for a sail.

"This is your boat?" Breegan had considered it carefully.

Embarrassed, Nigel defended his childish picture. "I've never painted a boat before."

"As I can see," said Breegan.

Nigel sulked in silence. He knew she was right. He should be able to whip up something a little more dignified. Obviously, his maturing Gift of Colors had yet to improve his artistic skills.

"It is acceptable," Breegan decided.

She had passed the paper to Padwick. "It looks like a sturdy vessel," he said.

When Nigel offered to try again, Breegan had said no. "It will serve as it is."

Now the boat waited for them.

"What do I do about this door?" Nigel called to Breegan. "Lock it or erase it?"

"Erase it!" she called back, anchoring the boat with her Aura.

"Paint it, erase it." Nigel dropped his haversack and knelt beside the door. As he pulled out his turpentine, Breegan came up beside him.

"Use a word, Nigel," she said.

"To erase a door?" He shook his head. "I'm not ready for that."

"Try." Her tone was encouraging instead of insistent.

Nigel faced his now incongruous boulder. It sat displaced upon the white beach like a wart. "Alakazam!"

The door disappeared in a puff of pink smoke. "Holy cow! This is amazing! Wow!"

Jumping up, Nigel almost hugged Breegan. He stopped still.

"I could just kiss you." Nigel grinned.

Breegan forestalled her next duty and indulged her sense of humor. She walked slowly around Nigel, looking him up and down. "I wonder what Judson would think of such an act? If you kissed me, he would sense it. Even now, he is waiting for my return. No doubt, he would consider your kiss an insult. He might even challenge you to a duel."

"I think I'll just pat myself on the back," said Nigel.

"Good. Now come." Turning, Breegan headed back to the ocean where Nigel's boat waited. "I have more to do."

"More?" Nigel asked Padwick as they followed Breegan to the water.

"Breegan wishes to inspect the Eras."

"Ah."

The ocean was warm against Nigel's legs as he and Padwick waded into it. Nigel splashed at Padwick, giddy with the success of his latest magical accomplishment.

Padwick splashed back, overjoyed to be in Atla again.

Breegan let them play until they accidentally splashed her. Saying nothing, she wiped the saltwater from her face and pointed at the boat. Nigel and Padwick sloshed toward it and climbed aboard like errant children. Breegan followed.

"We will circle the area and I will search for any trace of Siskis," Breegan announced. "There must be nothing left of Karn. Even a grain of sand will be unacceptable. I must be certain that the Siskis is gone."

"What about the archipelagos?" asked Nigel. In the distance, he could see several small islands of beach and cliffs stranded on the expanse of waves.

"Seven survived the *baskaray*," Breegan remarked. "They are safe."

"How do you know?" asked Nigel.

"Breegan's *zinahday* with Atla allows her to search for specific disturbances in the Eras," Padwick said to Nigel. "Not only evoking it, but controlling it. Remember?"

"Like the storm, of course," said Nigel. "I guess we'll get a good sailing wind."

Breegan sat in the stern of the ship. "I will evoke only enough Eras to sail the boat, Nigel. We will travel with the natural wind and I will focus my energy on my search."

Breegan waved her right hand and the sail billowed with her Agenta Magic. They left the emptiness of the beach for the loneliness of the ocean.

Even as Padwick dried them both, Nigel shivered. Despite all his paintings of seas and oceans, he had never actually sailed anywhere.

"Should we be watching for something?" Nigel asked, hoping for a distraction.

"Yes." Breegan scanned the waves.

"What?"

"Anything."

Unnerved, Nigel scanned the ocean's surface as Breegan made the ship zigzag across a long, wide area.

"I see only waves, Breegan," said Padwick as they retraced their course again. "And I sense nothing unusual. Oh!"

Nigel turned to where Padwick was looking. A large creature like a whale-sized dolphin blew spray at them. "Is that a *fekinat*?" asked Nigel, worried.

"It is a *yavanim*," said Padwick, excited. "Is she not beautiful, Nigel?"

Accustomed to his friend's exuberance, Nigel agreed. "You bet. Beautiful."

He looked to Breegan. "Should I be worried?"

"No," said Breegan. "It is a good sign."

The wind swirled about Breegan, drying her hair and warming her spirit. "I can touch her Aura," Breegan said. "She is strong and rich in Eras Magic. She would never swim where anything dangerous or malevolent existed."

Breegan pulled her hair over one shoulder and began braiding it. "We will head home now," she said.

***

Nigel trailed a finger in the bottle green water, creating a ripple in the reflection of Atla's two moons and recalling his first night in Atla.

"Two moons," he said.

Padwick, just drifting off to sleep, sat up a bit. "Pardon?"

"Sorry. Sorry. I was just thinking out loud. Go back to sleep."

Padwick stretched and rolled onto his side. "Sailing is good for thinking," he murmured, snuggling into his scarlet blanket. "And for sleeping. Sleep well, my friend."

Sleep? Nigel looked up at the moons. How could he sleep? It was their last night on the ocean. Tomorrow they would reach Eshref, the southern tip of Atla. Nigel was surprised at how disappointed he felt.

During the past six days and nights, he and Padwick had relived their adventure. Breegan steered the boat and occasionally corrected a detail in the storytelling. She continued to monitor the Eras, sometimes taking them off course and making circles of eight until Nigel felt dizzy. The Eras of Atla always passed the test. The Siskis was gone.

Padwick wanted Nigel to paint another door. "What adventures we could enjoy, Nigel."

"I'm not sure I'm ready to be an adventurer, Padwick. I'm sorry to disappoint you, but I'm an artist; I still want to paint."

"That is natural," Breegan said. "You have had much to learn, quickly, and under dangerous circumstances. Travel back to where you felt inspired or enjoyed a respite from care."

"The seashore world!" Padwick had looked hopeful.

"When you are ready to use your Gift," continued Breegan, "you will know."

How will I know? Nigel wondered.

He pulled his hand out of the water now, looking at the northern horizon.

"What are you thinking, Nigel?" Breegan asked. She sat in the stern, watching him.

Surprised, Nigel sat up straight. "It's strange that you can't tell anymore."

"Tell?"

"You know." Nigel tapped his temple. "No more *zinahdays*."

"No. No more *zinahdays*. Not with me." Breegan considered Nigel's demeanor. "What are you thinking?" she asked again.

"The adventure," Nigel confessed, feeling guilty after all his complaining. "I'm going to miss the adventure."

"Have another," Breegan said.

"What?"

"Quiet." She frowned. "You will wake Padwick."

Standing up, Breegan brought the boat to a slow stop and began to strip. "Come with me," she invited Nigel.

Not wanting to stare, Nigel took off his glasses. "Where?"

"For a swim. We can talk."

There was a splash. Nigel put his glasses back on.

"I'm not a good swimmer," he tried to whisper.

"But you are a good adventurer."

"I am?"

Breegan dove under a gentle wave, surfacing beside the boat. "You need practice," she said, half-serious, half-teasing.

This side of Breegan had been completely hidden during their time together. *Probably out of necessity*, thought Nigel. "It got pretty scary out there," he objected.

"Yes. It did. But it is not scary now." Breegan splashed at Nigel. "Come. Swim with me."

Nigel hesitated, feeling like the old, easily embarrassed human again. *Oh, what the hell*, he decided. Taking off his clothes, Nigel climbed over the side of the boat and dog-paddled around it, trusting Breegan to keep the ocean calm.

"Hey, Breegan?" Nigel managed to float on his back as Breegan swam effortlessly near him.

"Yes?"

"What happened to the contaminated Seers?"

"I know only that they are gone," Breegan answered, her voice tinted with sadness. The loss of her people, however necessary, was painful. "As the Siskis is gone."

"So Atla's, like, paradise now," said Nigel, trying to cheer her up.

"In what way?" She splashed at him.

"No more evil. You know, the danger's gone and everything's fine and dandy."

Breegan splashed at him again. "There is always danger, Nigel. Good is balanced by evil. But the Siskis, wherever it came from, is destroyed."

"Wherever it came from?" Nigel resisted the temptation to splash back at Breegan. "Are you saying it was never a part of Atla in the first place? Like an alien?"

"I am saying it did not belong here."

A shadow of something torpedo-shaped passed near the prow of the boat.

"What was that?" Nigel tried to tread water.

Breegan splashed and kept him buoyed with her Aura Magic. "A *fekinat*," she said, unconcerned.

"A *fekinat*!" Panicking, Nigel splashed wildly.

Breegan swam closer to him, her manner calm. "Splash at them, Nigel, or climb aboard the boat. You are safe. This is Atla. There are *fekinats*. They belong here."

"But you said they were aberrations of Siskis," Nigel argued.

He smacked the surface of the water even as he grabbed onto the side of the boat. "Take that," he said to the fish as it darted away.

Breegan splashed again. "That is not what I said. You assumed that. Not all of the *fekinats* were tainted by the Siskis. They are part of Atla's ecosystem. The Siskis was not. Therefore, some of the *fekinats* remain."

She pushed at Nigel with her Aura. "Climb aboard. It is late."

Nigel hoisted himself onto the boat, feeling awkward and scared all over again.

Breegan swam around the boat once then climbed aboard. She took the blanket Nigel handed her. "There will always be something scary in the world, Nigel," she said. "You must choose whether or not to let it frighten you."

Nigel noticed his skin was dry even as he pulled on his clothes. "Thank you," he said, not looking at Breegan as she dressed.

"You are welcome."

"No." Nigel sat down, forcing himself to look straight into the dazzling emerald eyes. "I mean it. Thank you, Breegan. For everything."

Breegan bowed her head a little. "Thank you, as well, Nigel Nessel. You will always be welcome at my door." Her voice was like a gentle kiss.

Breegan brought the wind back to the sail. "We will reach Eshref tomorrow." She spoke in her usual voice. "Go to sleep."

She's back in charge, thought Nigel. *Strong, confident and just a bit bossy.* He smiled, looking up again at the moons. *Who could sleep? I'll just rest my eyes for a moment*, he told himself.

The rocking of the boat soothed his nerves. He dreamed of flying *fekinats*.

Nigel felt something land on his nose. He swatted at it even as he jerked himself awake. Whatever it was dived-bombed him again as he pushed his glasses into place.

Squinting against bright sunlight, Nigel saw his attacker.

It was a large blue dragonfly. It soared past again, all the colors of Atla's sky reflecting off its magnificent wings.

Nigel ducked and the dragonfly landed on the sail.

We must be close to land, thought Nigel. "Where are we?" he asked.

"We are approaching the cliffs of Eshref," said Padwick, happiness making his voice shine.

Nigel watched the dragonfly lift off and head for home, flying low over foamy whitecaps.

"Wow." Nigel inhaled the scented air.

Two hundred yards ahead, the waves leaped to kiss the vines and flowers that trailed over the end of Eshref's peninsula. The cliffs, as Padwick called them, were only seven feet high, but their smooth, gleaming white surface made them look far higher.

"I don't see a beach," Nigel said.

"We do not need one," said Breegan.

She was standing in the stern of the boat, legs apart for balance as she steered it with her thoughts. The breeze ruffled her hair. Her emerald eyes danced like the waves. Lifting her right arm, fingers outstretched, Breegan smiled.

Nigel knew that smile. He had felt a fraction of its unbearably sweet touch.

For a moment, he wished he could be its recipient then he felt happy for Breegan. After all, she was the hero.

Nigel faced about, shouting a "hello" and waving as he recognized Ezamiah. Judson stood beside him.

Slowing the boat, Breegan brought it safely to the base of the cliffs.

Excited, Padwick stood on the prow and grabbed a vine that dangled above his head. He stepped off the boat onto the vine. "Climb the ladder, Nigel. Look up, not down."

"That's a ladder?" Nigel looked at the tangle of vines

"It is indeed, my friend." Padwick started to climb. "Hurry. Ezamiah is waiting."

Slinging his haversack over his head and across his chest, Nigel made a pass at a sturdy-looking vine. He gave it a wary tug. It held, and he noticed that it intertwined with other vines only a foot up.

Like a giant fishermen's net, thought Nigel. *And the flowers are the catch of the day.*

He put one foot on a leafy rung, stepped off the side of the boat, and clambered up the net before he could let himself think about what he was doing.

"Here he is." Padwick beamed as Nigel pulled himself over the top of the cliff.

Ezamiah bowed his head to Nigel. "You have done well, Nigel Nessel."

"Thank you." Nigel moved hurriedly away from the edge of the cliff. *Not exactly the hero's welcome,* he thought, *but then I'm not exactly the hero.*

He looked for Breegan. She was already pulling herself to safety. Tucked in her sash was Nigel's painting.

"Your boat, Nigel," she said. "It proved to be stronger than it appeared. As did your Gift, Nigel Nessel." A whisper of a smile lit Breegan's eyes. "As did you."

Nigel grinned. "Call me Buckaroo," he said.

Turning away from Nigel, Breegan paused to glance at Judson then strode on to stop in front of Ezamiah. He extended his right hand, palm up.

Breegan raised her right arm, lowering her palm above Ezamiah's palm. "Know this from me," she said, "and be content."

A purple mist obscured their hands for a long time. Nigel watched as different emotions appeared on Breegan's face and transferred to Ezamiah's: concern, pain, hate, despair, joy.

Breegan drew a long breath, releasing it as a single tear slipped down her cheek. "It is done. Atla is safe."

Ezamiah clenched his fist and bowed low before Breegan. "You have done well, Breegan."

She spared a smiled in Nigel's direction and nodded to Padwick. "We have done well, yes." Breegan turned away.

Not far away and yet not close enough, Judson waited.

Breegan walked slowly toward him, feeling his cheek long before she lifted her hand to touch it. "My heart follows yours," she whispered.

"And if your heart should stop, mine will beat for you," Judson answered, "because my heart follows yours."

He took Breegan's hand and kissed its palm. Their lips met gently, but their embrace was fierce. They held one another for a long time. When Breegan let go, she held on to Judson's hand. Together, they walked away, following the coastline.

Her laughter floated back to Nigel: sweet, happy, triumphant.

"Well, I guess I got my happy ending." Nigel couldn't keep the disappointment from his voice.

"Are you not happy, Nigel?" asked Padwick.

"Oh, sure. I am. Really. It's just … Well, what happens now?"

"Nigel." Ezamiah spoke with the faintest note of reprimand in his voice. "You must recall that you were in the midst of magical cirumstances long before you recognized them. Do not be so easily disheartened. More Magic will find you. Perhaps even an adventure."

"Really?" Nigel felt anticipation mixed with trepidation.

"An adventure!" Padwick stepped close to Nigel.

Ezamiah smiled. "You have the Gift of Colors, Nigel. Such a Gift stirs the soul. Magics cannot help but be attracted to you. It is your destiny. It is what drew Breegan's attention when she searched for help."

"No kidding." Nigel felt a rush of excitement. "I have a destiny?"

He looked at the spectacular green ocean he had recently sailed. A gift and a destiny.

"Scary," Nigel whispered.

He remembered his swim with Breegan the night before. There had been *fekinats* all around them and he'd stayed in the water and splashed. Well, one splash, but it was a start.

I guess it's like Breegan said, I just have to choose whether or not to be scared. *After all, the quest was successful. And I was brave; I even dashed around a bit.*

Nigel looked at the picture of a boat in his hand. *And I feel different. I feel better. I don't feel awkward or out of place. At least, not at the moment.*

What do I feel? Nigel asked himself. "Confident," he decided, saying it aloud.

Nigel undermined his choice of word for a second. Could it really be that simple?

The right answer is always the simplest, Nigel reminded himself. *It's like when I'm painting a complicated series of waves or a particularly unique sunrise. I always go for the simplest blue or green. The palest pink. And it always works.*

Maybe every time I made a spontaneous artistic decision, I was tapping into my Gift of Colors, thought Nigel. *Of course! Painting is focusing and projecting. The perfect practice for an Atlan. And an adventurer.*

Nigel rummaged in the right front pocket of his jeans and pulled out his keys. He released the mail key from the ring and held it out to Ezamiah.

"I almost forgot about this," Nigel apologized. "You wanted a talisman to *fairow*. I hope it works."

"I have no doubt it will," said Ezamiah, "but such an important talisman must be presented at the Council." He turned to Padwick. "Will you escort your friend to Biachin in six days time, Padwick?"

"Happily, Ezamiah."

"Biachin?" Nigel perked up. "That's my home province, isn't it?"

"Yes," said Padwick. "And Breegan's, as well. Perhaps we will see her there. To share the honor of your accomplishment."

"Our accomplishment, Padwick. Like Breegan said."

"Would you like me to summon *seniyas* for your journey across Atla?" Ezamiah offered.

"Oh, no. I mean, no thank you. Thank you very much. We'll …" Nigel lowered his voice and leaned over to Padwick. "How will we get there?"

"Perhaps you can paint something for us that travels on the ground?"

"Sure. Why not?" Nigel wondered if he could paint a decent car. He would probably have to settle for a horse and cart. Maybe a burro.

Ezamiah smiled and pocketed the talisman. "Come, Nigel. Come, Padwick. We will dine at the Inn of Eshref tonight and discuss your transportation."

Nigel neatly folded his picture of a boat and stuck it in a pocket. "Sounds like a good start, right, Padwick?"

Padwick grinned. "By the Light! It is indeed, my friend. A little practice for you. Perhaps a few weeks traveling about Atla. Then, through a door and into another adventure."

Epilogue

Nigel rolled over and fell out of bed. "Ow!"

He sat up and rubbed his head, then his right shoulder.

"Are you injured?" asked Padwick.

"Not much."

"You were dreaming again."

"Yeah." Nigel climbed to his feet. He pushed against the small of his back and stretched. "Same dream every night for two weeks. Purple. Purple people, purple sky, purple landscape. Not even anything I recognize, just shades of purple."

Padwick climbed out of his bed and looked out the window. They had spent the last three days at Satchi's house. He was a friend of Padwick's and an excellent storyteller. From his home in Sunderland, they could see the Emerald Sea.

The Hall of Doors is so close, thought Padwick. *Yet, we do not need it. When will Nigel feel brave enough to paint another door?*

"What do you think it means?" Nigel's question interrupted Padwick's thoughts.

"I do not know. We can cross the Emerald Sea to Jeraj. The desert people are very good at examining dreams."

"I don't need a psychiatrist," Nigel muttered.

There was a sharp rap on the door. Before they could answer, it was flung open. A tall figure stood silhouetted against the sunlight: long hair, long legs.

Nigel didn't dare hope.

"Breegan!" Padwick hurried toward her. "It is wonderful to see you. And at such a time."

"What time is that, Padwick?" she asked.

"Now. Nigel has been dreaming."

"Oh?" Breegan arched an eyebrow in Nigel's direction. "Of what?"

"Purple," Nigel blurted.

"Yes," said Padwick. "For two weeks now. You would know, Breegan. What is the meaning of purple dreams?"

"They herald the start of an adventure," she answered.

"It's about time," said Nigel.

Breegan smiled.

About the Author

Author of the award-winning short story, "The Ring of the Bell", Jenna Lindsey wrote her first novella at fourteen. Although hearing impaired and agoraphobic, Jenna hears her characters clearly and enjoys vicarious travels through her novels. Jenna and her husband live in Calgary, Alberta with three impatient cats.

LaVergne, TN USA
11 December 2009
166642LV00001B/6/P